FINDING GRACE

J. Q. DAVIS

FINDING GRACE

Never Pretend. Just be.

12 YEARS EARLIER...

Serena

IT WAS DARK. TOO dark. I didn't know that 1 a.m. could be so dark. I had never been out this late. Sometimes, I would stay awake past midnight, when it was hard to fall asleep after a particularly heavy night of screaming matches, but I was always in the comfort of my cozy little bedroom. Under the covers trying to weaken the high-pitched screeching my mother produced. Holding a flashlight with one hand and drawing a landscape on my sketchpad with the other. I liked drawing landscapes, even though I had never left this small town. My parents never took my brother, Charlie, and me on vacation. They could never afford it. And when Dad left, we definitely couldn't afford it.

My landscapes all bore my scribbled signature: Serena. Because who knows—maybe I'd be famous someday. I got most of my ideas for my drawings from textbooks. Or TV. Or the one framed picture hanging sadly on the wall at the office Mom and I went to every month to pick up a check from the government. The portrait was old; the glass clouded by years of neglect and the canvas faded from the sunlight shining through the window it faced, but I could tell it was once a really pretty painting. A lot of times, I got the ideas from my head. Landscapes were fun to dream up. I'd basically just throw a bunch of elements together:

1

water, earth, air... A snowcapped mountain surrounded by a calm lake underneath a sky with scattered white, fluffy clouds. Sometimes, I would imagine myself rowing down the lake in a tiny boat, taking in the sights. Smelling the sun on my skin. Listening to the sounds of a waterfall close by. Away from the yelling. Away from the cries.

It was cool outside. My arms were shivering. In my haste to get away, I had only grabbed a light sweater. The backpack slung over my shoulder warmed me a little, but not enough. It would only get colder throughout the night, which sucked because I didn't pack anything else but some underwear, pajama pants, my pencils and pads, a toothbrush, and a photo of my brother and me. It was my favorite picture of us, the edges worn from tucking it somewhere different every time I left the house. It always had to be with me. Either in my schoolbag, the back pocket of my jeans, inside my binder. It was what kept me safe.

The photo was of me and Charlie at the little park down on the corner of my street. That park was super small. There was a metal slide that burned our skin in the summertime and a rainbow-colored merry-go-round that didn't spin. If you went to the park after noon, chances were high that all the kid stuff would be occupied by sleeping homeless people. Which was weird. Didn't it seem like homeless people were always sleeping?

But Dad had rigged up a tree swing on the one tree standing strong in the center of the play area. He wasn't very good at it, though. The makeshift swing was made with an old rope from our shed and a long piece of plywood to sit on. You'd better hope you didn't slide your bottom across it the wrong way, or else a splinter would find its way embedded into your butt skin.

In the picture, Charlie and I sat on the flimsy wood, facing each other, both grasping on tightly to the rope.

Dad snapped the candid of us right before we moved our bodies back and forth, swinging sideways like some sort of floating seesaw, which was seconds before the wood cracked beneath our butts and the braids of the frayed rope gave way. We fell together onto the dying grass below.

I remembered that day like it was yesterday, because it was the last time I saw my brother alive.

Charlie was five years older than me, and he was the same age I was today when a stray bullet from one street over from our house penetrated his bedroom wall and found its way into his brain while he slept. The cops said it was a very unfortunate and tragic freak accident, but I didn't think so. It wasn't an accident that my parents were alcoholics who couldn't keep a job long enough to make the amount of money it took to get us out of this bad neighborhood. It wasn't an accident that the person who shot the gun that sent that bullet whizzing through the air into my brother's head was a stupid young thug playing around, showing it off to his buddies. Accidents happened, but not in this crappy town that was surrounded by crappy people who had no regard for authority or making the right life choices. I knew for a fact that if we didn't live here, if we'd lived a better life, Charlie would be here today.

Instead, he only got to live for fifteen years. But I was lucky enough to call him my brother. He was the best person I had ever known. The best friend I ever had. The only one who truly knew and understood how screwed up our lives were. When Mom and Dad were drunk and arguing, he'd come in my room to keep me company. He would turn the music up loud on his used MP3 player and we'd play with my Barbie dolls together. Thankfully, I had one Ken doll, which was always Charlie's choice. He was older, but he never minded playing with me. And when Mom and Dad were drunk and passed out, Charlie made sure that I was fed and showered and ready for school the next day. He took care of me, more than anyone else ever had.

Dad left when Charlie died. He still came around to see me sometimes, but not a lot. He and Mom would just fight, or he'd fight with whatever guy Mom was seeing that week. Most of the time I felt invisible—like I was just watching an episode of *Cops* because eight times out of ten, the police would be called to come break up all the brawls. My mom was an amazing actress, though. She might not have had an education or a job or the ability to cook anything other than mac and cheese, but she sure could cry and tell a fake story on the spot. Whenever the cops showed up, she'd pretend to be sober, like Dad and her boyfriend were the ones causing all the ruckus. They'd be asked to leave, and then I would find my mom in the living room all alone, cradling a bottle of vodka in one hand and a cigarette in the other, crying her mascara right down her cheeks. That wasn't fake. That was real Mom.

Child Protective Services came one day when I was twelve. They asked a ton of questions. Questions about Dad leaving and Charlie's death and Mom's boyfriends. They wanted to know about me. About my school and the food I ate and the things I liked to do. I answered every question expertly. It helped that Mom and I had practiced before on what to do in this type of scenario. She warned that they would try to take me away if they felt like I was unhappy. Take me to some kid jail where I'd have to share a room with five other girls, and those girls might not even be nice. We'd probably have to shower together, too, and I didn't want to be naked around a bunch of mean girls I didn't know. Mom promised they would make fun of me because of my bright red hair and freckles, reminding me that there weren't many girls who shared the same qualities. And I really didn't want to be made fun of.

The CPS agents just so happened to make an unannounced appearance when Mom was in her in-between stage—in between a hangover and her first whiskey-laced cup of coffee. That coupled with her acting skills led them to believe that things weren't so bad for me. So they left, fortunately. Or unfortunately.

I shook my head at the unpleasant memories. Eventually, I'd have to let them go. The streets at this time of night were dead. I felt really vulnerable. Really lonely. Folding my arms over my chest to try to keep the nippy air from seeping through the thin fibers of my clothes, I began to walk faster. I wasn't even really sold on where I had decided to go. It was an option. Maybe even my only option.

The idea of running away had been on my mind for a while. Ever since Charlie died and Dad left. Ever since Mom started drinking in the shower and her revolving boyfriends started sleeping on our beat-up couch every other night. But I was always too afraid to leave the comforts of my brown paneled walls and stained carpets. Before, when Charlie was around, he had gotten the brunt of Mom and Dad's wrath. They screamed at him to do all the chores. To do all the things *they* should have been doing as parents, like grocery shopping and cooking and cleaning the toilets. But now that he was gone, and Dad was gone, Mom needed someone to take care of her. To clean up her sick whenever she consumed more alcohol than food. Or her blood whenever one of her boyfriends didn't like something she said or did.

I was scared, but I was more scared of losing myself. Missing out on life because I was too busy trying to survive it instead of living it. I didn't want to eat peanut butter sandwiches for dinner anymore. I didn't want to watch my mother cry anymore. Charlie never said it out loud, but I knew he wanted to leave. He had to. If this was what he dealt with, he had to. But he didn't because of me. And something inside my heart was forcing me to walk down these dangerous streets alone in the chill of the night. I had a feeling it was Charlie. He wanted me to get away. To go find a better life for myself because no one else would help me.

The sound of sirens pulled me out of my thoughts. I turned to see blue and red lights heading toward me at a high speed and prayed that it wasn't coming for me. But then I remembered that Mom was passed out cold when I left, so I was sure she didn't already have a search party out looking for her daughter. Who knew if she ever would, anyway.

The cop car zoomed past me, and I exhaled the breath I had been holding in. I was glad to continue running away. It shouldn't be too much longer before I got to the bus station.

We didn't have a computer at home, so I had gone to the library the other day and searched the Internet for bus ticket prices. It cost ninety-three dollars for a one-way ticket to Florida, and that exact bus left the station at 3:15 a.m. I figured I would at least try to make it there as if it was the place I chose to go. I didn't know if that was where I really wanted to end up, but at least I had an idea of how much money I needed. Mom kept a wad of cash in the green cracker tin on top of the fridge. It was a long shot. Her hiding place wasn't exactly hidden from some of the deadbeat boyfriends who rummaged through our cheap stuff in search of something to steal. But I got crazy lucky when I found a hundred-dollar bill rolled in with some ones. Could have been luck. Could have been that she was too drunk to notice. Could have been Charlie. Either way, I didn't feel bad about taking it. She'd figure out how to pay rent. She always did.

I crossed a deserted intersection and passed a gas station that had a half-lit sign advertising gas, cigarettes, and fried chicken. There were no cars, just a couple of guys drinking from a brown paper bag, standing right outside the entrance. Keeping my head down and avoiding any and all contact, I stared at the ground and scurried past. Thankfully, they didn't even acknowledge me. Before I left the house, I swore to myself that I wouldn't speak to any creepy or sketchy strangers. I wasn't a kid anymore, but I felt like that rule applied to anyone, at any age.

The bus station wasn't that much farther. Our town was tiny, and I remembered the way to get there because it was in our "downtown" area, right next to the free clinic where Mom would take Charlie and me whenever we were sick. I hated that place. The lines to see a doctor were always out the door and there were coughy, snotty babies everywhere. We'd end up spending pretty much the entire day breathing in germ-polluted air, all to see a doctor with a heavy accent that we could barely understand. He would stick us with a needle and send us on our way, then we'd have to walk home in the heat or snow because we didn't have a car, and Charlie and I could never catch a cold on the days when the weather was nice.

The only overpass in our town came into view and anxiety started to make my stomach churn. It was really dark under that bridge—I could already tell. There could be anything hiding in its shadows. And weird sleeping homeless people. But I had to be brave. It was the only way to get to the station.

I stepped out of the security of the streetlamps and into the uncertainty of what might be hidden in the darkness. My eyes were bulging, struggling to acclimate to the sudden change in light. They say you could never really feel your ears, but I could in that moment. Every slight noise made them twitch involuntarily, as if they were searching for the source on their own. I flinched at the sound of a glass bottle rolling on concrete to my right, then jumped at the hushed voices to my left. My feet couldn't move any faster. I didn't want to run. For some reason, I was afraid that something would start chasing me. About a minute later, the longest minute of my life, I was finally out of the unknown and onto the other side. The bus station sign was now visible and just about two more blocks away.

The automatic doors slid open and I stepped through into an almost-empty wait area. The seats all faced the ticket booths and the enormous passenger information display screen above the glass partitions. My gaze traveled to the one man working behind the window, then over to the seats. A bearded guy lay on his side on top on his luggage, across a bench made for two. His arms were crossed over his chest, which pulled up his plaid flannel shirt and revealed his over-sized belly. It hung off the side of the seat like he had too much to eat. Or like he was pregnant. A dirty baseball cap covered his eyes, and I assumed he was sleeping. Or dead and no one knew it yet.

All of the middle rows were completely vacant, except the second row from the front. There was a man. Or rather, a boy. A really tall boy with long legs stretched out straight in front of him. He was wearing gray sweatpants and a blue sweatshirt, and he was really lanky with long arms. His hair was short and messy and spiky, and he looked like he might have been sleeping, too. He rested back into the chair as if he was relaxed and comfortable, his hands in his pockets and his eyes closed—like he could have been lounging at home in front of a TV.

Picking a chair directly in the front, I set my bag on the floor, sat down, and glanced up at the display screen. There were numbers and letters and names of cities I'd never heard of, all lit up in reds and yellows and greens. An overwhelming sensation flushed my face, and I questioned whether or not I should even be here. In the middle of the night. Alone. With barely any money. What was my mom going to do in her in-between stage, when she sobered up enough to realize that the only kid she had left was gone? Part of me felt guilty. Would she think that I had died, too? But another part of me felt stupid for even caring about how she felt, because chances were, she wouldn't care.

I hadn't the slightest clue of where I should go. Or what I would do when I got there.

My attention was fixated on the board when suddenly, my chair bounced slightly. I immediately turned to my right and realized that Tall Boy had moved closer to me. Like one seat away. Worried that he would steal the few possessions that I owned now, I picked up my bag and squeezed it tight against my body. Tall Boy was kind of cute, but that didn't mean he couldn't be a thief.

I tried my best to forget he was even next to me and looked back up at the board. I had to figure out what I was going to do. But he kept shifting in his seat, making it hard to ignore him. I turned in his direction again, and this time we made eye contact. The corner of his lip turned up before he took his earbud out, which was obscured before because the wire was tucked inside his sweatshirt.

"Hey."

Don't talk to strangers. Don't talk to strangers.

"Hi." I couldn't stop myself. His smile was too nice. His eyes were too soft and friendly. His voice was too deep and smooth at the same time.

"Where are you headed?"

Don't tell him you don't know.

"I don't—"

"Attention, passengers. The 3:15 bus to Tampa, Florida will be boarding in twenty minutes." I peered at the booth clerk behind the glass window, who stared back at me and Tall Boy as he spoke into the microphone in his hand. "Fifteen minutes," he monotoned.

"That's me," Tall Boy said.

"Me too." What? I had no idea why I said that, but he raised his eyebrows as if intrigued.

"Do you have family there?"

"Um...yeah. My brother," I lied. "He's...he's in the Marines." There. That should scare him enough to stop him from trying to kidnap me or something.

"Really? Wow. I'm actually going to be shipped out to boot camp soon. Where did your brother go to boot camp?" he asked, seeming to be genuinely curious.

I didn't know how to answer him. I knew nothing about the Marines, except that they were supposed to be the best of the best. "I...uh...wait, how old are you?" He couldn't be much older than me. He was really tall, but his face... He looked like he could possibly go to my high school.

"I'm about to turn eighteen in a few days."

"Do you go to Kennedy High?"

"Oh, I don't even live here. I'm just waiting on the next bus. I'm from Detroit. My mom lives there, but my dad lives in Tampa. I'm going to spend some time with him before I have to leave," he explained.

I nodded and faced forward.

"What's your name?" Tall Boy asked. It was too late to ignore him now. I thought about giving him a fake name, but out of all the names in the world, I couldn't think of one.

"Serena. You?"

"I'm Julian. It's nice to meet you."

"You too."

He glanced down at my hands. "Do you have a ticket yet?"

"Uh...I don't. I should get one, huh?" I chuckled nervously. Crap. I didn't even know if I wanted to go to Florida. What the hell was in Tampa? Definitely not my Marine Corps brother.

"Well, you better get one before it's too late. You have a few minutes before boarding starts."

I grabbed my bag and hesitantly approached the ticket window. The thought of just running out of the bus station crossed my mind, but then, where would I go? I could wait outside for ten minutes until Julian got on his bus, but I really didn't want to go out into the night again.

The ticket guy didn't even look up at me and pressed a red button that made a loud clicking noise. "Where you headed, ma'am?" he asked, clearly not really caring what place I picked.

"Um...I'll take a ticket to—"

Click! "Can you speak up?"

I cleared my throat. "I'll take a ticket to Tampa, please."

Click! "That'll be ninety-three dollars," he blurted, as if that number was just sitting on the edge of his tongue and waiting to be rolled off. I bent down and pulled the hundred-dollar bill out of my sock. The man took the cash, punched some numbers into the computer, then a piece of paper popped out through a little metal slit on the counter. He tore it away and dropped it into the dip under the window. *Click!* "Have a safe trip."

"Thank you," I said, sliding the ticket out. I turned back and sat in my seat.

"Is this your first time traveling alone?" Julian asked.

"No." I was lying again. I didn't want him to know that this was my first time traveling ever. He might not have been that much older than me, but he was still a stranger. I didn't want him to somehow take advantage of that information.

"Cool. Do you mind if we sit together?" He held up the wire to his earbuds. "We can share some music."

I bit my bottom lip and struggled to make a decision. But when his hazel eyes bore into mine, patiently waiting for an answer, I finally said, "Okay."

He smiled. "Serena. I like that name."

I smiled back. "I like your name, too."

We sat silently for a little bit before the overhead intercom screeched and the voice of the window ticket guy echoed around us again. "The bus to Tampa, Florida is now boarding."

Julian grabbed the handle of his duffel bag and stood up. "That's us. You ready?"

I stood up, suddenly feeling like a little kid next to him. He was a giant compared to me!

We walked out of another set of automatic doors that led us outside to a long line of buses. It reminded me of the line at school behind the gym when the last bell of the day rang. Only, these busses weren't yellow and there weren't gangs of people enthusiastically piling into them, ready to be free from the eight hours of learning. Not that anyone really learned anything at our school. The teachers were always too busy breaking up fistfights and hushing rowdy kids in class.

When we reached the bus, Julian stepped aside and raised an arm, gesturing for me to go in first. *This is it*, I thought as I climbed up. I was leaving this place behind. This depressing place that held both good memories and bad. I didn't feel like I would miss my mom as much as I would miss Charlie. He had been gone for five years, but being home, in a place we both shared, kept him close to my heart. A slight tug pinged in my chest at the thought of abandoning our memories here together. We had no memories together anywhere else. But I had to believe that my brother wanted me to leave. That somehow, he was the one who urged me from the beyond to pack a bag, steal Mom's money, and find my way to the bus station through the darkness.

I picked a random seat toward the back of the bus. Julian followed close behind, and when I sat down, he took my bag and placed it in the overhead bin before plopping down next to me. He pulled out his iPod and the blue screen illuminated. I eyed it enviously. Charlie had a little handheld MP3 player that we shared, but Dad eventually sold it at the pawn shop for drinking money. The iPod Julian had was one that I'd been secretly coveting for a couple of years, but there was no way I could have ever gotten one unless I stole it.

"Do you like Paramore?" he asked.

My heart started to race. It was one of my favorite bands. "Yeah."

"I thought so. You kind of remind me of her. You know, with the red hair?"

He was referring to Hailey Williams. I didn't think I looked like her, but I could see why he'd think so. My hair was almost unnaturally red.

Julian passed an earbud to me before he stuffed his into his right ear and leaned his head back. I mimicked him, placing mine into my left ear and leaning my head back, trying my best to just relax. This wasn't so bad. For this being my first time ever traveling, I was happy that it was with someone at least close to my age who was about to go off to the military. The best of the best of them, too.

Julian pressed the big round button on the iPod and a quick drum riff pounded in my ear. He twisted his gaze to me, our eyes locking. His head bopped to the beat and he grinned. I grinned back and followed his rhythm with my own head. The weight of the bus shifted, and I anticipated seeing more passengers enter the bus, but it was only the driver. He sat down in his seat and played with a bunch of buttons before turning the wheel. We accelerated, as did my heartbeat. We were all alone in this huge bus. And it was happening. I was really leaving.

Hailey from Paramore kept singing the word *crush* in our ears, and my cheeks flushed.

School popped into my head. I had to finish school somehow. There was no way I would allow myself to be a high school dropout. That would probably guarantee going down the same path my parents did. And if Charlie were here, he'd encourage me to finish. I wondered what he would think of all this. Would I even be running away if he was alive? Would we have run away together?

I hadn't noticed my leg bouncing nervously until Julian placed his hand over my knee, as if to calm me. And almost instantly, I became calm.

The driver turned the wheel again, and we were now on the overpass that I had walked under just a little while ago.

"You okay, Serena?" Julian whispered. His voice was so low, I could barely hear him over the hum of the bus engine and the melody of the music in my ear. I sucked my lips in, biting down on my bottom lip before answering.

"Yeah. I'm okay."

He nodded and smiled. "Don't worry, we'll have fun. I have lots of music on this little thing."

For some reason, I believed him. I didn't have to worry because he was with me. They were both with me. Julian... and Charlie.

THE JERK
Present Day

IT WAS CLOSING TIME, but a couple walked in through the restaurant doors. They approached the hostess stand as if to be on a mission. Carrie, the hostess, grabbed two menus and escorted the man and the woman into the dining room. I stalked them from the bar, silently praying that Carrie wasn't picking a table in my section. The man looked like he had a permanent scowl on his face and the woman's shoulders hunched forward as she followed close behind him, as if the man had an invisible leash tethered around her neck.

I almost did a celebratory foot shuffle when it looked like Carrie was leading them toward someone else's section, but then she made a beeline straight to one of my empty tables. Bitch. She was new. She didn't know me well enough yet. I would have to take the time to pretend like I wanted to be her friend. That way, I could manipulate her into never giving me the last table of the night again.

Taking a deep, irritated breath in and exhaling it with a forced smile, I approached the table.

"Hi. My name is Serena. I'll be your—"

The man cut me off. "I'll take a coke. She'll have a sweet tea."

I bit my bottom lip and gripped my pencil tight. Interrupting my greeting was a huge pet peeve.

"We'll start with the fried crab claws," he said.

"John, could we try something different this time? We always start with the crab claws, honey." The woman sitting across from him glanced over at me and smiled weakly. I assumed she was his wife. They were both wearing wedding rings. "How is the shrimp cocktail?"

Before I could answer, John raised his voice. "We'll start with the crab claws," he said firmly.

I peered over at the too-eager-and-disrespectful man's wife, who lowered her eyes back down to the menu.

"I'm sorry, sir, but we seem to be out of fried crab claws. Would you like to start out with—"

"How could you be out of crab claws?"

"John," the woman hissed closed-mouthed. She was clearly embarrassed.

"No, I would like to hear this." He set his menu down and pushed his glasses up the bridge of his nose before folding his arms over his chest. "There's an ocean blocks away full of crabs. How could you be out of crab claws?"

I grinned and pressed the tip of my pencil down so hard on my notepad that it broke.

"They decided to take the day off." I fake-laughed and shrugged as if I had no control over what the crabs did on a Wednesday evening. This seemed to amuse the woman and she giggled, but behind that phony facade was fear, which was made clear when the man shot her a dirty look. She stopped laughing immediately.

"You have never been out of crab claws before."

"Well, sir, I honestly don't know what to tell ya," I said in the nicest tone possible. "But if you'd like, we do have a great shrimp cocktail that I can start you out with."

"I don't like shrimp cocktail," he snapped back, chopping at the table with his hand. I took a deep breath in, incredulous at his behavior over some crab claws, and glanced over at his wife again. She furrowed her brows, returning an apologetic frown.

"Sir, I'm sorry about the crab claws, but we do have other great items on our appetizer menu. Maybe your wife would like to pick something out herself." I smiled and gestured to the lady.

His eyes widened and he sat back in his chair. "I would like to see your manager."

Of course. I nodded enthusiastically, as if it was a totally normal thing to request my manager, then put a hand on the woman's shoulder. "I'll be back with your drinks."

I sashayed away from the patrons, careful not to give away my frustration in the way I walked. Megan and Mia, the bartenders, knitted their brows together sympathetically when I passed the bar. Somehow, as if it were the unspoken language in the hospitality industry, they could tell in my face that these people were annoying and I was ready to leave. The two girls were already cleaning up the bar, and there were only three servers left who hadn't been cut to go home. The nighttime manager, Joe, assured me that the reason why I never went home early was because I was his "best" server. He claimed that no one else knew how to close up the place as well as me, but I honestly thought it was because I was the only one who didn't bitch about it. I needed the money.

I walked past the dishwashing station and the kitchen to get to the manager's office. I could see Joe through the window blinds on the door, shuffling through receipts and punching numbers into a calculator. I knocked before barging in.

"Joe," I exhaled. "Table four wants to see you."

He released an agitated breath of air. "Serena, what did you do now?" he asked without looking up.

I rolled my eyes. "Nothing! This guy is a jerk! I mean, his wife is terrified of him and he speaks for her. You know how much I hate that." And men who were disrespectful and controlling. I had dealt with my fair share of them.

He stopped to look up at me. "Do you ever wonder if maybe she likes it?"

I paused and narrowed my eyes at him. "Joe, no woman likes to be treated like shit. Oh, and by the way, I told him we were out of crab claws."

"We aren't out of crab claws, Serena."

"I know."

Joe exhaled before placing his hands on his knees to help himself stand up. I stepped out of the way to let him pass. My five feet and eight inches towered him. He was plump and stumpy and short. Apparently, he was a horse jockey back in his younger years. From what I'd seen, those guys were super short and fit. But it seemed those years were long behind Joe and all he had left were his three consecutive years of championship, a divorce settlement that left him broke, two kids who hated him, a dead-end job, and his emasculating height.

I followed him out into the dining room.

"Serena, you have been here too long. I shouldn't have to be doing this," he whispered as he walked toward the table.

"Yes, too long," I muttered under my breath. I stopped at the bar as he reached the table, then watched his hands express sincere apologetic gestures. Joe immediately went into ass-kissing mode, and I rolled my eyes. That man certainly didn't deserve it.

"Hey, Dan's coming on again in about five minutes," Mia said from behind the bar as she dried a wet wine glass.

She nodded at the TV screen hanging on the wall. It was almost time for the 10 o'clock news, and Dan was due to make his report about something weird that happened at a grocery store downtown, though nobody was sure what. At least, not yet.

I sat down on one of the stools and stuck my hands into my apron. "Yeah, he's been at the hospital all day."

"I don't have a good feeling about this supermarket thing," Megan chimed in. I shrugged my shoulders in reply.

Megan and Mia were by far the hottest brunettes I had ever seen in my life. They were not related, but probably could have passed off as twins with their equally long, dark hair and caramel complexion. Their makeup always looked like it was professionally applied, and they both liked to flaunt their exceptionally large breasts by leaving too many buttons undone on their uniform shirts. These girls were just what guys wanted to stare at while they sat at a bar after a long day's work. We liked to call these Latin ladies the M&M's.

A hand touched my shoulder and squeezed, then another hand met my other shoulder. The fingers dug gently into my sore muscles and massaged for a minute before stopping abruptly, forcing me to grunt and pout. "Don't stop!"

Julian sat down on the stool next to me. He pulled out a large bundle of cash from his apron and started counting.

"You did well tonight," I pointed out.

"Nah. Half of this is for the house. Oh, hey!" He stopped counting and glanced over at me. "Did you find that color you were looking for to finish your painting?"

I rolled my eyes. "No. Janis is still out of it at the shop, and I can't find it anywhere online. Every time I walk past the damn thing, I want to cry. It's just sitting on that easel, begging to be finished."

It was true. My watercolor of the view of downtown Tampa overlooking the bay at midnight was nearly complete, except for one finishing touch—a particular color that I couldn't seem to find anywhere! It was a purple hue, perfect for the reflection of the Sun Trust building's luminous roof on the water.

Julian frowned. His brows rumpled and he pursed his lips together. His top lip hid under a trimmed mustache that connected to a short, polished beard. The recessed lighting above the bar made the few strands of gray stand out more than usual. It was crazy to think he had so much gray hair now, but I always found the salt and peppery look to be kind of sexy. He was only three years older than my twenty-seven years, but the gray made him look distinguished.

He ran his fingers through his wavy locks. "That sucks. It really does." Then, he reached inside his apron and pulled out a little bottle. The glass pinged on the bar top when he set it down in front of me. "So, it's a good thing I found it for you."

I gaped at it in disbelief. "Jules," I breathed. "How did you find it?"

"I know a guy."

I gave him a skeptical glare. "You know a guy?"

"Yeah, a dealer. An art dealer," he answered, trying hard not to crack a smile, but after a second, failed miserably.

"How the... When did I..." I was speechless. Art was my livelihood. My passion. I knew from time to time I would drone on about it to him, about how I'd been searching for this stupid color for weeks now, but I didn't think he was actually listening. I should have known better, honestly, because he was Julian. My best friend. He knew how important my craft was to me. He knew it was the way I escaped the realities of the world.

He stood up from the stool and tucked a loose strand of my long, fire-red hair behind my ear, the soft skin of his fingertips slightly grazing my cheek and sending a tingle down to my neck. "See, I listen to you."

Julian DeLuca turned out to be one handsome man. He was worlds away from the lanky giant I'd met in that bus station so many years ago. His stint in the Marine Corps changed his body. Somehow, he managed to gain a couple more inches of height, and if it wasn't for my growth spurt right around my seventeenth birthday, I could have probably passed for his teenage daughter whenever we stood next to each other.

He was really muscular and tanned now. He filled out his clothes in all the right places, where it really mattered on a man—like his arms and his chest. Pretty much all the girls who worked here drooled over him. I would have to admit, I was kind of attracted to him, too. But Julian and I could never be like that. We could never be in an intimate relationship. He was my family. My only family.

I picked up the bottle of paint and mentally cursed at it. *Where have you been, you jerk?*

"Thank you so much, Jules," I said.

"You're welcome," he replied. We stared at each other a moment, silently, and blood rushed to my cheeks.

No, there was nothing between us. Julian had been in a dedicated relationship for a long time with a girl he met right before he left the military. Her name was Lenora, but she went by Lenny. She liked to smoke cigars and did CrossFit six days out of the week, her calf muscles bordering the same size as Julian's. But her facial features were very feminine, with eyebrows arched to perfection and high cheekbones that girls often tried to emulate by caking on tons of makeup and using the contour technique.

"Have you talked to...?" I absentmindedly started but stopped, sneaking a glance at Julian. He and Lenny had recently broken up, and my train of thoughts had made me forget that detail for a minute. But he seemed to know what I was referring to.

"No. She came by yesterday to grab some of her things, but we didn't say anything to each other." He sounded sad, disappointed. Not angry, despite the fact that the reason for their split was due to Lenny cheating on him.

I couldn't blame the guy, though. Lenny might be an idiot for letting Jules go, but in all the times I knew her, she was also very sweet and kind and thoughtful. One day, she'd overheard me complaining to Julian about how I was having a hard time sleeping. Then, the next day, she and Julian came over for game night with a gift. She said she had a friend who was into oils and aromatherapy, so she bought me a diffuser and a few different oils that were known to relieve stress and stimulate restful sleep. It was a very kind present, but Lenny didn't know that my sleepless nights had more to do with the years of mental anguish I'd endured than just simple everyday stress. There was only one person who knew about the hardships of growing up with an alcoholic Mom and Dad, losing my brother at a young age, and running away from home with no place to go. And even Julian didn't know *everything*. He'd probably freak out if he did.

I didn't tell him the truth about Charlie or my family or the fact that I was running away to nowhere until he returned from boot camp, and it still wasn't the entire truth. He didn't know I was homeless for the longest time. I was too ashamed. Too embarrassed. And maybe a part of me was too embarrassed to admit it to myself. Here was Julian, who came from a loving family. Even though his parents were divorced, he told me on our sixteen-hour bus ride that his mom and dad still got along really well. They even competed with each other on who could treat their only son the best, showering him with gifts and pretty much anything he wanted. Meanwhile, I dealt with parents who forgot my birthday every year because they were too drunk to remember. So, there were never any gifts. Not from them, anyway. Charlie always picked up a cupcake from the grocery store and made me a present, like a homemade journal or something.

Julian was a lot like Charlie, in a way. Maybe that was why I felt a connection with him in the bus station that night. Maybe that was why we got along so well for twelve years now. He was always looking out for me, just as Charlie did.

I remembered when we arrived in Tampa from that bus ride how he had given me his cellphone number right before he got into his dad's car. He also offered to stick around and wait with me when I lied and told him my brother was running late to pick me up, but I insisted that he didn't. It wouldn't be until a little over twelve weeks later that I would get the nerve to call the number he'd given me. By then, I was making the streets of Tampa my home, holding up a WILL WORK FOR FOOD sign and having people eye me with pity as they dropped quarters into my cup. I used those quarters to call Jules from a pay phone, until one day, realizing that he might try to call me first and find out that it was a pay phone's number, I stole a cellphone someone had left behind on a park bench. Okay, technically, I didn't steal it. It was left there, unattended, for a long period of time. Our friendship flourished with those constant conversations over the phone, but I still didn't divulge the fact that I was homeless.

I used to worry that Julian would someday run into me, all homeless and begging for food and money. But he ended up getting sent off by the Marine Corps to live somewhere else for two years, and by the time he came back, I was no longer sleeping under overpasses. Oh, and I was no longer scared of overpasses. Side note—homeless people slept a lot because it was exhausting to be homeless. All the walking and lack of food and energy and uncomfortable cardboard beds weren't good for our bodies.

"Serena, I'm going to have someone else take that table," Joe informed me as he walked past to get back to his depressing office, interrupting my thoughts.

"Yeah, I figured." I wouldn't have expected any less. Chances were that John-the-Giant-Tool requested to have a different server, which was fine by me considering it was my last table and he would have probably tipped me less than ten percent. So, I wasn't losing anything.

I glanced at Julian again, the memories of our past flooding back. When he returned to Tampa after the two years away, we finally upgraded our friendship from phone exclusivity to actually hanging out since I finally found somewhat of a decent place to rest my head. My situation had changed, but it wasn't *that* much different. I was still on the poorer side of the spectrum. When Julian found this part of my life out, he tried and tried to offer to help me financially, but I refused. I was stubborn and determined to make it on my own. And he didn't fight me on it. He understood it was what I needed to make me feel better about abandoning my crappy life and drunk mother. My mission was to prove that I could be better than my parents.

Over the years, Jules would have to travel and live in different places for work for short periods of time, but we always kept in touch and always reconnected when he returned. He became pretty much the only friend that I'd ever been able to keep close to me, even though most of the time he physically wasn't present. This was how I knew our friendship was genuine.

Harley came to mind.

"Hey, how's Harley? Are you going to see her this weekend?" I asked, pushing the nostalgia aside for a moment. Harley was Jules' little seven-year-old surprise, when four years ago, a woman showed up on his doorstep and claimed to be his baby mama. Not even kidding, I wanted to rip her to shreds for popping into Julian's life that way and for keeping him away from his kid for so long. If Julian hadn't made me promise to be nice, I might have done something that I would later regret. Or not, if she deserved it. Instead, I urged Julian to get a paternity test because...bitches be crazy. When it came back positive, I vowed to help him in any way I could.

And this was why Julian was working here with me—to have another job in order to make extra money for his daughter. His other job, the one he acquired after leaving the military, had something to do with logistics.

"She's good. Loving the paint set you gave her," he said. "She says she wants to be just like her Aunt Serena."

I smiled. Harley and I weren't terribly close, but I helped out with carpooling here and there. Having kids of my own was never an idea I entertained, and Jules knew that. Therefore, he didn't ask much from me when it came to his daughter. But he was my dearest friend and I felt it was my obligation to be there for him whenever he needed me. He was too good a person not to be.

"Are we still taking her to the art museum, then?" I asked, mentally going through my calendar.

"Yup, next weekend. If you're still up for it."

Being with a seven-year-old all day long wasn't exactly how I wanted to spend my Saturday, but Jules would be with us, so it should be tolerable.

"Yes, sir," I affirmed. "I'm up for it."

Our eyes remained locked for a beat longer and my heart fluttered.

"Serena, Dan's on," Megan announced, forcing me to finally unlock my gaze from Julian's. I promise I wasn't secretly crushing on him or anything, even though it would totally be justified if I was. But sometimes, I truly felt lucky to have him in my life and I couldn't help staring at him. I hoped that he could read in my eyes how much he meant to me.

Besides, I was completely in love with Dan.

My attention went straight to the fifty-inch TV hanging on the wall in the corner of the lounge. Gale Walters was delivering the news from her desk at the station. I'd only met her a few times, but I wasn't a fan. She was kind of snooty.

Mia turned up the volume.

"Residents are still urged to stay indoors and to be on alert for any signs of illness. The supermarket will remain quarantined and the CDC is working diligently to get those folks tested. Let's take it back to Dan Michaels one last time at Tampa General Hospital. Dan, there were some attacks being called in at the hospital. Can you tell us a little more about that and what the scene is like there tonight?"

My heart skipped a beat, as it always did when Dan was being introduced. I glanced down at my engagement ring and smiled. I couldn't wait to marry that man.

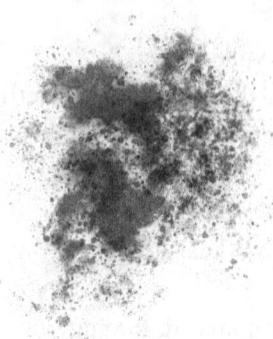

THE
SILHOUETTE

I LOVED WHEN PEOPLE asked how Dan and I met. Most of the time, I tried to forget the things that I had been through. But meeting Dan was a bright spot. The calm eye in the hurricane that was my life.

Begging for money in my vagabond days wasn't the only way I managed to get by. One of my fellow hobo buddies suggested that I start selling my drawings on a busy corner in the business district next to a popular coffee shop. My artwork was sub-par at best because I couldn't afford better quality sketch pencils, but they weren't bad. So I picked up my dirty backpack and tattered sheets and moved over to that part of town. It turned out that people actually enjoyed stopping to watch a young, poor girl draw landscapes right before their eyes, and I sold lots of pieces.

One day, a man named Jimmy, an old hippie-looking war veteran with a long white beard and a ponytail, stopped to admire my work. He was so impressed, he offered to hang some of my art in his gallery. They sold pretty fast, and it wasn't long before Jimmy offered to kind of take me under his wing. For many years, I became his art apprentice while getting my GED and living in the extra space in the back of his gallery. It was barely a studio apartment. There was no kitchen or wall between my bed and the toilet, but it was a hell of a lot better than having to pop-a-squat in between two cars, hoping no one would catch me.

Jimmy put his blood, sweat, and tears into the place. Literally. He built it all by himself. He had owned it for a very long time, and it housed many paintings from fellow artists around the city. Fast forward a few years after I moved in, when the recession hit, Jimmy was left broke. No one was interested in buying art, and he struggled to keep the gallery going. When some investors came in and offered to buy it, he had no choice but to sell. Little did he know, their plans were to knock it down and replace it with yet another coffee shop franchise.

Several local artists, including myself, banded together to protest the demolition. It was all over the local news, and Dan was assigned the field reporter for the story. The whole incident landed me my third visit to jail—the first and second were for disorderly conduct and panhandling—but it was also when I met my future fiancé.

I sat in jail for five hours before someone came to bail me out. I had no idea who it could have been. I hadn't made my one phone call for someone to come rescue me, which would have been Julian, but he was out of town so my next call would have been Jimmy. But when I was released, there Dan was, the last person I ever thought I'd see. I thought maybe he was there to interview me about the art gallery demolition. Turned out, he was so intrigued and fascinated by my devotion and passion for art that he felt like I didn't deserve to be behind bars. It was a pretty risky thing for a guy to do just to get a date. Thankfully, he allowed me to pay him back for the bail money.

Sad news, though—Jimmy died from a heart attack two days after his gallery was torn down. I lost someone and something I cared deeply about within a week, and it added to all of the heartbreak I'd already been through.

"Yes, Gale. I'm at the hospital where earlier today, we received word that there was some sort of commotion happening on the floor where the sick individuals were taken for treatment. We are currently awaiting a press conference from the Centers for Disease Control and the chief of the ER department at Tampa General, who are going to tell us a little more about the incident and the current condition of the patients."

Dan stood in the spotlight of the camera with the hospital as his backdrop. He seemed a little tired. I knew that he had been on this case ever since he got the call early yesterday morning. We were in bed when the newsroom phoned to inform him of breaking news at a downtown supermarket.

I had grown accustomed to his line of work. He was always called in at all hours of the day. Truthfully, there was no set schedule on when crime and things like that were supposed to happen. The news was unpredictable. But I'd seen Dan tired before and this was different. He was normally upbeat and alert for the camera, even when he was exhausted. But now, his eyes were drooping, his speech almost sluggish.

Dan usually made sure to keep up his appearance for television. He dressed in stylish suits and ties. He was always well-groomed. You could even say he was a metrosexual of sorts. And he wasn't a hairy guy, at all. So he always had that fresh, clean-shaven, and perfectly groomed look. However, tonight, he had a five o'clock shadow going on. He was disheveled and rough-looking. I wasn't sure if I liked it on him or not. On Julian? Sure. He was more rough and manly and rugged. But on Dan? Not so much. He was prettier and more high maintenance, which was not my usual M.O. Somehow, I tended to attract the bad boy jerks who rode motorcycles and rocked sleeve tattoos. Didn't mean to stereotype, but it was the truth in my life. Maybe it was my athletic build or tough-girl persona that attracted them to me. And maybe it was why I loved Dan so much. He was different in a great way.

"Dan, can you tell our viewers, again, what exactly happened at the supermarket today?"

He paused for the delay and nodded his head slowly.

"Yes, I arrived at the scene at Publix Supermarket on the corner of Bayshore Boulevard yesterday regarding an attack by an unknown man. Witnesses stated seeing this individual stumble into the store, bleeding from his eyes and ears and mouth. A clerk immediately ran to his aid, but the individual attacked her. After wrestling the woman to the floor, he rushed toward another customer and attacked her, too."

"Dan, how was this man able to attack five people without anyone else intervening?"

He paused again before answering. I could tell by the way he was slightly swaying that the fatigue had truly set in.

"Witnesses described seeing the man move from one person to another in quick motions. So, he basically attacked one person, and when another tried to stop him, he switched his attention to them."

"Did he have a weapon?"

Dan lifted his hand and pressed down on his ear, mimicking some sort of secret agent. He closed his eyes as if it could help to hear her better. *"What was that?"*

"Did the man have a weapon? How exactly did he go about attacking these people?"

He paused again before answering, then coughed.

"Uh, it seems that the assailant was unarmed, Gale. Witnesses say they did not see him carrying any weapons, and that he bit the victims on their neck and arms."

"Wow. This sounds like something you see in the movies, Dan. We're going to hear more about the status of the attacker by the chief of the Tampa PD in just a moment. But, Dan, before we move on to that, can you tell me what the scene is like there at the hospital?"

Delay.

"Yes, it seems to be quiet right now, Gale. Just a couple of hours ago, there were more attacks reported in the ER, but things seem to be under control. I was able to interview a witness in the emergency room and she stated that she saw one of the victims go into some type of shock. A sort of catatonic state before attacking a nurse, similar to the way the assailant attacked victims at the supermarket. But we'll be able to get the full story during the press conference."

"Yes. Thank you, Dan. We'll take a quick break, and when we return, a word from Tampa Police."

Megan muted the volume. "Um...does this not sound like a zombie attack? Remember that guy who attacked a homeless person in Miami?"

"That guy was crazy drugged out," Julian responded. "He wasn't a zombie. But I did seriously think that my days of playing video games all hours of the night were finally going to pay off."

"There would never really be zombies, right?" I asked. "I mean, that's like movie stuff."

The zombie genre seemed to have exploded over the past few years. It had come a long way since *Night of the Living Dead*, but it wasn't real. Just like werewolves and vampires. It was fictional sci-fi crap.

Megan grabbed the tip jar and began organizing the cash. "Hey, I believe in it. Why else would the CDC be involved? Obviously, there's something crazy going on."

"Meg, you really believe in that shit?" Mia snorted. "Come on! They said earlier that the CDC was there because the man at the store was clearly sick. He could have had rabies, for all they knew."

Megan pursed her lips and squinted at Mia. "You never know!"

Julian turned to me. "What do you think?"

I opened my Waiter Wallet and soothed the crinkled edges of the old picture of me and Charlie. I brushed my thumb over Charlie's teenage face before removing the photo and stuffing it into my back pocket. This was the same ritual I had been performing for a while now: place the picture in my Waiter Wallet before my shift, remove the picture from my Waiter Wallet after my shift. It never got old.

I pulled out my stack of receipts and cash and started sorting. "I think I'll get more details when Dan comes home tonight."

"Well, you better text me. I want to know, too."

I chuckled. "Of course!" Whenever Dan was on a big job, such as breaking news, he always came home with much more information than what was actually reported to the public. Most of the time it was confidential—like police or coroner reports. But he told me, anyway. And Julian was the only person I had ever shared that information with. Dan could probably get into major trouble for telling me, but he trusted me, and I trusted that Julian wouldn't tell anyone else.

I left the bar and focused on getting through the rest of my shift quickly. John the Asshole and his wife were still eating in my station. I had no doubt that he knew the restaurant was closing soon. He ate his food slowly, just as some kind of revenge on me. Having to deal with these types of people really made me want to walk back to Joe's office and quit. Although, that probably would not have been the best idea. I still sold paintings, but not enough to live on. My homeless days were behind me, and Dan and I lived pretty comfortably now. We could probably live on only his income, but I wasn't the type of woman who would allow my boyfriend/fiancé/husband to pay for everything. It was important that I contributed. There was no way I'd ever allow myself to be some deadbeat like my mom.

As I walked past the dining room, John and I made eye contact. I wondered if I could get away with dropkicking John in his face, then telling his wife to move on and never look back. Go find a real man who didn't have to treat women like shit to compensate for his tiny wiener.

I finally got to our condo right after midnight, which was my usual time. As I walked up the stairs, I could feel the weight of the double shift on my lower back. Years of working out kept me physically fit, but nothing ever seemed to prepare me for an entire day of standing, bending, and carrying trays of food.

My thighs screamed one last time before I reached the top step of the third floor. The brisk wind from the bay swirled around my face, and it felt nice. When you live in Tampa, you either live near the ocean or near the bay. This was according to my standards, of course. No one else followed this rule, that I knew of. Water was one of my most favorite elements. It was my favorite to draw. Maybe because of the various ways water could be captured— calm or flowy or turbulent, depending on my mood. And while the ocean offered a beautiful view to wake up to in the morning, the bay seemed to satisfy my artistic needs more appropriately. The buildings and the bay and the reflections went well together.

I opened the door with an eager pit in my stomach. The need to get out of my work clothes and the seafood stench was strong, but the desire to see my future husband was stronger. I parked right next to Dan's car in the parking lot, which was surprising to see because I thought he'd still be working.

"Hi, babe," I called out, shutting the door behind me before locking it. There was silence. This struck me as a bit odd. Normally, I could hear the faint sound of the news coming from our bedroom at the end of the hall when I came home. Whether Dan was sleeping or not, the news was always on around him. Also, his laptop bag would be on the kitchen counter, along with a blazer hanging off the back of the dining room chair. But neither of those things were there when I walked past.

"Dan?" I called out again, this time a little louder.

Nothing. Did I mistake his car for someone else's? I thought I'd seen his news station ID badge hanging on the rearview mirror. It had to be him. I picked up the pace down the hall, peering into each darkened room in search of Dan. My keys were still in my hand. Gripping them tight, I wedged one key between my fingers to simulate a claw. Living on my own in the streets had forced me to become more aware of my surroundings. I wasn't sure if that was a good or bad thing. It was the result of finding myself in some unsafe situations involving homeless muggers who were so desperate that they'd try to rob their own.

I finally reached the bedroom, which slightly illuminated by the light from the walk-in closet. It was purposely left on in case I got home late at night and Dan wasn't here. The door was partially closed, and I put a hand on the knob to push it open but stopped when a strange sound reached my ears.

It was breathing. Heavy, rapid breathing.

Instinct—a paranoia ingrained within from experiences throughout my life—told me to turn around and run out of the front door. But my mind told me I was being ridiculous. It had to be my fiancé. The man I loved. Maybe he was asleep. Maybe his allergies were acting up.

And then came the more sinister thoughts. What if something was wrong with him? What if he needed my help? What if someone was choking him at the same time I was trying to figure out whether or not to swing this door open?

Not only was my awareness heightened because of the years of solitude and slight addiction to watching crimes shows late at night before bedtime, but the whole supermarket ordeal was kind of freaking me out. Or maybe I was just being silly. Dan looked so worn out on the news earlier. Maybe he just came home and simply passed out on the bed.

I tightened my fist and opened the door completely. My eyes darted over to the bed, which was still neatly made from this morning. My peripheral vision caught a glimpse of a silhouette, someone sitting in the chair near the window. My heart began to race.

I flicked the light switch on the wall. It was Dan. He was sitting in the chair with his arms hanging off either side and his head slumped down to his chest. His legs were bent in an unnaturally awkward position. He was still dressed in his suit, blazer and all. I didn't call his name again because, clearly, he was out. I suddenly felt awful for him. He must have worked so hard and so long that he just couldn't take it anymore. That chair was where we sat to take our shoes off. I imagined he left his bag in the car, came in to sit and take his shoes off, but fell asleep in the process.

I walked over and knelt down in front of him, unlacing his dress shoes to help him get comfortable and into the bed. But before I could pull his left shoe off, he lifted his head in one quick motion, as if I'd abruptly awoken him out of his deep sleep.

He glared at me, and I flinched at the sight of him. "Dan? Are you okay?"

THE DAUGHTER

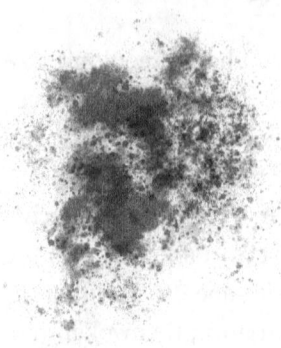

BLOOD WAS GUSHING OUT of his nose. A trail of it leading out of his ears and down his jawline and neck had already coagulated. His skin looked like it was painted a sick shade of nude, and his eyes were bloodshot...and empty, as if all the life had been sucked right out of him. His tie was still knotted and his dress shirt was still buttoned, but it was all drenched in red. He tilted his head to the side and gargled, blood dripping out of the corner of his mouth. He opened it slowly, revealing his teeth to me, and a growl escaped his throat.

We stared at each other, and I struggled to understand what he was doing. Whatever it was, I knew it wasn't right. And when my brain finally registered what was going on, I started to back away from him just as he lunged toward my neck. Before he could reach me, I swung my fist at his face, completely forgetting that the exposed key was still clutched between my fingers. It stopped him in his tracks. A gash about an inch wide and four inches long appeared across his cheek. It instantly began oozing blood, and the skin around the wound stretched farther apart as he opened his mouth wide and bellowed out a loud and strained moan. He lifted his arms and tried to charge at me again, but I pushed him back into the chair and got to my feet as fast as I could. I ran out of the room and down the hall, reaching the front door and unlocking it as if my life depended on it. My legs practically grew wings and flew down the stairs, skipping two and three steps at a time. When I finally reached my car, I jammed the key into the ignition and threw the gear into reverse. Before backing out, I took one last glance at the stairs. He wasn't there.

Was this really happening? Did Dan really just try to attack me?

I slowed my breathing and waited. I didn't know what I was waiting for. Maybe I was waiting to see him, to see if my future husband was okay. But I had been in too many situations where I waited around to see if the guy was really going to hit me or not, and ninety percent of the time, he did. As much as I made it a point not to become my mother's daughter, somehow, we seemed to have the same taste in abusive boyfriends. A couple of my low-life exes had gotten a lick on me, one even managing to give me a good right hook to the jaw. Don't worry—my left hook busted his nose pretty good.

I was an idiot back then and learned from my mistakes. And Dan was different than those other guys. He would never hurt me. Never. Something had to be terribly wrong.

Gale's voice popped into my head—the signs of illness. His nose and ears were bleeding. He didn't talk. He literally growled at me!

My hands shook as I gripped the steering wheel and peered out of the windshield. There was still no sign of him. The deafening silence in my car made me even more nervous. Thank God I hadn't taken off my crossbody purse when I initially entered the condo. I reached inside to pull out my phone. The first person to come to mind was Julian, but I didn't dial his number. My fingers glided across 9-1-

1 instead, then the speakerphone button. A busy signal echoed loudly into my quiet car and I hurriedly shut it off, afraid that the sound might alert Dan. How the hell was 911 busy?

I backed out of the parking spot and began to drive out of the complex. When my eyes traveled to the rearview mirror again, my foot involuntarily slammed on the brakes.

There he was.

I twisted around in my seat to get a better view. Dan stumbled down the steps, off the curb, and seemed to be walking aimlessly around the parking lot. His feet were shuffling, and his arms hung at his sides as if he didn't know how to use them. I didn't stick around any longer. As much as it pained me to leave him like that, I had to get the hell out of the parking lot. I stomped on the gas and finally made it out onto the main road. There wasn't another car in sight. It was past midnight now, but it was still unlikely that the roads would be this empty. I remembered Gale urging residents to stay indoors.

It was safe to say that Dan was infected. But how? Did he come in contact with one of those people from the supermarket or the hospital? I knew how demanding and important his job was, but I always worried about him when he had to report something serious. I wanted to believe that Dan was smart enough to be careful when he was on the scene of a crime. He told me himself that safety came first, no matter how big the story was.

I reached a stoplight and glanced down at my phone. My hands were still shaking, but my fingers managed to dial Julian's number. It rang. No answer.

Hi. You've reached Julian—

I hung up. Leaving a voicemail might be pointless. I needed to talk to him now! Maybe he would text me right back.

Serena: *Julian, please call me. ASAP.*

A bang on my window made me jump in my seat and I immediately leaned away from the door.

"Please! Please, help me!" a woman cried, both palms of her hands pressed against the glass. I quickly examined her, trying to find any signs of whether or not she was infected. No bleeding from her nose or her eyes. She didn't appear to be growling. Actual words and sentences were forming from her mouth.

"My boyfriend! He tried to kill me! I think he's sick! I ran away and I just need to get somewhere safe! Please, just give me a ride!"

I glanced at her wrist when she began thumping on the window in hysterics. It was bleeding from a wound in the shape of a mouth.

"I'm sorry," I said, feeling horrible. "I can't."

Her cries got louder as she pleaded, "Please! Please! Don't leave me here! He'll find me!"

The light turned green, and even though my heart ached for this woman, my mind told me to get the hell out of there. She had clearly been bitten, and I couldn't let her in this car.

I turned my gaze straight ahead and slammed on the gas. The tires of my car screeched against the concrete road.

"Please!"

Her screams followed me down the street a few blocks until they faded, and soon I could no longer see her in my rearview mirror. If this was anything like a zombie movie, I did the right thing. That wound could have been anything else, but I wasn't going to take my chances. If I could leave my fiancé behind, then there was absolutely no way I was about to pick up a total stranger who could have been infected with some contagious virus.

Julian didn't live too far from me. I focused on getting to him as quickly as I could. It was certainly helpful that there was no one else around, including cops.

The M&Ms came to mind and our conversation at the restaurant bar. I hadn't been able to really speak to Dan about this whole situation since the attack at the supermarket. He had been on the scene the entire time, so I hadn't gotten my usual dose of extra information. I knew as much as the public did at this point, which was that some guy—who was probably drugged out—walked into the supermarket and began attacking people. Those people who were attacked were brought to the hospital, where they attacked more people. The victims became the attackers, and I assumed that this kind of thing worked like a domino effect. Sooner or later, it would get out of control and would be harder to contain, and then BOOM! We've got ourselves a zombie freaking apocalypse. I hoped I was wrong, though. There was no way that zombies were real.

I pulled up to Julian's little one-story bungalow a few minutes later. He was one of the people who preferred to live near the beach. I hopped out of my car and hurried up to his doorstep. There was a light on inside the house, but his truck wasn't in the driveway. Shit. He must not be home. I knocked anyway.

No answer.

And right as I looked down at my phone to send another text message, the headlights from his truck lit up the front of the house. Julian jumped out of the driver's seat without shutting the door behind him and jogged over to me.

"Serena," he huffed, putting one hand on my shoulder and one on my face. He turned my head from side to side, examining my skin and my eyes. "Are you okay?"

The feel of his concerned hands searching my face threatened to force my emotions to spill over. I couldn't remember the last time I cried. This wasn't by choice. I had become immune to disappointment and loss over the years, and it seemed like all my tears had just...dried up.

I swallowed hard. "I'm okay," I lied. A scratching noise forced my glance over at his truck. "What was that?"

His hands dropped to his sides. "Serena, this is serious."

"What exactly is happening?"

A helicopter, flying lower than I'd ever seen before, hovered directly above our heads. I looked up but couldn't tell what kind it was. It could have been a news chopper or police, but it was too dark to make it out.

"It's a zombie outbreak," he said.

"That's crazy, Julian!" I knew it had to be true, but I just couldn't wrap my head around it. Another clamor from his truck interrupted, followed by what registered in my brain as rattling chains. "What is that noise?"

He grabbed my hand and yanked me toward the back of the truck. I peered over the edge and noticed some movement under a green tarp that covered the entire bed.

"Julian?"

He unlatched the door and pulled it down before climbing in to uncover what was underneath. I gasped.

Harley, his daughter, was lying flat on her back, her wrists and feet bound by chains. She didn't appear to be trying to get out of her restraints, but rather, she seemed to be sort of squirming in slow motion. Her little pink nightgown was coated in blood, and I hoped that it wasn't her own. She moaned and snarled as she stared pie-eyed at the sky.

"Julian," I rasped. "Is she... How did this happen to her?" He bent down near her bare feet and touched her toes. I wanted to touch her, too. Make sure I was really looking at a little girl in chains. But I didn't.

I usually wasn't too fond of children, probably because I never had friends that we kinds my age when I was growing up. No one wanted to be friends with the girl whose parents were always drunk and belligerent. And during my homeless time, I wasn't exposed to a lot of kids.

But Julian's daughter had always held a special little place in my heart, probably because *he* meant so much to me. She was his mini-me. A tiny female version of Julian. They looked so much alike that it was kind of scary—the same long body, mocha-colored hair, hazel eyes, squared, strong jawline, thick eyebrows. They also acted the same. Harley was still young, but she possessed the same determination and warrior mentality that the military had drawn out of Julian. At the same time, both of their hearts were sweet and innocent and generous, which overpowered everything else. I sometimes worried that the women Julian dated would take advantage of his soft core, and I hoped that Harley might grow up to have a little more gall. It wasn't okay to be an asshole all the time, but it might be necessary in some life situations. Maybe it was something I could teach her because I had lots of nerve collected over the years, which was distributed evenly to people who deserved it.

"Is she...infected?" I whispered, worried that Harley would hear me and get scared by the word *infected*. Leaning in closer, I inspected her body. Her pale skin was almost translucent and the blue veins in her arms pulsed rapidly.

She stared up at the sky, her eyes bloodshot and making swift movements, as if to be counting the stars. Dried blood left a trail from her nose and ears down her neck...just like with Dan.

"I'm pretty positive she is," Julian said as he knelt down beside her.

"Jules, this can't be a zombie outbreak. That can't happen. It's not real."

"It is, Serena. I drove downtown. It's already crazy there. The cops don't know what they're doing, and people are already rioting and turning."

"Turning? How did this happen so quickly? I just don't understand how this could get so out of control so fast."

Julian tucked his arms under his daughter and lifted her up as if she weighed no more than a sack of potatoes. She continued squirming and bit at the space between his face and hers. He leaned his head back, but he didn't seem afraid at all.

He jumped down from the truck. "Grab my keys and unlock the door," he instructed. I did what I was told, following close behind him as he walked in and set Harley down gently on the couch. Julian wrapped the chains that restricted Harley's motility around the couch's feet, furthering the hindrance of her movements. "Vanessa was supposed to meet me here after her shift at the hospital. She was letting me have Harley a few extra days this month because she and Tommy made plans to take a vacation."

Vanessa and Tommy were Harley's mother and stepfather. The three adults who cared for this little girl had a pretty good relationship. When Vanessa had shown up to tell Julian he was a father years ago, they had both agreed to do what was best for their daughter's happiness. None of the holding grudges crap. Harley had been born out of a one-night stand, and Julian had told me that he and Vanessa were not compatible at all—which was why they never rekindled any romance between them. Besides, Tommy, the stepdad, adored Harley, treating her as his own. So it all worked out anyway.

As silly and ridiculous as it sounded, being that I was a woman almost in her thirties, I kind of envied Harley for having three parents who cared so deeply for her, when I had none.

Julian continued. "But when she didn't show up, and they didn't answer any of my phone calls, I got worried because of all the attacks Dan was reporting at the hospital." Both Tommy and Vanessa were nurses at Tampa General Hospital. "I jumped in the truck and drove down to their house to make sure everything was okay." He took a blanket off the back of his couch and covered Harley with it.

"You found her like this?"

"She was kneeling down over Vanessa...eating..." He choked on his words. I took a step forward and rested a hand on his shoulder, but before I could offer any comfort, Julian shook his head and took a deep breath as if to try to erase that memory. "This is happening so fast because it's zombies, Serena. It's exactly what we see on TV. It's a highly contagious virus, and no one was prepared for it."

"Well, what are we going to do?"

"I don't know. But I have to take care of my daughter. If there's a cure or something, she has to get it."

"How are we going to keep her safe?"

He turned toward me and wrinkles in his forehead appeared. "Wait, where's Dan? Is he still at the hospital?"

I glanced down at floor. Again, my emotions threatened to break down my wall, but I didn't allow it. Julian knew exactly what had happened without me saying a word, and before I knew it, his strong arms were wrapped around my body. His warmth felt comforting, but I pulled away.

"I left him at our condo. I tried calling 911, but all I got was a busy signal. I didn't know what else to do, so I came here."

"You did the right thing by leaving him. I mean, look at what she did to her own mom." He took my hand and guided me to the loveseat against the wall, parallel to the sofa his daughter was on.

"So, do we leave?" I asked, genuinely confused. I had no idea what we should do next. I was prepared to take care of myself when it came to being out on the streets. I was mugged a few times—held up once by gunpoint—back in those homeless days. When I got older and could afford it, I took self-defense classes. My purse always had two essential items: the picture of Charlie and me, and mace. When I felt like the time was right, I purchased a legal firearm, which was kept in the glovebox of my car. I sometimes wondered if that was the reason why guys felt prone to physically hurting me. Maybe they were intimidated by me. Fearful that I had the ability to kill them if I really wanted to.

But what the hell was I supposed to do to a zombie? From everything I'd seen, the most popular way to take them down was a shot to the brain. But having to kill someone? It was something I had thought about on more than one occasion. It was what came along with surviving on the streets. There were many times when a hobo friend of mine was found dead in the gutter. Death was too close for comfort for a long time. And while I was pretty sure I didn't have a problem pulling a trigger to protect myself and my best friend, it was still a scary concept to take a life—sick or not.

"I think we should stay here," Julian suggested. "At least for the first few days. Chances are, the roads and main highways to get out of town are already congested. And it just seems riskier if we leave now. With the looters and zombies roaming around, it's even more dangerous to be out in the streets."

He had a good point.

"Well, aren't people going to help? What's the news saying? What about the military?" I assumed this was one of those situations that called for armed forces. Julian had been out of the military for a few years, but he still had friends who were active. They might have had some information that could benefit us.

He stood up and walked toward the front door, moving the curtain that covered a small, rectangular window near the door. He peeked outside.

"I don't know. I could try to call Sergeant Gomez or someone to see if they can tell us what to do. I tried to turn the news on earlier, but all the channels show that blue emergency message. We only have the radio."

Harley let out a long, deep moan and I glanced over at her. I wanted to ask Julian what his plans were with her. Was he going to keep her chained up? Did he plan on feeding her? If she was a zombie, they had to eat, right? But they ate living things. Wasn't he scared?

He rushed over to her side. "We can stay here. We have time to get what we need to secure the house. Maybe some boards for the windows. Some food and water. This thing just started. I'm sure the looters haven't gotten everything yet," he said, combing his fingers through Harley's hair.

I still couldn't comprehend how this happened. Just a couple of hours ago, I was at work and everything seemed normal. How does a city go from normal to on the verge of being overrun by zombies in such a short period of time?

The restaurant came to mind, and I wondered if Megan, Mia, and my co-workers were okay. Something told me that being belittled by an asshole customer was much better than my current situation.

THE PASSWORD

WE SAT IN THE living room, quietly watching Harley as her little-girl monster-ish groans filled the space.

"Dan's laptop," I mumbled, breaking through the ominous air Julian's daughter was forcing around us.

"What?"

I stared off into the distance, picturing the laptop. It wasn't in its usual spot on the kitchen counter. It had to be in his car. He must not have gotten really sick until he got home. Otherwise, he would not have been able to drive. So he had to have left it in his car.

"His laptop. When he gives me all that extra information on breaking news, it comes from his laptop. I think he documents everything on there. Maybe we can find out what's really going on."

"Serena, it's clearly a zombie outbreak. I know it's hard to believe, but this is no shit really happening."

"I know it's happening, Jules. But maybe he had some important information that wasn't reported to the public. Maybe there could be some place for us to go. Some place to get help. I don't know. There could be anything. Dan has friends all over the place, including government friends and police force friends. Maybe they can help us."

He glared at me as if I was nuts. "You really want to go back there?"

I paused and thought about it. I really didn't want to see Dan as a zombie and risk being attacked by him again. But there might be something useful on his laptop.

"Dan is all about his work, you know that. He takes notes constantly. Every little thing he does, every conversation, every phone call."

Julian stood up and left the living room. Two minutes later, he returned, snapping a clip into the magazine well of his pistol before tucking it into his jeans.

"Where's yours?"

"Right here," I said, pulling the handle out of my purse just enough for him to get a peek. I might have been distraught by Dan's attack, but I remembered to pull my .380 semi-automatic out of the glovebox before knocking on Julian's door. Julian actually picked this one out for me. I normally carried a smaller pistol, but he insisted that I needed something with more power. We went target shooting once every two months, a hobby that we both enjoyed doing. He taught me a lot about how to handle a firearm—not that it was really that hard to do. You point and shoot. But it was much better when you could point and shoot and actually feel confident about what you're doing. Julian also taught me how to respect a powerful weapon that could kill you...even when you were unsuspecting and sleeping soundly in your bed. I didn't want Charlie's death to affect me that way. I didn't want to allow an inanimate object to harness a deep fear. So, with my best friend's help, I learned to hone an appreciation for something that could possibly save my life one day. Dan wasn't into guns as much as Julian and I were, but he entertained me by accompanying us every now and then. And I adored him for that.

"This is what we're going to do," Julian began. I trusted Julian with every ounce of myself, so I listened intently. "You know the garage around the corner where I work on my truck?"

I nodded. An old man named Barnaby, who was always high from prescribed medical marijuana cigarettes, owned the shop, and for a small fee, allowed Julian to tinker on his vintage truck there. Sometimes, when Dan was working and I needed a break from painting, I'd sit on a spare tire and incorrectly hand Julian all of the tools he called out to me from under the engine.

"Barnaby went on another one of his gambling vacations to Vegas, but he left me the keys in case I wanted to work on the truck while he was gone. We can't take Harley with us on a supply run. It's too dangerous right now for us to try to protect ourselves and her. I know it's not the conventional thing to do but locking her up seems to be our only option to keep her safe. I can't leave her here and risk looters or the cops busting in and harming her. Let's hide her there while we go get what we need."

He seemed skeptical of his own plan. I was sure that he questioned whether or not he was being a good dad. I tried to back him up on it.

"Yeah, I think that's a good idea."

"After we drop her off, we'll head over to your condo, pick up the laptop, stop at a store to get some supplies, then pick up Harley and get back here."

I nodded in approval, although the number of things we needed to do worried me a bit. He leaned over the couch to scoop Harley up into his arms. I opened the front door and stepped aside while he carried her out to the bed of the truck. She continued to growl and snap at the air, breathing heavily and generating a sound that no human being should be able to make. My heart ached for Julian's poor little girl.

Julian and I hopped into the old truck and drove off down the street. The garage was exactly around the corner from his house—a small, single-story establishment that could only fit two cars at once. It was one of those places that was tucked away behind more prevalent businesses. You wouldn't know it was there unless you actually knew Barnaby, who shortened his client list years ago when he got too old and tired to work on cars. Now, he just rented the space and his tools to close friends and spent most of his time in out-of-town casinos, trying to pick up cocktail waitresses who could be young enough to be his granddaughter.

Julian cradled Harley in his arms while I worked to get the padlock opened. Glancing around first to make sure no one was sneaking up behind us, I lifted up the latch and rolled the metal door up. Darkness enveloped us as we stepped inside, and the smell of aged and oxidized tools coated the inside of my nose.

"Take that and lay it down on the floor behind those boxes," he instructed, pointing his chin at the dirty sheet that partially covered the only vehicle parked in the space. "We'll try to conceal her the best we can."

I laid the cloth down and moved out of the way so he could set Harley on top of it. He did it ever so gently, as if she were made out of glass.

"We'll be back, baby. I promise," he whispered softly to her, caressing her forehead. She obviously had no clue what he was saying and only tried the best she could to reach his hand with her mouth. He stared at her for a moment longer before standing up and punching the wall next to him. I jumped at the forceful bang of his fist meeting the sheetrock, which made all the tools hanging on the pegboards shake and bounce. I didn't say anything, realizing that he just needed this moment to release the frustration that must be gnawing at him.

Julian was not one to get angry. He had a forgiving heart, which I both admired and loathed at the same time. There were times when I'd wake up in the morning and tell myself, *You'll be kinder today. You'll be more understanding and more positive.* On good days, I managed to live by these affirmations. Julian and Dan actually had a huge hand in my happiness. But then there were the bad days, when I'd be in my head and the only colors I'd use for my paintings were from the darker shades of the palette. I would struggle to smile because my heavy past never ventured too far from my thoughts. And if it did, it wasn't for long.

But Jules always had a good attitude. About everything. All the time. Even when he learned that Vanessa had kept Harley from him all those years. Even when he got medically discharged from the military for blowing his knee out, which was pretty disappointing because he loved his job. He didn't anticipate leaving the Marine Corps until he was forced to retire. I loved his positivity, but every now and then it would get under my skin. No one could be that happy all the time. Or rather, it was unfair, and I was jealous.

After about five minutes of watching Julian pace the dank garage and shake off an explosion of fury, he finally came to his senses.

"Ready?" he asked as if nothing had happened.

"Yeah."

He rolled down the door and secured it with the padlock.

"Do you think anyone is going to come loot this place?"

"Probably not. We'll try not to be too long, anyway."

We reached the truck as quickly as we could. We were both on high alert, scanning our surroundings in search of zombies or people with ill intentions. It always seemed like the bad people came out when there was a crisis. Kind of like how cockroaches only came out in the dark. And looting always seemed to be a major issue. I recalled watching footage of Hurricane Katrina on the news and seeing people run down the streets, lugging big-screen televisions and mink coats in the pouring rain. What was the point in that? Did they think they were going to turn around and sell it for money? No one wants a TV without power and a mink coat in August!

There were also reports of shootings and crimes happening during the disaster. Having lived around criminals, hobos, and addicts most of my life, it wasn't hard to imagine people acting this way during a catastrophic event. Hell, I might have participated in the hoodlum activity if I were still living on the streets. Only, I would steal things that I could have used, like food and water.

The drive to my condo was quiet for the first five minutes.

"Do you want to take Dan to my house? We can keep him safe there," Julian asked, breaking the silence.

"I don't know. Would we only be endangering ourselves? We don't know when this thing is going to get better...or if there is a cure or something." I hesitated before saying that last bit. I knew the whole reason Julian captured his daughter and chained her up was because he held out hope for some kind of cure. I didn't want to discourage him.

"You never know, Serena," he said dryly. I recoiled back into the seat at his tone, which was a lot more salty than he'd ever spoken to me before.

"Are you okay?"

He nodded.

I turned toward the window and stared out into the vacant streets. Every now and then we would pass a few people standing out on their porches or packing up their cars. But for the most part, this area of the city seemed pretty empty.

"Where is everyone?" I whispered my thoughts out loud.

"This is only the beginning. It'll get worse."

I didn't respond. I contemplated his words. *It'll get worse.* Funny thing was, it made total sense to me. The whole state was going to catch wind of what was happening at the hospital in Tampa. People would become afraid and panic, and things would get chaotic. But I still couldn't understand how we were suddenly in the middle of a zombie outbreak. How could this be real? How were Dan and Harley infected?

He turned the old radio on in the restored 1950s truck and tuned the dial until there was the sound of a news anchor's voice.

"*...this warning. Do not panic. The CDC and Tampa Police are requesting that all residents stay indoors. As of right now, it seems the threat is mainly isolated at Tampa General Hospital.*"

Julian let out a throaty, sarcastic chuckle. "They obviously don't know shit."

"*The hospital has been quarantined temporarily. It seems right now that this unknown virus is not airborne. The CDC states it is too early to tell exactly how this disease is spread, but by the rate of infection and some of the events that have taken place, they are certain it is not spread through the air.*"

"No shit!" Julian yelled at the radio.

"If you or anyone you know has symptoms of aggressiveness; bleeding from the eyes, ears, or nose; vomiting; nausea; or diarrhea, please dial 911 and help will be sent—"

He turned it off. "That's obviously a recording."

I pulled out my phone. "Maybe we should try to call again. For Harley and Dan."

"It's pointless. The hospitals are going to be overrun soon. And I won't put my daughter there. It'd be like I'm sending her off to die. I would rather keep her safe myself. Ride this thing out and survive until there is a cure."

Julian's way of thinking worried me, but I had to believe he knew what was best for his daughter.

We pulled into the condo complex cautiously. I told Julian to drive slowly and to keep his eyes peeled for Dan, as this was the last place I'd seen him. But when we got closer to my building and the parking spot, there was no Dan in sight.

"Do you think he would have gone back into the condo?" I asked, but I already knew the answer to that. Chances were that whatever sickness he got had disabled his way of thinking. He wouldn't have thought of going back into our house. Zombies moped around aimlessly, with no particular destination in mind.

"No," Julian answered as he pulled his gun out from behind him. "He probably doesn't even know where he is right now."

I used my spare key to Dan's sedan to retrieve his laptop bag. Thankfully, it was where I had suspected.

We walked up the stairs to the third floor. The condo door was still wide open. Before I could cross the threshold, Julian snatched a hold of my wrist.

"I'm going in first," he said, holding the gun out in front of him. He stepped in slowly, similar to the way a cop would before entering an unknown and dangerous environment. But Julian did know this place. He had been here plenty of times with his girlfriend (ex-girlfriend now) for dinner parties and game nights. If I wasn't with Dan, I was with Julian, either here at my house or his.

I pulled the gun out of my purse, clutching the pistol grip tight as I followed close behind him. The inside looked the same as it did before, completely untouched. There was no sound. No heavy breathing. No moaning. I peered into the kitchen to ensure it was safe before setting the bag down on the counter.

"Go ahead. I'll check the rest of the place," Julian said.

I clicked around Dan's computer and searched. Julian came into the kitchen a couple of minutes later. "It's all clear."

It didn't take long before I found a folder titled *WORK*. After double-clicking on the icon, an obnoxious ding sounded from the computer, followed by a popup window that demanded a password.

"Damn it. Do you know it?" Julian said.

I closed my eyes and pictured Dan sitting on the bed next to me, partially covered with the blankets and his computer on his lap. He always did work in bed before we turned out the lights. I tried to envision myself watching him click into this folder and typing in the password, mentally picturing his fingers moving across the keyboard and the sound of his fingertips clicking the letters.

And after he was done working, he would lean over to turn his lamp off on the nightstand, then scoot closer toward my lips to give me a sweet goodnight kiss before nuzzling up to my body. My heart tightened with sadness at the thought of never creating new memories with Dan like that again.

Clenching my jaw tight and shaking my head, I fought off the emotions. Suddenly, there it was. In my mind, clear as day.

I typed *0607Brooklyn* into the little window—the date of our first kiss and the city where he first told me he loved me. The screen changed and I was in.

God, he loved me so much.

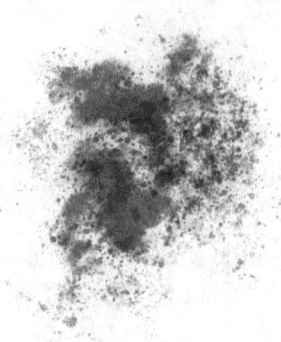

THE DOCTOR

JULIAN AND I BOTH leaned in to analyze the information. The document contained pages and pages of words. Sentences. Paragraphs. Notes. Phone numbers. Dates. Times. It seemed disorganized, which was very unlike Dan. He was clean and meticulous at home. But I figured work would sometimes be too busy and hectic for him to keep things in order.

The feeling of being rushed loomed over me, so I skimmed through his words as quickly as I could.

> ***Wednesday 1/31***– *A call was made to 911 regarding an attack at the Publix supermarket on the corner of Bayshore Blvd.*
>
> ***On the scene 3 p.m.*** *– 5 people were attacked by one man. Appears to be in his late 20s. Caucasian. No weapons involved. Witnesses state seeing the man biting victim's neck, face, and arms. Assailant bleeding from ears and nose. Victims were taken to Tampa General Hospital. Assailant detained and taken to Tampa General.*

Okay, these were all things we already knew.

> ***Tampa General 5 p.m.*** *– Victims are held in the emergency room for evaluation of wounds.*

Major blood loss. Assailant is strapped down and on 50/50 hold. Assessed for source of bleeding. Not complying with police.

6 p.m. – *Witnesses state one of the victims attacked nurse in the ER. Nurse is in critical condition.*

6:15 p.m. – *Witnesses state other 4 victims are showing signs of aggression. Commotion reported in the ER involving other patients, as well as doctors and nurses. Same symptoms as assailant. Bleeding from ears and nose most notable.*

6:30 p.m. – *CDC is requesting everyone stay indoors. Diagnosis of some kind of virus. No drugs in victim's toxicology report. Awaiting press conference.*

7 p.m. – *Received return phone call. Dr. Julie Gaines of the CDC states too early to tell where this virus began.*

7:30 p.m. – *Spoke to Jay Inglewood. States possible unknown connection to a doctor by the name of Mark Walker. Awaiting return phone call from Dennis for info.*

9 p.m. – *Gained access to emergency room before lockdown. Multiple victims. Few fatalities.*

That was it. No more information. This must have been when he was attacked. My stomach did a sickening roll as I imagined how it could have happened. Where had he been...bitten? I didn't remember seeing any wounds on his body. Then again, I was too busy running away from the man I loved so much before he could dig his teeth into my flesh.

Julian unexpectedly slammed his fist into the granite countertop before storming off in a huff. I flinched at his sudden fit of rage, but I understood. Dan was his friend, too.

I remained quiet. If I were to speak now, tears were definitely going to follow. I had to do something else to distract my mind. I minimized the folder and clicked the Internet browser, which already had a few tabs opened. My finger glided over the mouse pad and tapped the first one. A page that looked like a newspaper article appeared with the headline: ***104-Year-Old Woman Says She's Ready for Her Next Adventure***. Below the bold letters was a picture of an elderly African American woman with a silver bun on top of her head, smiling wide as she stands next to a piece of furniture filled inch by inch with picture frames. They were mostly black and white photos, all capturing the woman at varying ages of her life. Some candids and some posed. The woman playing the piano. The woman sitting on an elephant. The woman surrounded by little children wearing only underwear to cover their genitals. The woman standing on the ledge of a cliff, gazing out onto a seemingly never-ending mass of mountains.

Skimming through the article, I could tell that this was just a puff piece about the oldest woman to ever live in the small town of White Water Creek, Arkansas. It was the story of her life and all of the things someone could do in one hundred years. It was odd, but there had to be a reason why Dan did a search for this woman.

I clicked on the next tab, which opened to a picture of a man wearing a white lab coat with his arms folded over his chest, giving the camera a sideways glance and showing all of his teeth in an over-exuberant grin. His pose was the quintessential "Hi. I'm a doctor, and I can help cure you." His short, dark hair was parted, combed over, and gelled like he was ready for a noir film, and his round gold-rimmed glasses sold the need to prove that he was a medical physician. Underneath the creepy eagerness behind his eyes was a pretty handsome man. I stared at the picture for a moment before reading the caption that accompanied the photo: *Dr. Mark Walker, MD, PhD, Biochemist, Author, Philanthropist.* There were a couple of links to books he had written and phone numbers and locations to his offices.

"Serena, we should really get going before people start looting all the stores," Julian warned, poking his head in from outside the front door.

"Okay." But I didn't stop. Hoping to find a headline that read: *How to Kill Zombies in Tampa, Florida*, I hurriedly scrolled through the rest of Dan's Google searches. Maybe there was some other information somewhere. How to stop the infected? How not to get infected? Would there even be any stories written and published yet? I wondered why Dan was reading this particular information. What did this doctor have to do with anything? Or the old lady? If my fiancé was trying to find things out, then it meant that other news anchors and news stations were right behind him. Because that was how the news worked. In the end, it was all just a competition.

Finally giving up when I realized there was nothing else to find, I closed the laptop and placed it back into the bag. I glanced around the kitchen, realizing that this was probably my last time in my home. At least for a long time. The idea of leaving felt heavy on my body. It took so much work to get to this point in my life. To a point where I felt comfortable and accomplished and happy. Now, it all seemed so fragile. Like if I blinked, I would be right back in that crappy neighborhood, listening to my crappy parents spit out vile curse words to each other through the walls of my bedroom.

I jogged into the bedroom and pulled a suitcase out of the walk-in closet. Opening every drawer, I grabbed handfuls of clothes and crammed it all into the bag. Dan would have had a fit if he were here watching me do this. It seemed like only yesterday, he had given me a class on how to efficiently pack a travel bag. I loved how passionate he felt about everything. Even unimportant things like luggage organization.

I walked back into the kitchen to find Julian pulling items out of the pantry and placing them into a grocery bag. "We need to stock up."

I nodded in agreement and started helping him.

Once we packed as much as we could, Julian and I both carried everything out of the condo and down the stairs. It was silent outside, which was surprising. I would have imagined people filling their cars with all of their valuables just like we had seen earlier on our way here, but it seemed no one in the area was even awake. Cars were still parked in the lot. It was a small complex, with only two buildings that were three stories tall. There were about fifty occupants in each. Maybe they were all just listening to what the news said and staying indoors.

Julian placed the bags in the bed of the truck before reaching over to take what I was holding in my hands. I walked around to the passenger side and pulled the handle. But before I could open the door, a force on my back shoved my body against the metal frame. I winced at the pain of my breasts smashing into the window. The sound of heavy breathing resonated in my left ear and I spun around as fast as I could. It was Dan. His mouth was covered in blood and it dripped down to his neck and shirt. But it wasn't dry. It was wet and fresh.

He opened his mouth wide and hissed. I tried to step away from him as quickly as I could, but he instantaneously brought his hand up and pinned my shoulders against the truck, restricting my movements. He was somehow incredibly strong.

"Serena!" I heard Julian's muffled yell from inside the truck.

Recalling the many hours spent with my self-defense instructor, Officer Grant, at the YMCA, I brought my fists together. While Dan's arms stretched straight out ahead of him and his hands pushed on my shoulders, I lifted my arms up between his and separated them outward in a rapid motion, causing him to release my shoulders and lose his balance a bit. At the same exact time, I kicked my leg up and rammed my foot right into his crotch. Instead of the usual hands-to-the-groin reaction, he simply fell to his knees. There was no pain-stricken expression on his face. No sound. Nothing. It was as if it didn't even happen.

Julian came around the truck with his gun in hand, aimed and ready to fire.

"You okay?" he asked, his eyes shifting from Dan to me, then Dan again.

"Yeah." I looked down at Dan, who was now on all fours and struggling to get to his feet. He seemed helpless, as if he were a little toddler learning to walk again. I squeezed my eyes shut, feeling my heart tighten. I knew what had to be done.

"Just do it," I urged Julian.

"Serena, we can just leave him. We don't have to—"

"If you don't, he'll hurt someone else. Just end it!" I turned away but could feel Julian's eyes on me. And then, not a minute later, the gunshot rang through my ears.

This was it. This was the moment, after more than a decade, that my emotions were finally going to break the barrier. The tall wall that I had successfully built to protect myself from getting hurt. There was no way I could hold my feelings in any longer.

Julian wrapped his arms around me from behind and squeezed, which only forced a powerful surge of tears to overflow. I leaned forward and bawled uncontrollably, my body heaving in desperate attempts to breath normally. I could feel Julian's arms tighten around my waist every time I nearly fell to the ground. The man I loved was just killed. My life. My family. My everything.

When my throat finally started to burn too much from all of the wailing, I quieted down and wiped my nose with the back of my long-sleeved work shirt, sucking in a large breath of seafood stink before pushing Julian's arms away from me. As much as I was grateful to have him with me, I suddenly felt like I didn't want to be touched.

Julian stepped back, giving me space. "You okay?"

"Yeah," I mumbled. I kept my eyes away from Dan's body, afraid that seeing it lifeless on the ground would only cause another violent crying episode.

"Should we take him with us?" Julian asked in a low voice. I knew why he asked that question and I felt exactly the same. I didn't want to leave the love of my life out in the middle of the road. Dead. But I had no idea what we could do with him. How could we could even bury him? And what about a funeral? How could we have one in the middle of a zombie apocalypse?

I was speechless. But Julian must have sensed my inner turmoil because he said, "Get in the truck. I'll put him in the back."

We stepped over Dan's body, and right as Julian was opening the passenger door for me, a long and agonized roar came from below us.

Julian's eyes widened in sheer shock. "What the hell?"

THE
STORE

DAN WAS LAID FLAT on his back with one arm stretched out high above him, grabbing at the air. His lips receded back, revealing bloodstained teeth. There was a bullet-sized hole in the side of his head, but it was barely wet with blood.

"Shit! He's not dead!" Julian yelled and pointed, as if I wasn't already gawking at the same thing.

"Why not?" I asked, confused and freaked out. The whole world knew how to kill a zombie. The universal standard was to shoot, stab, bludgeon—anything that resulted in penetration to the brain. Julian shot Dan right in the skull. I was staring at the proof. But Dan wasn't dead. He was moving and moaning and now trying to stand up. "What do we do?"

Julian yanked me away before Dan could swipe at my ankles as he absentmindedly shambled up to his feet.

"I have no idea!" Jules grabbed my arm and pulled me around to the driver side of the truck before opening it and practically throwing me inside. I slid over to the passenger seat and watched Dan finally get to an upright position. He slowly ambled over to my window and pressed his hand up against it. I stared straight into his empty, red eyes. They were lost, as Dan was lost. He was no longer in his body.

There was no life left in him. As he moaned and pressed harder against the glass, I placed my hands over his, the see-through barrier protecting his clawing fingernails from cutting into my skin. My heart broke with every bite he took at the air. The cries and screams erupted out of me and I was unable to contain my ache for him. I knew I was losing him. The undeniable instinct threatened to make me gag. I knew that this would be the last time I'd ever see him again. It was the last time he would ever look like the man who chose to love me unconditionally, even with all of the baggage I carried every minute of every day. Through all of my mood swings and highs and lows. He would never love me again, and I was afraid he was my last chance at happiness.

I wanted to hug him so badly. Rid him of this disease. Nurture him and bring him back to life—the same way he brought me back to life. But he was glaring at me with menace, and I knew he only wanted one thing. To kill me.

The sound of the old truck engine coming to life roared over my tortured sobs, and sooner than I wanted to, we were backing up and driving away from my Dan. I howled and cursed and beat at the window, not completely believing that this was what I had to do. Julian rubbed my back and stayed silent, allowing me to bawl into the vinyl seat. He let me cry until my breathing slowed and my heart stopped racing from the agonizing loss of my future. He let me cry until I finally closed my heavy eyes and gave in to the grief.

My eyes rolled back into focus as a hand gently nudged my shoulder.

"Serena," Julian whispered.

Exhaustion weighed down on my head like an anvil. I stretched my body as much as I could in the seat and glanced out of the windshield in front of me. We were parked in front of an *Ace Hardware* store. The parking lot was completely secluded, and we seemed to be surrounded by trees.

"Where are we?"

"I had to drive us out a little ways to get somewhere safe. All of the other stores in the city are being looted."

Did he take us to another state? I couldn't recall ever seeing a lone hardware store in the middle of a forest in our city. But I didn't question him. I didn't really care. I was still groggy from emotional sleep.

"How are we going to get in? There's probably an alarm," I said, hopping down from the truck. Before I could even think of any clever ideas to enter the store without setting off an alarm system, Julian flung a large rock straight into the front glass door, shattering it into a million pieces. The alarm instantaneously sounded and red strobe lights danced around the darkened interior.

"Come on!" he yelled over the loud noise, grabbing my hand and tugging me with him. I stepped over the shards of glass and followed his pace. "Grab what you can! Batteries, hammers, tools! Anything you think would be useful!" he barked before running deep into the store. Panic and fear washed over me. Or maybe it was adrenaline. I felt like a criminal. A rebel. A vigilante.

Thieving wasn't foreign to me. It was how I survived for many years. But most of the time, I stole from people. You wouldn't believe the things people would forget on bus benches and on top of their cars. All I had to do was keep my eyes peeled and to pay attention. Small convenient stores were good places to swipe things from, too. Well-known establishments like these were risky. I had never done anything this major...or sloppy.

My heart thumped inside my chest. I picked up a woven basket as I rushed down the aisles and began following Julian's orders, thinking about what we needed as best as I could despite the loud alarm blasting in my ears. It reminded me of a show on *The Food Network*, where I had to rush to beat the clock by collecting ingredients for the delicious dinner I had to cook for judges.

I tossed items into the basket. Flashlights, batteries, first aid kits, rope... Anything that seemed just a little bit helpful. I concentrated on the stuff that I would probably buy in the event of a hurricane. Things that would be useful in case of a power outage. Tools needed to prepare our home for high winds.

I wasn't completely sure if these things could be of use for a zombie outbreak, though.

After finally filling the basket, I rushed over to the front doors. Julian wasn't anywhere in sight. I ran to the truck and emptied my goods into the bed before jogging back into the store. My eyes began to burn from straining to focus with the bright red lights blinking around me, and the screech of the alarm was making my emotional headache worse.

"Serena!"

I could hear Julian's faint call over the noise. Fearful that he may be alerting me of cops or something, I stopped what I was doing to head outside. He was placing several 2x4s into the bed.

"We've got to head out. I'm pretty sure the cops are all downtown, but just in case. And we still have to make a food run."

I had hoped the supermarket wasn't far from where we were. It was nice that there was no one else around. I couldn't imagine having to fight people over lighters and pocketknives. I hadn't seen downtown and all the chaos yet, but I wouldn't want to be in the middle of it.

We got into the truck and drove down the road. Five minutes later we were at the grocery store. It was pretty small. The green sign out front read *Mabel's* and definitely had a country feel to it. Stacked bales of hay and barrels aligned the storefront as decorations, and it looked like a log cabin. It was obviously a Mom-and-Pop shop, and a part of me felt guilty for having to throw a rock through the glass window to gain unauthorized access. It could have been owned by an old married couple who inherited the business after years of being passed down through generations. I might have been ruthless when it came to living on the streets and holding my own, but I still had morals.

There was no elegant alarm system with strobes lights in this one. Only an obnoxiously long, old timey ringing that made my head vibrate. The plan was the same as the last heist. We went our separate ways and crammed as much food and water into our baskets as possible. We spent a little more time in this place because we knew we would need much more food than tools to survive an unknown amount of time.

I jogged down each aisle, then paused when I reached the *Sanitary Napkins* section. Yes! I scooped the entire display of maxi pads and tampons into my bin. A woman could never have too many of these. Julian was already at the truck when I got back. I handed him my items and he glanced down at it before chucking it into the bed, biting the inside of his cheek as if to hold back a grin.

"Stop it," I ordered.

"I didn't say anything!"

I smiled, but it hurt to do so.

We loaded ourselves into the truck and made our way toward Harley at the garage. Julian switched the news back on the radio.

"*...and the city of Tampa is issuing a curfew effective immediately. The Mayor is strongly urging residents to follow this curfew and to stay in their homes. Violators will be arrested and...*"

He switched it back off. "This is only going to get worse."

"How do you know that?" I asked, a little frustrated that Julian was suddenly the Nostradamus of Tampa, Florida. How could he possibly know what the outcome of this will be?

He pointed to the windshield. "That's why." I followed the direction of his finger and my jaw dropped. We were still about ten miles away from downtown, but we didn't need to be down there to assume the worst. Helicopters were circling the bay and the metro area. The yellowish-red hue of flames in about five different areas lit up the night sky. Even though we were still miles away, the smell of things burning came in through the air conditioning vents of the truck. I rolled down the window because, honestly, I just didn't know what else to do with what I was looking at. Even with the distance in between, I could hear the sound of sirens, gunshots, and desperate screaming.

"Julian," I breathed.

"Serena, it's going to get worse," he repeated.

"How did this happen? How *could* this happen?" It completely confused me. How could a very established, well-known city get so out of control?

"Apparently, it spreads fast. You get bit and then you turn into one of them," he stated.

I peered over at the outbound traffic to the left of us. It was bumper to bumper, hundreds of headlights gleaming back at us.

"Shouldn't we be leaving?"

Julian kept his eyes on the road ahead. "No, I'm getting my daughter and we are staying at my place. There's no way we're going to get through that traffic or out any other way, for that matter. Everyone's trying to get out of the city."

A huge part of me didn't want to stay. Had I been on my own, I would have tried to flee the city. But I felt safe with Julian. His experience with this might not go any further than late-night video game sessions, but I trusted that he would protect me. Maybe it was because he was tall and burly. Maybe it was because of his years in the military. Or maybe it was because he had a daughter and I knew he would move mountains to keep her safe. But he was my Julian. And I believed that he would move mountains for me, too.

I grabbed his hand into both of mine and held it up to my chest as I watched downtown Tampa collapse before my very eyes.

THE JOB

THERE WAS A WAY to get back to Julian's house that involved going through the downtown area, but we completely bypassed it. I was glad, but I was still curious to see for myself what exactly was happening. Were zombies already roaming the streets?

We finally reached Barnaby's garage. As we pulled in front of the garage door, a gang of young kids came barreling down the side of the building. They were carrying boxes and chairs, laughing as they tried to keep their pants above their waists as they ran.

"No... No, no, no, no!" Julian scrambled out of the truck without setting it into park, and I immediately pulled the gear handle up as he rushed to get inside. Whipping my gun out of my purse, I stepped off the truck and stood close to our vehicle. We had a bed full of supplies that could be stolen, and I had to protect it. But I kept one eye on Julian's silhouette in the dark repair shop. Not two minutes later, he walked out of the shadows with Harley in tow.

"Is she okay?"

"Yeah, they didn't break in. Hey, we should grab some of Barnaby's tools and get back to the house and start securing it."

Harley was still bound by her hands and feet, still pale, and still yearning to reach her dad's face for a bite of his flesh. He placed her in the back, then we both worked together to grab some tools. My eyes darted to a sword-like object hanging on the wall inside a glass display case. "What's that?"

"Oh, it's Barnaby's prized possession. He said he made that machete himself and used it in Vietnam to cut through the jungle...and the enemy."

I studied the wooden handle and black blade, imagining a young Barnaby slicing plants and bodies. We kept the lights off in the garage for safety, but the silver edge of the knife caught the reflection of the streetlamp and glistened behind the glass. "Do you think he'll miss it?"

"I honestly don't think he'll be coming back. You want it?"

"Kind of."

Julian picked up a wrench and gently pushed me aside, then with one quick punch with the tool, the glass on the display case broke into several large pieces. He grabbed the machete and handed it to me. "It would be really good to use if these zombies are attracted to sound. I always use melee weapons in video games."

I took the handle into my palm, getting a feel for the weight. It was lighter than it looked, and the handle fit into my hand perfectly. I couldn't imagine having to use this on a person, so I silently promised myself it would be a last resort.

We finished packing some more things into our vehicle and got back to the house. Julian's neighbors were outside loading up their minivan. We sat in the truck and waited until they got in their car and left. Julian didn't want to risk being seen with a sick little girl in his arms.

Once inside, he placed Harley back on the couch, and we began our mission to make his home more secure.

"Let's just concentrate on getting the windows and entrances boarded up for now. We can worry about putting everything else away later," he insisted.

For the next two hours, we worked diligently to get the 2x4s nailed over windows and doors. I lived in Florida long enough to know exactly what this felt like—preparation for an impending hurricane. But no one ever had to have it done on such a time constraint. We usually had, at the very least, a day to get ready before the storm. Now, it felt as though the zombies were breathing down my neck, groaning at me to hurry up and finish or else they were going to eat me alive. Thankfully, the hours seemed to fly by, and when we were done, I plopped down on the recliner in Julian's living room to rest my muscles.

"You okay?" he asked, walking in with a hammer and a box of nails.

I closed my eyes. "I'm just tired...and starving."

"Well, we can chill for a bit now. I'm going to put Harley in my bed. Then we can go ahead and put the food away."

I nodded and began carrying our rations into the kitchen. I wasn't the most organized person in the world, but I tried to arrange everything in its respectable category. Most of it consisted of dried and canned foods. This was Hurricane Preparedness 101. The power goes out, you have no electricity. No electricity, no fridge. No fridge, bad food.

I did, however, grab a few packs of ham and cheese from the condo. The electricity hadn't gone out yet, and sandwiches were my comfort food—light but filling and could be eaten at any time of the day. Also, it was really cheap. And for tonight's 3 a.m. feeding, it was going to be a turkey sandwich. I fixed myself one and another for Julian—extra mayo because he loved it. He entered the kitchen just as I sat down at the counter. His house was too small to have a dining room or a place to even put a table. Two stools for the countertop were all that would fit.

"Thanks," he said, pulling up the stool next to me. My mouth was too full to answer back. I gave him a head's up and concentrated on not gagging. My stomach was hungry, but my mind was not happy with eating. I was still on the verge of crying my eyes out with every minute that passed by. Dan's lifeless eyes kept flashing through my thoughts. His pale, bluish skin, the gunshot, and the sound of his body hitting the ground all kept replaying over and over again in my head.

After our meal, I showered. The stench of fried seafood was still in my hair. And I figured I better use as much water as I could before that luxury was gone. Julian showered after me. We didn't dress in the usual pajama attire. He suggested that from here on out, we should always be prepared in case we had to leave in a hurry. Jeans and T-shirts weren't always my thing, especially to sleep in, but I guess I would have to get used to it.

I was an artist. Not only that, I was a starving artist who had, for a very long time, lived in dirty, stinky, ripped-up clothes found in random garbage bins around the city. Now that I could afford to be picky, my fashion choices leaned toward the bohemian/hipster side. Sure, my interior was tough—it was my difficult life that molded me that way, and there was nothing I could do about that. But I liked to express the softer side of my personality through what I wore. Neutral, earthy tones on long, flowy skirts, scarves, kimonos, and wide-brimmed hats. In the wintertime, I loved to pair combats boots with jeans. But my tops were floral and light-colored. It was all about balance.

So, you could imagine Julian's reaction when he realized this was mostly what I'd packed in my rushed state back at the condo. He watched dumbstruck while I sat on his couch with my suitcase and attempted to organize my girly clothes in the dimly lit living room.

"We're going to have to get you some better clothes."

"Sorry," I apologized defensively. As if I knew I was going to be in the middle of a zombie apocalypse when I went shopping for all of this. He lowered his head back down to the task at hand, which was writing things down on a notepad.

"What are you doing over there?"

"I'm making a list of things that we still need," he responded without looking up. There was tension lingering around us for some reason, and I didn't like it. Julian and I have gotten into some disagreements over the years, but we could never stay mad at each other for too long.

"Are you mad at me?" I couldn't imagine why he would be. He stopped writing and glanced up at me.

"No."

The low light softened his rugged facial features. He stared intently at me for a moment, then his eyes filled with sincerity right before he spoke again.

"I'm sorry. I'm...I'm just worried about Harley. And I shot Dan. But he didn't die, and this is all just crazy."

A part of me understood him. It must have been horrible to see his daughter in such a ghastly way, and I was certain that the only thing on his mind was whether or not she was going to live through this. My years of loss and pain have fine-tuned my way of thinking. There were always more negative thoughts than positive, and I was used to it. And I wholeheartedly understood how shooting Dan could make him feel horrible. I would be devastated if I thought I had killed my friend. Then finding out that they didn't actually die would wreck me all over again.

The picture of Charlie and me stared up at me from my suitcase. As much as I just wanted to curl up into a fetal position in a darkened room and cry until I became dehydrated, I couldn't. Charlie would not have wanted me to. And neither would Jules. He was all I had left now, and I needed to dig up some hope for the both of us.

"This thing could end tomorrow. There may be something someone could do to make her better. This can't be it."

He placed his notepad and pencil to the side and leaned forward. "Serena, you don't understand. What's happening...it won't end soon. This isn't even the beginning. This is just one city, one place in the whole world. Soon, it will be multiple cities, and before we know it, this virus will have plagued everyone everywhere. We won't see a cure for a while."

His ominous tone and matter-of-fact demeanor unnerved me. I was in awe at how he didn't even blink once as he spoke, but afraid of how he might know this information to be absolute.

"How are you so sure?" I asked with an unintentional crack in my voice.

He licked his lips and took a deep breath in before leaning back into the loveseat. After a short pause, he began, "When I was stationed out in California for those two years, I met a guy at the bar I was bouncing at."

"A place called One Eyed Jack's. I remember you telling me about that job." It was a while ago, but I remember Julian felt all badass because he was a bouncer and could actually break up fights without breaking one of his own lanky arms since he'd finally gained some muscle.

"Yeah, and it was awesome because I was making a little extra cash. You know we didn't get paid well as grunts.

Anyway, this man approached me and offered some kind of security job. Said he was a doctor who traveled a lot and needed me to tag along with him. It was strange. I didn't think a doctor would need a bodyguard. But he was offering a helluva lot more money than I was making at the bar. I told him I would only be able to help on the weekends when I wasn't working on the military base, and he was okay with it."

"You never told me about this security job," I interrupted, feeling a little resentful that he'd never mentioned it before. There were some things that Julian didn't know about my life on the streets, but I had only omitted those details to protect his heart. He could get very protective of me at times.

A flashback of the night Julian and I were out at the bar down the street from the restaurant replayed in my mind. We frequented the bar quite a bit with our coworkers. One night, a bunch of drunken frat guys decided to grace us with their loud mouths and obnoxiousness. One of them was coming on to me, relentlessly refusing to leave me alone even after I'd rejected him several times. That was when Julian stepped in and clocked him right in the face. I had to literally pull Julian off the poor boy, whose nose was no longer in its natural place. I was upset with Julian for not considering that I could take care of myself. He knew how capable I was. And for starting an unfair fight. The boy had no chance against Julian's Herculean stature.

But I couldn't stay mad at Jules for long. He was really drunk. Otherwise, he would not have intervened. The sweet Jules that I knew who normally avoided confrontation would have just discreetly grabbed my elbow and pulled me away from the asshole.

He shook his head. "I didn't tell you because I only went on two jobs with this doctor before I realized that it would conflict with my other job. But the whole thing just seemed to rub me the wrong way, anyway. Kind of shady, you know. He told me he needed some assistance with his patients. That they might get aggressive at times, which was a side effect from this drug that he was injecting them with."

"What was the drug?"

Julian squinted as if to be thinking really hard. "I don't remember. It was some kind of serum, I think. But I went to Atlanta with him for the first trip and we did house calls. It was me and another guard...Gino or something. Some guy from New York who also served as a Marine."

"Who does house calls anymore?"

"That's what I thought, too. But we went to a couple of people's houses. I waited outside the patient's home while the doctor and his team went inside and did whatever they did. The other security guard mentioned that the doctor was saving lives. He talked about how smart and amazing he was."

There was something about this story that didn't sit well with me. "That's a good thing, right?"

"You'd think so. But on the next trip, I overheard someone say something about 'time of death' and 'time of resurrection.'"

I tucked my chin toward my chest and drew my brows together, attempting to understand what Julian was saying. The only time I had ever heard the word *resurrection* was when it was pertaining to Jesus or zombies in a horror movie. And some people even claimed Jesus was a zombie. "You mean, someone died and was revived? Like by CPR, or something like that?"

"I don't think so, Serena. At least, now I don't think so. Back then, I thought it was a weird choice of words. But now...I think I know what's happening."

"You do?"

"I'm not one hundred percent certain, but Dan's documents. He mentioned Dr. Mark Walker. That's the name of the doctor I worked for. It can't be a coincidence."

"Are you suggesting that this Dr. Walker guy is the one who started the zombie outbreak?"

"I'm saying that it's possible," Julian countered. "I'm not sure exactly what this medication was, but it just makes a little bit of sense, don't you think?"

I shrugged. "I guess." Maybe it did. Only Dan knew why he wrote *Mark Walker* into his notes. There was something in my gut that was telling me there's some relation, but how many other Dr. Mark Walkers were there out in the world? In the same breath, Dan and Julian were both very smart men. Dan was good at his job: reporting and investigating. And Jules was good at thinking logically. Between the two of them, they could probably crack a cold case.

Julian's little fits of rage throughout the night were suddenly making sense. "Are you upset that if this is the same guy you worked for, you could have stopped him or something?"

He glanced down at his hands shyly. "No. I don't know. It just bothers me that I might have known the guy who made my daughter this way. You didn't see her, Serena. When I got to Vanessa's house, I wasn't sure what had happened at first. It looked like maybe Tommy came home from work at the hospital sick. He might have bitten Harley and Vanessa fought back. Tommy wasn't there, but I'm just assuming this is how it happened." He glanced up at me, and his eyes welled with tears on the brink of brimming over. "How am I going to tell her that she killed her mother? How am I supposed to explain why she did it?"

I had no idea how to answer that. Did she already know what she did? There was no way to tell if Harley would remember her actions once she got better. We just didn't know enough about the virus yet. But judging by that glossed-over daze in her eyes, I had a feeling this disease was going to affect her mind long-term.

I stood up and sat on the coffee table in front of Julian, placing my hands on his knees. "We'll figure it out together. I'll help you. But you could have never known that that doctor was going to start this. You don't even know for sure if it's the same doctor you worked for." Right as the words came out of my mouth, I realized that Julian was probably right. Why else would Dan have been researching for a Dr. Mark Walker? I may not have had much family, but the two men I *did* have, I trusted to have good instincts.

"Serena," he whispered. "It only makes sense. Dan was on to something. How many other doctors out there were talking about resurrections? I don't know the specifics, but this medication he was helping people with could have been defective. You know?"

As I bowed my head in understanding, a wave of fatigue suddenly fell over me. It all seemed like too much to bear at the moment, and I felt too tired to keep talking. Julian must have realized as much, and he gently combed a piece of my long hair away from my face with his fingers.

"We should get some sleep," he said, his voice almost a hum.

"Yeah, we should."

I stood up, but before I could take a step away, Julian grabbed my wrist. "Serena."

With my eyesight lowered to our feet, I allowed myself to collapse into him. My body, my feelings, my heart... it all seemed too heavy to keep upright anymore. One of

Julian's long, brawny arms wrapped around my body, the other found its way into my hair and gently guided my head toward his heart. His chest rose and fell with every breath, and his heartbeat lulled my eyes shut. I didn't want him to say anything. He didn't have to. Julian knew me well enough to know that I needed this moment of silence to figure out what to do with my emotions. He knew me well enough to know that when one particular bad thing happened, it would easily elicit *all* of the bad things that have happened over the course of my life. And when I'd get into that mindset, it was like falling into a deep well with no way out. The sadness would turn into depression, then self-loathing, then anger. Eventually, I'd find my way out, but not without trudging through the dark, twisty trail of psychological torture first.

Julian held me for a while. Perhaps it was grief. Maybe fear of what was in our future. But whatever it was, we were comforted and protected from the unknown in our embrace.

I pulled away first. "I'm going to bed."

We got ourselves situated in the living room. Being that Julian's house was so small, any strange noises could easily be heard from the bedroom where Harley had been chained up. But I could already tell that the mixture of hollow silence in the house and Harley's little sweet, diseased moans would make it difficult for me to fall asleep.

Even though my body felt tired, my mind was definitely not. After about twenty minutes of tossing and turning, I became frustrated. Julian's gentle snoring confirmed that he had already fallen asleep. I tried to focus on the light rumbling coming from his lungs, but Dan's strained groans and bloody mouth kept flashing over and over in my brain. My whole body ached for him. I missed him so much already. The love of my life. The one person that I wanted to spend the rest of my life with was gone.

Dickhead John, the customer from the restaurant earlier, somehow made an appearance in my thoughts. I thought about his rudeness and wondered where he was. Maybe his wife turned into a zombie and ate his sorry ass.

Then, Dr. Mark Walker's photo from the Internet infiltrated my mind. The thought of him angered me. I was mad that this was all happening. Upset at Dan for not being safe. For being too tired, which probably caused him to make a bad judgment call. Resentful that he wasn't here with me and that I would have to survive this thing without him. Pissed that Julian's daughter was sick. Irritated at the fact that Julian now felt the burden of having to protect both me and Harley.

I was furious at that damn doctor. There was certainly no proof in front of me that showed he had anything to do with this, but I still believed that it was all his fault. He did this. He was the reason why Dan was out there right now, dead and suffering.

Hatred for this Dr. Mark Walker began sticking to the sides of my stomach as the tension in my body finally started to relax. And as I drifted off to sleep, the wheels in my head kept turning. If this doctor was responsible for this mess, we had to do something about it.

THE CLEANUP

Grace

"SONNY, WHEN IS THE boat scheduled to dock?"

Sonny flipped her blonde mane away from her face and switched the phone to her other ear. "Seven," she whispered.

I nodded. "Ian, how are the newcomers?"

"They're okay, love," he answered in his sexy Australian accent. "Eating dinner in Newport now."

I took a deep breath to remember what I was doing. I hadn't had a full night's sleep since the outbreak began a few days ago. Everything had been a blur—like it was all one long day of cleaning up the island, planning, and figuring out what our next move was.

It felt like years had passed since the first time I docked at Everlasting Paradise. I tried every day to forget what led us to this conference room in the Z lab. The loss of Tristen, Maddi, Charlie, Estelle, Destiny, and Agent V left a hole in my heart. It hurt all of us, everyone who managed to escape Dr. Walker's wicked plans.

Even when the rest of his staff and employees heard about his passing, a sense of relief seemed to float around the island. I didn't actually think that they hated him as much as I did, but they certainly had issues with his plans. They didn't completely agree with selling Serum Z on the market, promising a life of immortality without informing the public of one major side effect: that they would crave human flesh. They also didn't agree with his plan to harvest humans and secretly sell human meat as if it were regular food. If it wasn't for Dr. Walker's promise of money and threats to ruin anyone who leaked his diabolical plans, most of his employees would have quit a long time ago. It was like they were stuck.

Serum Z saved a lot of the people on this island, but it was now on the verge of harming the world. We were on the cusp of a zombie apocalypse, something I knew Dr. Walker and his colleagues certainly did not anticipate happening.

A zombie apocalypse. I couldn't even believe it was really happening! It was still hard to grasp the fact that I was half human, half zombie.

With all of my years of watching horror movies, of being obsessed with zombie films and television shows, and even wanting to become a horror movie makeup artist, you'd think I would actually be excited that it turned out to be real. But excitement was the furthest emotion I had. It was fear that consumed me now. Fear that we weren't going to figure out a way to clean up Dr. Walker's mess.

And here I was, a teenage girl sitting at a desk, directing people on what to do and how to save lives. Seriously?

"Well, I don't give a shit! Tell him he's either with me or he's not! I'm running the show now!" Kate slammed her phone down on the big, shiny wooden table. The same table where the scientist sat before I bit him...and killed him. Ian was kind enough to finish him off and clean up all the blood. Otherwise, I couldn't bear being in this room. I still felt awful for what I'd done.

"Ugh! You'd think they would be happy and willing to figure this whole thing out. I don't get it," she complained as she took a seat.

"Another one?"

She lowered her head, suggesting that the answer was yes. Another employee had decided to challenge Kate as their boss. She wasn't even in her thirties yet, and I knew the burden of running her late father's former evil empire was hard to handle. Kate did spring into action when we were sure that the patient recently injected with the mutated Serum Z was the one who attacked those people at the supermarket in Florida. She began making phone calls and informing Dr. Walker's staff that he was dead. She kept semi-true to the story we initially came up with—that his "turn" didn't end so well. Only in this version, he didn't just die. He was injected with the serum and came back to life. He brutally attacked his two VIP colleagues, Dr. Charles and Dr. Tamma, and so Kate had no choice but to kill him. This really derailed anyone's suspicion over the whole matter.

We were able to keep most of his other staff members. The agents/bodyguards agreed to stay on the island after we assured them that we had no intentions of following in Dr. Walker's footsteps. A lot of the doctors and scientists were more than happy to help fly as many Zombrids from around the world as they could to ensure their safety and take care of them. And the Zombrids were more than happy to give us their blood for research, in hopes that we could find an antidote to this mutated serum.

But there were a few staff members who didn't want to have anything to do with his corporation anymore—like Robin. We could stand to lose her because she was just a receptionist, but Kate was trying her hardest to keep *all* of the doctors and scientists. The qualified people who could really be useful.

"You know what? It's fine. I'm not even going to argue with them. If they want out, they want out. My dad might have been manipulative and persuaded them to stay by offering them money and threatening their lives, but I won't do it."

"Have we figured out what we're going to do about the media?" I asked. As of right now, the world didn't know about Everlasting Paradise or its location. Dr. Walker employed many people, but he somehow managed to keep this place and his plans for world domination a secret. And now that we were able to keep most of his staff, they agreed to keep our discretion.

He did use intidimation and blackmail to get what he wanted out of his employees in the past, I learned. Kate said it was not an easy task. It involved legal forms and loads of money. Money that had to be used as an incentive for his staff to stay loyal to the island. And sometimes Dr. Walker would go further than that, threatening lives and families. She refused to go into any details when asked, but honestly, I didn't want to know. As long as we weren't doing it anymore, it didn't matter. I didn't worry about our staff tattling on us now. They were probably scared about being blamed for all of this. I was scared, too.

Over the past few days, the CDC, government, and pretty much everyone managed to figure it all out pretty quickly. Dr. Walker's face had been plastered all over the news. I guess it wasn't too hard to piece together since he was a well-known doctor who injected about a hundred people all over the world. It didn't seem like a big number, but somehow...it was. I guess when you consider what he planned to do, it made that number more significant. No one knew about his future plans except for us, but there were some "subjects" who came forward and confirmed being treated with an experimental drug that brought them back to life. We weren't upset with them or anything. They were just telling the truth.

Kate's phone dinged and she glanced down at it.

"As long as the press doesn't know where we're located, we should be okay. All of Dr. Walker's clinics and offices in the States have been raided by officials, which is also how they were able to confirm the Serum Z theory. They found loads of documents about it." Kate didn't like to call her father *Dad*. I wondered if she ever did. "We've just got to continue to work on a cure and try to keep quiet. If they find out about us, they'll intervene and probably take all the Zombrids that are here, our doctors, everything. We just need everyone to stay focused and worry about their tasks."

"Are we going to have enough to keep the newcomers fed in The Safe Zone?" Ian asked. The Safe Zone was his temporary name for our island. A safe place for the Zombrids to convene and get what they needed, away from the apocalypse. Ian argued that we might be influenced to act the same way the crazed zombies did. This made sense. Every time we even talked about food, it seemed to awaken my hungry stomach. Seeing those zombies eat humans might force our minds toward the dark side.

Kate looked at him, then her eyes shifted to me. She knew how much I disliked what I had to do to stay sane. To stay normal instead of a flesh-eating monster.

"We should have enough for a while if we're smart about rationing. But we're eventually going to begin the process of coming up with a more...kosher way to feed the need."

A twinge of hunger shot across my belly. It was my time to eat.

The hunger didn't change over the past few days. It hadn't gotten any stronger, but it hadn't let up any, either. I still craved human blood and flesh and followed the schedule Dr. Walker had given me. Now that I knew that Dr. Walker was lying about feeding us animals, and that we were eating *actual humans*, I felt like I was somehow craving it more. When Sonny, Ian, and the others found out that they were all eating humans instead of wild boar and other island animals, they were pretty okay with it. Maybe even a little too nonchalant about it. Ian even joked about wishing he had reached the point of hunger that I was in so that he could eat more often. It was only a matter of time, though. Eventually, all of the Zombrids would need to eat frequently to keep from becoming VIP members of the Donner Party.

This serum mutation gave me the heebie-jeebies, too. I worried that eventually the formula that was in my blood would transform and turn me into one those maniacs roaming around Tampa. But Kate and the other doctors insisted there was only the one formula that could do that.

Another hunger spasm forced a grimace that I hid behind my hand. I knew I had to get to the mess hall, but I hated having to sit at the booth with an empty seat across from me. My feeding partner, Estelle, was dead, and it made me sad before and after I went into the food coma.

Kate stood up and directed a question at me. "Have you given any more thought to what we talked about the other day?"

I rolled my eyes. Not at her, but because I wasn't comfortable with what we talked about the other day. "Um...yes. I did."

"And?" she asked, raising her eyebrows in anticipation of an answer.

I ran my fingers through my long, curly hair, trying to come up with an answer. She set her palms on the table and leaned in toward me. Her sleek ponytail rested on her right shoulder and her beautiful face relaxed. My eyes wandered away from hers in hopes that somehow, she would just forget I was sitting there.

"Grace, I know it's tough. But she can really be useful here. She knew my father, maybe even better than I did. She knew about your condition and she has the knowledge that might very well lead us in the right direction toward finding a cure. She can even help us figure out the food situation. Besides, you have to be worrying about her safety."

Kate might have been far different than her father—morality-wise—but she did have the same persuasive, and maybe even manipulative, abilities. The apple didn't fall far from that tree. I knew what I had to do. But was I ready to face the woman who lied to me my whole life about pretty much everything, including the death of my father, and sent me to live with a homicidal maniac who killed my boyfriend and made me eat him? And the verdict was still out on whether or not she even had anything to do with Tristen's death.

"She's fine. There haven't been any attacks in New Orleans." I wasn't giving in so easily.

"Grace, you know as well as I do that if we don't find a cure, this thing is going to spread fast."

I contemplated this deeply. I didn't want my mom to die. As much as she pissed me off, as much as I didn't want to even see her face, I didn't want her to be eaten.

"Yeah. Okay. Fine. I'll call my mother."

Kate didn't smile. She simply nodded and turned to leave the conference room. She knew how I felt. She knew exactly what it was like to be betrayed by a parent.

ONE MONTH LATER...

THE POSER

THE ACTIVITY AROUND US increased over the next month. Every day was new and interesting. We worked hard on keeping The Safe Zone safe and our new guests comfortable.

On a sunny and breezy afternoon, I sat on the porch of the Laguna hut and watched my fellow Zombrids get acquainted with Everlasting Paradise. Ian stood in the middle of the yard, pointing over to the Malibu hut and explaining the island grounds to the final group of Zombrids that had just arrived this morning. There were about five in the group, two girls and three guys.

There was a group of about three Zombrids standing outside of the Newport hut, probably waiting for the lunch buffet of innards and flesh to open. Two more Zombrids seemed to be relaxing underneath a palm tree, and four others sat at one of the picnic tables, laughing and chatting. Scenes from Maddi's birthday party flashed before my eyes and sorrow filled my chest. I was very skeptical of this place in the beginning, but that particular memory was a happy one. I imagined how different things could have been if the island really was a sanctuary from the start. It could have been a place I could call home.

"Grace!"

I turned to see Sonny waving her hand in the air at me. The stub of her other arm dangled at her side. This new flawed Sonny was still tough to get used to, considering I was the reason behind it. But as I watched her jog toward me with a smile, her long, perfect blonde hair swaying effortlessly with the breeze from the ocean, I was reminded of how much she had changed. Of how much losing her arm had affected her as a whole. She wasn't as stuck-up as before. She had her moments, but she seemed to be more humble now. Even sweet.

She finally reached me. The afternoon sun kissed her tanned skin just enough to cause a glowing effect. I had to stop myself from complimenting her beauty. She could still be bitchy toward me at times, and I didn't want to give her the satisfaction.

"Grace, are you heading over to the Z lab?"

I nodded. "The meeting starts in about ten minutes. Did you already eat?" It was kind of hard to believe that I even cared about whether or not Sonny had eaten. She had been my mortal enemy for so long. Now, we were immortal frenemies. We would never have the bond that Phoebe and I had as besties. We may never be Sisters from Another Mister or soul buddies or friends who shared our deepest, darkest secrets with one another. But there was something about losing someone we both cared about and having to escape the wrath of a maniac together that took our relationship to a whole other level. I could actually tolerate her now.

She flipped her hair over her shoulder and began walking with me. "Yeah, Ian and I ate before the newbies. Ew! Did you see some of these people? I know Dr. Walker was, like, injecting whoever he wanted, but come on! He could have at least picked *some* good-looking people. And

I bet none of them have even heard of *Chanel*. There's no way I'm going to eat with them."

Maybe I spoke too soon. I tolerated her as much as I could, but I still wanted to punch her in the throat sometimes.

"This isn't high school anymore, Sonny. And not everyone can afford overly expensive clothes and makeup to cover up their flaws," I scolded her. She rolled her eyes.

Of course Dr. Walker didn't pick and choose his patients that way. Not too long ago, Kate had given me a little feedback on how he worked his way and the serum into people's lives. She explained that in the beginning, his plans to actually help people were real. He legitimately wanted to create a drug that could increase the chances of survival during the process of reviving someone in cardiac arrest. He worked tirelessly to find the perfect formula. When he injected me, the serum had only been tested on animals. And when it actually worked on a human, Dr. Walker knew he had something amazing on his hands—something that could change the world.

When he tested Serum Z on my father, he truly had no idea that it would kill him.

"I'm really sorry about what happened to your dad, Grace," Kate had said during our conversation. "But I didn't know anything about it until much later. Nobody knew that injecting the serum into a live person would kill them."

I nodded. Dr. Walker had kept the whole incident under wraps from everyone. Along with my mother, apparently.

After learning that Serum Z was causing his "subjects" to crave a certain kind of food, he had panicked. Kate said that Dr. Walker didn't sleep for weeks, trying to figure out how to fix that side effect. He was so disappointed that his magic potion had a serious flaw. But when he realized there was nothing he could do about it, he just...rolled with it. Instead of stopping the production and administration of the serum, he came up with an entirely different plan—one that resulted in riches and power. For him.

He decided to manipulate the first few injected patients into coming to Everlasting Paradise. This way, he could do whatever he wanted to them without question— examine their bodies, perform procedures, secretly experiment with their food by feeding them dead/living things. It bought him time to figure out how to distribute the medication, make money off of it, and feed the growing population of Zombrids without them knowing what they were really eating. If anyone happened to figure out the truth or stumble upon it, he either paid them an obscene amount of hush money or...killed them. Yes. He killed more people than we initially thought. And not just to turn them into Zombrids.

Since Serum Z was considered an experimental drug, and since he couldn't necessarily get the consent of a patient who was already dead, Kate said he visited hospitals and did house calls all over the place and posed as a physician called in to further investigate a medical case. This wasn't very hard to do. He was well-known in his field of medicine. He was a best-selling author and philanthropist. The hospitals, and people in general, actually welcomed his presence. His expertise. They trusted him.

During his unsolicited visits, he would approach the most terminally ill patients (ages varying) and either persuade them to join his elite Zombrid society, or worse... just kill and inject them. Kate said some were aware and agreed to euthanasia. But some had no idea. He would claim that he was helping them, but it was clearly murder.

When Kate told me all this, I was left speechless for a moment. Then the questions started coming.

"So, what did the patient do when the craving for human flesh struck them?" I had asked Kate, wanting to know as much as I could about what Dr. Walker did. "Did they even understand...or could they even explain their overwhelming desire to eat something with a pulse?" The thought of my very first craving came to mind, remembering just how insanely confused I felt about it.

Kate had sighed wearily. "Well, he did try his best, I'll give him that. He went above and beyond to make sure his patients were appropriately fed from the moment they were give Serum Z. And later on, when he began injecting patients but didn't require them to come to the island, he made sure that they were sent packaged meals to feed their need."

"Is that where he got his idea—"

"Yes. He soon realized that was the key to hiding the truth. He decided he would create 'subscriptions' for *Z meals*, meals that were masked as regular food."

I nodded, understanding that to a Zombrid, if it tasted like what they wanted, they wouldn't give a crap what it really was or where it came from. It would be like those weight-loss commercials you see late at night. Those companies send out already-made, low-fact, low-carb meals. Dr. Walker was planning on doing exactly that. Only these meals were ready-to-eat humans.

Most of the first thirty patients who were sent to Everlasting Paradise met their untimely death, again, here on the island when Dr. Walker decided to experiment with the chemical properties of the serum. The altered serum turned them into true zombies (Ian called them TZs). So, he decided to burn them all. But there were still about seventy more Zombrids out in the world. We had managed to get all of them. Except one. You could probably guess where that last one was.

"So what's this meeting about, anyway?" Sonny asked, breaking my train of thoughts.

"I'm not sure. Kate mentioned something about a breakthrough on the phone."

We reached the steel door to the Z lab. In the Walker days, this door would have been sealed shut. The only way to gain entry would have been with a keycard, a password, and a button pushed by the lovely receptionist, Robin— Agent V's secret crush. It saddened me to think of that. Robin was very upset when she learned about V's demise. She was one of the first people to opt out of working here ever again, and I didn't blame her. The idea that she might blab about where the island was located did worry us, but she promised not to tell if we promised to find a cure for the outbreak.

As we stepped out of the elevator onto the second floor, I glanced at the empty desk in front of me. It belonged to Beverly, Dr. Walker's dedicated secretary, who had been a part of his team since the very beginning. She believed that what he was doing—euthanizing and injecting and harvesting humans—was the best thing that could have happened to this world. In fact, she was so dedicated that after learning about Dr. Walker's death, she killed herself. We found her lifeless body in her hut along the beach, hanging from one of the rafters. It was extremely unfortunate, and dramatic, but Kate said she wasn't surprised at all. Beverly had no other family back in the states. The island and Dr. Walker were all she had.

I'd hate to say it, but it was for the best. If she was that devoted to Dr. Walker and his plans, then she might have spoken to people about our whereabouts out of spite.

I pushed open the glass door, and Sonny and I took a seat at the conference table. About a minute later, Ian strolled in. His bright yellow tank top matched his flowery surfer shorts, and he gave us a sexy, mischievous side smile before he took a seat at the end of the table. Sonny twirled her hair around her finger and returned a flirty grin. I rolled my eyes. At her, not him. Ian might have been a little womanizing and cocky, but I didn't blame him. He *was* pretty hot. And I definitely didn't regret our little tryst in the jungle that almost led to the loss of my virginity. However, I cringed at the thought of Sonny and I both having some kind of chemistry with the same boy...again.

I didn't think of Ian in that way, though. Tristen was still heavily on my mind. Especially after learning that he had passed through my lower intestine.

To be honest, I didn't think Ian was interested in me that way, either. Or Sonny.

Kate walked in, paperwork in hand. The two new senior doctors on the island, Dr. Sharma and Dr. Kamini, followed her into the room. They both sat down, and Kate spread her documents out on the table. Then, a woman I had never seen before but who looked oddly familiar to me, came in. Her eyes widened when she saw me and her hand shot up to her mouth, as if to cover a gasp. And as soon as she found her seat, someone else strolled into the conference room. My heart stopped. Completely and totally stopped beating for a brief moment. I wanted to sink down in my chair, all the way under the table. But it wouldn't have helped. Our eyes met and I froze. It was hard to look away.

THE MAP

I DIDN'T CALL MY mother when Kate told me to. Instead, I gave her the green light to do it for me. I was probably being a coward, but I still didn't feel ready. I'd heard rumors that she finally got here about a week ago, but we hadn't crossed paths. And it wasn't by accident.

Her eyes were warm. They were familiar, comforting, nurturing...all of the things I missed and needed the most at this time in my life. She stood in front of me. She had such a statuesque physique and poised posture. I sat upright in my chair, trying to match her elegance. She looked exactly the same as the day I left home.

Kate introduced her to the group. "Okay, guys. This is Dr. Eve Shelley."

It was still strange to hear her true name. But not *that* strange. I never called her Veronica, anyway. She was always Mom to me.

"And this is Dr. Shelley's sister, Megan," Kate said. I shot a glance over at the woman I had hung up on months ago when I called the phone number I found in my mother's closet. The woman who claimed to be my aunt. She really was my aunt. My long-lost family. "Dr. Shelley and Megan, this is Sonny and Ian. And you know Dr. Sharma and Dr. Kamini. And you obviously know Grace." She whispered that last part. Mom was going by *Dr.* now? She hadn't practiced in her field of medicine in a long time.

My mom tilted her head slightly and gave me a half smile—a smile that spoke a thousand words.

"You're Grace's mum?" Ian asked, seemingly surprised.

It was like it hurt her to turn away from me. "Yes, I am."

"Wow. Very nice," he said, eying her up and down.

"Really, Ian?" I snapped.

"What?"

Kate sighed. "Please excuse him. Unfortunately, the intellectual benefits of Serum Z didn't stick."

Ian narrowed his eyes at Kate playfully and she glared back at him. I had become convinced there might be some sort of romance igniting between those two. My mom took a seat across from Sonny and me. Her eyes locked onto mine again.

Kate began. "Okay, let me start by saying great job on locating all the Zombrids and getting them back to the island. We were really lucky to have them all agree. Some of them we had to convince, but most were willing. Regardless, you're all doing a fantastic job of getting them settled in. I want this place to feel like their home. A sanctuary where they can receive the proper food and care and know that they are safe. And we're grateful to them for agreeing to help us find a cure. So far, I think things are going really well. Dr. Sharma, how are we on rations?"

Dr. Sharma and Dr. Kamini were newcomers to the island. They had been working for Dr. Walker for some time, but at one of his clinics in the States. Dr. Sharma was probably one of my favorite doctors here at the moment. He was young and smart and funny. He was cute in a cool, hipster doctor kind of way. He even had one of those hipster haircuts—the one where the sides were shaved and the longer pieces on top swooped over his forehead.

Dr. Kamini was older. She was loud and nerdy and frumpy. She never wore makeup and always looked scattered-brain, despite the fact that she was actually smarter than her colleague. She was also Indian with a very heavy accent. She enunciated her English words properly, but it was still difficult to understand her when we first met. Eventually, I did get used to the way she said things.

Dr. Sharma thumbed through his papers. "Yes, we still have enough to feed the new Zombrids. We have about a months' worth of frozen food. Now, we can try the raw animals, but the animal population isn't big enough on this island to last a long time. And we aren't even sure if it will meet the needs of the Zombrids. Switching from human meat to animal meat might affect them negatively."

Dr. Walker and his crew had lied and said they were feeding us dead island animals. But it wasn't true. We all needed to eat something fresh and barely dead, and some of us—by that I mean only me—needed to eat several times a day to keep from becoming a TZ (true zombie). Eventually, everyone would get to the stage I was in.

Kate leaned back in her chair and chewed on the head of her pen thoughtfully. "Okay. Can we maybe try it? We can see if any Zombrids want to volunteer. We'll transition their food and monitor them closely to see if it does affect them."

Dr. Kamini shrugged. "We can try, but chances of the Zombrids being able to live on only raw animals are slim. Eating human flesh gives them the nutrients they need and replaces the part of the body that is dead. It helps them to function the way a normal person does. Without it, they would go hunting for it, unconsciously and aggressively."

"And once their minds go there, there is no coming back from it," Dr. Sharma added. "Not unless we have a cure."

I shivered. The idea of becoming a TZ scared the crap out of me.

My mother spoke up. "I can organize meal plans for the Zombrids. Maybe help ration what we do have left. I can also work with the chefs and help with transitioning whoever volunteers from human meat to animal."

"Yes, Dr. Shelley. I feel very comfortable with having you in charge of the food," Kate said. This made sense. The woman did manage to make some delicious dishes using human remains. "And Megan as well, seeing as how you own a farm back in the States."

"I know quite a bit about animals. Cooking humans... not so much." Megan smiled and giggled, but in a really nervous and uncomfortable way. God, she resembled my mother so much. The fact that they were sisters was unmistakable—same dark hair, elegant facial features, perfect posture. Megan just looked like a younger version of my mom. But I couldn't really focus on the fact that my estranged aunt was sitting so close to me. Not while my mother, the woman who claimed to care so much about me but continuously deceived me my whole life, was staring holes into my head.

"I'm on board for trying an animal diet with a Zombrid or two. But we have to keep in mind that it might not work. The fact is that the human species would be better suited for the Zombrid's needs, as it would be providing the exact components that they're missing," Dr. Kamini informed us.

"They are human, therefore, they should be fed humans," Mom stated.

"Yes. Precisely. It's better for their overall health because it's similar to their specific body functions. Animals are simply not the same as humans. Our anatomies are not the same—"

"But we'll have to be sure to check their blood chemistries and brain waves constantly," Dr. Sharma interjected. "If someone turns into a True Zombie, that could be disastrous for the island community. Maybe even traumatizing for some people."

I shifted uncomfortably in my seat, imagining how this little experiment could go wrong. Abby had looked so tortured in that jail cell at East Cocos. And V had eaten his own kind! Not to mention, having to eat human meat was traumatizing all on its own for me. I mean...I wanted to, but I didn't want to. It was an agonizing moral dilemma.

"So, like, what's going to happen?" Sonny asked. "If animal corpses aren't good enough, where are we going to get humans when we run out of what's in the freezer?"

Kate took a deep breath in, releasing an obviously distressed huff. "There's the issue. I honestly don't know. I *do* know that the harvesting-humans plan is not going to happen. It may have been Dr. Walker's vision, but it isn't mine."

"There is something I could do," my mother asserted, like she had been waiting to say it. "I've thought about this a lot and I think we might be able to somehow have the public help us."

"Oh! Oh!" Sonny squealed. "We could see if people want to donate their bodies when they die. You know, like how they put that little red heart on your license for organ donor?"

Mom smiled and pointed at Sonny. "That's exactly right, actually. Well, I don't know about the little red heart idea, but we could see if people would like to donate their bodies after death."

"Like for science?" Ian asked.

"Essentially." She shrugged. "Only, we would be using their recently deceased bodies to feed the Zombrids. I also worked as a medical examiner. I have friends who own funeral parlors. There are so many people who die and don't have families, which could be a reason why they would agree to donating. As long as we receive their bodies immediately after death and with prior consent, of course, it should still be fresh enough for adequate nutrition."

Kate shuffled the papers in front of her. "That is definitely something we can explore further. Thank you, Dr. Shelley. Now, let's discuss what's happening out there."

"Where is that guy?" I asked, curious to know what happened to the Zombrid who started the outbreak.

"His name is Jason Castro. He's a twenty-seven-year-old male who was initially admitted to the hospital for pneumonia. He was very, very sick at the time."

"And he died?" Ian queried.

Kate didn't look up from her papers. "He...he was euthanized," she said with a sigh. I could tell she was ashamed. Kate had told me that she was never the one to push the euthanasia drugs into the patient's veins, but she was remorseful for what her father did. She said she felt responsible, partially blaming herself for the outbreak.

"Why didn't Dr. Walker stop injecting people with the mutated Serum Z after what it did to Abby and everyone at East Cocos?"

"He did. And we thought we had gotten rid of that formula and..." Kate's voice trailed off. "It was really an accident."

Everyone at the table grew silent. What a terrible, unfortunate accident.

Ian decided to break the uncomfortable silence first. "So, we know that Jason changed about a week after he was revived with the messed-up serum. But when someone is bitten, they turn in…minutes?"

"Correct," Dr. Sharma answered. "The serum mutates inside the bloodstream and it takes about a week or so. It turns into a virus, attacking and contaminating everything in the body, including the saliva. When a person is bitten, saliva transfers through the victim's bloodstream. And this particular virus is fast-acting and very potent. It's like a Zombrid on steroids. They are aggressive and their hunger is insatiable. All reasoning is lost in their brain. All of their urges are uncontrollable."

"And you're sure Jason is the only one?" I pressed. We had to be completely sure.

"Yes. I have reviewed our files on everyone Dr. Walker dealt with. Besides, we would know by now if there were others injected with the virus."

"Man, this one guy caused the zombie apocalypse?" Ian stared off into the distance as he said this. I wondered if he was imagining what it was like to be Jason Castro. To be honest, I kind of was myself.

Kate pulled out and unfolded a large color-coded map. "Here is where the outbreak started," she said, pointing to Tampa, Florida. We all leaned in and followed her finger. "Tampa is wiped out and considered Ground Zero." She traced her finger along the rest of the state of Florida, which was colored red, along with all the states that aligned the Gulf of Mexico. "These are also wiped out." She moved her finger to the northeast, which was shaded orange. "These places are not as infected as the south, but it's getting there fast." She moved across the map, which had a mixture of green, yellow, red, and orange states.

Finally, she rested her finger on the West Coast, which was colored mostly yellow and orange but splashed with a few large red spots. "These places are moderate-to-severe. It won't take long for the west and northeast to fall because of the population. So, as you all can see, this virus has spread all over the country already. The military has pulled out completely from the red zones, with the exception of the quarantine line, which runs along state lines and the ocean. No one gets in, no one gets out. They're trying to control the other zones, but it looks like by the rate of infection, those orange and yellow zones are going to turn red quickly."

"What about overseas?" Ian asked quietly. There was concern in his tone. Could he still have family in Australia?

Kate breathed in and smiled slightly. "Thankfully, it hasn't reached overseas yet. Because of the fast rate, the FAA was able to issue a travel ban soon enough. But that doesn't mean they are completely out of the woods. It could still happen. We have an overseas team of doctors who are prepared to do whatever we tell them to."

Kate stared at Ian for a moment longer after she spoke. She must have felt his worries.

"It's only been a month. How did this happen so quickly?" I asked, finally able to speak. It was all so overwhelming. So heartbreaking. This color-coded map in front of us was like looking at a graveyard. How many people were dead out there? Zombies were roaming the streets and people were getting eaten alive by the minute. It made my stomach turn. But the disturbing part was that I didn't know if it was truly because it made me sad...or hungry.

Kate glanced up at me, nodded, and bit her bottom lip. I was sure she couldn't believe it, either.

This was it. This was a horror movie. *My* horror movie.

THE CURE

I DIDN'T LIKE THIS movie. I didn't like seeing dead people. I didn't enjoy eating fresh human flesh. Well...I did. It tasted like nothing else I ever imagined! It was the holy grail of food. But the act of eating it was disgusting. It broke my heart. It made me feel like a monster.

This real-life apocalyptic movie was the scariest one I'd ever seen. And I wasn't sure if it was because I felt terrible for those people who had to live through it, or because I felt guilty. Guilty because I had the capability of being on the other side of it. It could be me wreaking havoc in those red splotches on the map.

"You know, I bet people think they can just shoot one of those TZs in the brain and be done with it," Ian said. "But it's not how it works. That might be another reason why this has spread so quickly." Ian's comment sent feverish goosebumps down my back. He made a good point. Thanks to pop culture and its definition of zombies, these people were fooled. The TZs needed to be decapitated or burned to ashes. It was the only way to make sure they were dead for good.

Kate cleared her throat. "Listen, it's going to be okay. We've got this. There's another reason for this meeting. There has been a...breakthrough in our research for a cure."

Ian, Sonny, and I peered over to her at the same time. Kate stood up and pushed the chair away from her. She walked the length of the long table with her hands behind her back. Kate was nothing like her father, but she was a lot like her father, too. She carried his determination, his energy, and his undeniable hunger to be in control. But his way of thinking lacked her sense of morality. She might have wanted to take control, but it was in a good way. She wanted to control the safety of our country.

"Our team of agents managed to capture a couple of the infected at Ground Zero."

I winced at the word *capture*.

"We've been testing their blood, matching it to the Zombrid's blood and finding the differences and similarities. I won't get into the scientific and chemical properties or details, but I will tell you that we believe we have found the cure," said Kate, displaying obvious enthusiasm in her tone.

I could feel the excitement inside myself, too. "Well, what are we waiting for?" I asked eagerly. "Let's get them cured."

Dr. Sharma leaned back in his chair. "It's not that simple."

"Why not?"

"Sweetie, a lot goes into it," Mom answered. I kept my eyes away from her and glanced down at the table. I didn't want to give her my full attention. "There is research and preparation and monitoring... It could take a lot of time to ensure this is the right antidote."

"Dr. Shelley is right. And then we have to think about distribution," Dr. Kamini added.

"The world doesn't know about Everlasting Paradise and we want to keep it that way. If the media and the government learn of our location, we run the risk of them invading the island. As of right now, my fa—" Kate stopped, then corrected herself. "Dr. Mark Walker is a wanted man. They believe he is behind all of this. That he did all of this intentionally. They figured that out right away when they tested Jason's blood and found Serum Z. But no one besides the people on this island know that he is dead. And we want to keep it that way. At least for a little while longer. We just can't risk losing anyone on our team. Not when we are on the cusp of fixing what Dr. Walker started. If the public finds out, they might come in here and try to run the show. We need our independently run company to stay independent. The second we mention we may have a cure, the CDC, FDA, and all kinds of government entities will be on our asses."

A cure. A cure? Could this be a cure for all of us?

"What do you mean by cure? Is this only for the TZs?" I had to ask. A glimpse of living a normal life flickered before my eyes. I was aware that it'd be a long time before anything could go back to normal—if normal even existed anymore—but if it meant that I didn't have to eat humans ever again, then where did I sign up?

Kate sat back down. I knew the answer before she even spoke. The disappointment in her face said it all. "Unfortunately, this would not be a cure for all Zombrids. This antidote will only cure the TZs and turn them into Zombrids."

That wasn't a cure at all. That was a curse.

"They would turn into us?" Ian asked.

"Yes. Right now, the symptoms of the virus are what you all would have if you didn't get your daily nourishment. It's almost like they skipped straight through to that part. They'll try to eat anything and anyone who has a pulse.

Whether or not their state of mind could ever come back from that with this antidote is something we're exploring with testing. We believe it will, but we aren't one hundred percent certain. It's why this is all going to take a little time to figure out."

"Okay, so let's say we can turn the TZs into Zombrids, how are we supposed to feed all of those people? There are thousands of people infected. How are we supposed to—"

Kate interrupted my panicked rambling. "There will be millions soon. And then, there may be more true zombies than humans in the United States. But we can stop that from happening. Maybe, eventually, we can find a definitive cure for all Zombrids. But, Grace, this is the best we can do at the moment. And it's better than nothing."

"So, like...is there going to be another race?" Sonny asked. It sounded like a stupid question, but it wasn't. What if there was never a definitive cure? Would Zombrids co-exist with the humans? Could that even be possible? Who the hell would even trust a Zombrid? I could barely trust myself sometimes. I mean, I guess there were ways. That donor idea wasn't a bad one. Instead of the little red heart on someone's license, there could be a little red zombie.

"It was Dr. Walker's vision and it looks like it might come to fruition. We have to at least try. People are dying out there. I know this is not our fault. I know Dr. Walker left us drowning in shit, but I'm ready to make this right," Kate declared.

Ian immediately responded. "I'm in. Let's do this."

"Hey, I might be able to get a new arm once all this is over with. I'm definitely in," Sonny affirmed. Of course. She always thought about what was best for Sonny.

Everyone's attention was suddenly on me. Their eyes all gazed expectantly into mine. I tried to fight the urge to stand up and leave the room. Honestly, what choice did I have, though? I was Patient Zero. For all intents and purposes, I was the unspoken leader of our small Zombrid community. Dr. Walker wanted me to be the face of Serum Z. Would it be a bad thing now that we weren't intentionally killing people and actually trying to save the world?

My fingers fidgeted and my palms became clammy. Then, I answered. "Yeah, I'm in."

Kate smiled. "Great, Grace. I'm glad, because we need you. You and Sonny and Ian. If we wind up creating a whole new race of people, you three are going to be very important. And Grace, you are doing more than you even know."

I tilted my head at her. "How?"

"Well, it's you. You're the cure for the true zombie virus."

I could feel everyone's eyes on me as I sat there, trying to understand what Kate meant by her statement. Finally, I shook my head in confusion. "I...uh...what? How is that possible?"

"When we tested some of the blood you had donated with the TZs we captured in the States, it changed them. They became less aggressive. Less volatile. Obviously, it'll take a little while to determine the full effects of your blood over time, but we feel like this could definitely be it."

I brought my arms up and folded them across my chest, suddenly feeling uncomfortable and self-conscious. Like I was the one being hunted. "I...I don't understand." Thoughts of someone breaking into my room as I slept and stealing an over-sized mason jar filled with my blood crossed my mind. I instantly felt violated.

Kate spoke softly to me, as if she sensed my vulnerability. "We tried everyone's blood. We tried a number of different compounds and mixtures and formulas. And then when we transferred your blood into the TZ's circulation, it caused really good reactions. They have showed positive signs of revitalization."

"Why isn't Sonny's or Ian's blood good enough?" I asked defiantly, gesturing to where Sonny and Ian sat.

"Your blood seems to be the purest. We're not completely sure why. It could be because you're the oldest Zombrid here. Estelle might have been another candidate, but she's...no longer with us."

"How were the blood chemistries of the TZs you have tested so far?" Mom asked.

"All of the numbers were still out of whack," Dr. Sharma replied.

"Yes, but they seemed to be trending in the right direction," Dr. Kamini concurred.

The doctors spoke amongst themselves for a moment. I stood up and walked over to the window, peering down into the courtyard below. The new Zombrids were scattered all over the courtyard, and I watched as they laughed and talked and relaxed under the palm trees and cloudless sky. They all seemed to be happy. They all seemed to be comfortable in their skin and accepting of who they were.

Could I ever be like them? Could I ever truly be accepting of who *I* was?

I could hear the conversation at the table stop behind me, and then Kate said, "Grace, if you're okay with it, we need you to donate some more of your blood."

"What?" I asked, turning to face her again.

"We need more of your blood."

"How much more?" Were they just going to drain me until I was dry and shriveled up?

"We're working on a way to synthesize your blood. By doing so, we would be able to manufacture as much as we need to order to issue blood transfusions to all of those infected. But we need a foundation to start with."

"Kate, how much of my blood do you need?" I was tired of her beating around the bush.

"About fifty percent," she spit out.

"Kate, that would kill her!" Mom croaked.

"Actually, it wouldn't," Dr. Sharma corrected. "Grace is a Zombrid. She cannot die unless decapitated or burned to ashes. As long as she gets the correct quantity and quality of nourishment, her body will replenish all the cells and fluids it has lost. As a matter of fact, maybe even quicker than it would take a normal human being considering her healing abilities."

"You would be taking all of my blood. Wouldn't that make me lose the serum?"

"Serum Z is already part of your body. It has merged with your molecular chemistry and DNA. You will never lose it. Your body is now basically producing it."

"The only exception would be the side effects," Kate announced.

"Which are?" I sat back down. I needed to sit. I didn't smoke or drink, but somehow, I felt I needed a cigarette and some alcohol, too.

"You might feel like you are dying, but you won't be. Just as long as we take care of you afterward. We'll make sure we have exactly what you need to get better."

"And this will be the only time?"

"As soon as we create the correct formula that'll allow us to successfully synthesize your blood, we won't take any more of it. But that will take some time."

Well, this all made perfect sense. It was the perfect twist in my horror movie. I was the monster, but the monster was the answer to it all. The monster was going to save humanity.

"Fine," I mumbled and shrugged. I really didn't have much of a choice, did I? I didn't look at her, but I could feel my mother's stare on me from across the conference table. Sonny rested a hand on mine, and I appreciated her moment of selflessness. It was certainly rare.

"Grace, just remember that we'll be saving many lives. And we'll take good care of you throughout it all. All of you." Kate waved her hand across the three of us. "We're going to get the first round going in about an hour. That'll give us time to set everything up and make sure we've got some food for you after the blood draw."

I knew what she meant. All of this blood loss was going to require human meat. It was unfortunate because I was actually considering being one of the volunteers for the animal diet. But as much as I didn't want the human stuff, my mouth watered at the thought of it.

Sonny squeezed my hand and I glanced at her. "I'll be here with you, Grace."

I smiled at Sonny's unusual kindness, then gave a long and intentional glare at my mother. I had the urge to run to her with open arms. I wanted her to hold me. Nurture me. Tell me that everything was going to be okay. But I wanted her to feel my pain through my stare. I hoped that somehow, she would telepathically hear me curse her out and tell her that she was the reason why I didn't even want her to touch me. That it was because of her lies and betrayal.

Instead, Sonny and I stood up, linked arms, and walked out of the conference room. And I didn't even look back.

TWO MONTHS LATER...

THE CLERK

Serena

WARM BLOOD SPRAYED THE side of my face. I always tried to remember to turn my head after every dispatch. I didn't want to risk the infectious fluids making contact with any of my orifices.

The hard thud at my feet was confirmation that he was down, but not for long. I pulled my machete out of his skull. It was in there pretty good. I pressed my foot down on his shoulder, and with one powerful tug, I was able to retract my melee weapon. I learned to drown out the disgusting sound of piercing skulls, stabbing flesh, and even what I was about to do next.

I knelt down next to him and raised the machete up high over my shoulder behind me with two hands to be sure I could gain good momentum. After a second, I came down swiftly, the sharp blade splicing right through his neck. When I felt that I'd hit the ground, I knew that I had decapitated him. I cursed under my breath every time I had to do this. Why the hell weren't these things like the ones on TV? A shot to the brain wasn't going to stop them. We had our suspicions when Dan came back to life after Julian shot him in the head. Our suspicions were confirmed when we found ourselves in a sticky situation during a run for supplies.

We had managed to find a *Dollar General* a few miles east that happened to be unscathed by looters. Upon entering the store, we took out the four Creeps shuffling around the front door, aiming for the brain. We went on with our mission to scrounge up anything we could find. But when we returned to exit the store, all four Creeps were up and about again, threatening to attack us.

After we took them out a second time and waited around out of curiosity, Julian and I were in awe of their determination when they rose from the dead...again. Julian became pissed and decided right then and there to just chop one of their heads off. It worked. They didn't somehow manage to regrow a new head. So from then on, we made sure to decelerate and decapitate.

I stared at the Creep's face. Dark blood pooled around the open space between his head and his neck. His skin was pale and wrinkled, as if he were a hundred years old. His lips receded back, revealing black and decaying teeth. The man's head was severed but his eyes were still open and gazing back at me, red and empty.

He wore a uniform—gray slacks and a white collared knit polo. The name tag stitched over his left pec read *Clerk Johnny*. This guy was just a cashier trying to make a living. I desperately searched for that part of me, that nerve in my brain that was supposed to be struck when something sad happened. The little twinge of guilt for having to completely end someone's life. But there was nothing. These people were dead way before I even touched them. I just made it permanent—giving them a chance to finally rest instead of their constant, aimless shuffling through deserted streets.

I knew that my unfortunate experiences throughout my life had made it hard for me to connect with my feelings but living in a world like this didn't make it any better. It only enhanced my disconnection and reassured me that this place would always be screwed up, one way or another. Apocalypse or not.

I thought I could be happy. Dan had me believing there was hope. But he had tried to kill me, and even though I knew it wasn't really him, it still added to the series of unfortunate events that have plagued my life. I sometimes wished I could just die so that I could start all over again.

"Serena?"

Julian saved me from my macabre thoughts, and I stood up from the corpse. Julian was carrying a crate with one box of cereal and two tubes of toothpaste. "You okay?"

"Yeah. I'm fine. Are you ready?"

"We can head back. There was nothing else. Already been looted," he stated, disappointment crossing his face.

I took the crate from him. "It's fine. It's getting dark, anyway. We should head back and try again tomorrow."

I began to walk ahead of him and toward the front of the convenient store. But before I could exit, his hand pulled slightly at my upper arm. "Hey, you sure you okay?"

An exasperated sigh escaped my throat. It wasn't because I was annoyed with his question. It was actually quite flattering that he even noticed something was on my mind. It just meant that he knew me so well, and I loved that.

"I'm okay, Jules," I lied. The truth was, I was in *that* place again. That place in my brain that had me questioning whether or not I even wanted to be here anymore. It was a place that I'd visited before when all of this started, but I found myself frequenting it more often these days.

He took the crate from my hands and set it down on the floor. His tall, lean body hovered over me, and as much as I wanted to run away from the conversation we were about to have, I knew he wouldn't allow me to.

Julian placed his large hands on each of my cheeks, inspecting my eyes as if he was going to find something in them. "Serena, you know you can tell me anything. I've been giving you the space you need because I know that you lost Dan, and I know that everything around us has crumbled. But now it's time. You need to talk to me."

His voice was deep and soft at the same time, but I wasn't having any of it. I pushed his hands away. "Julian, there's nothing to talk about."

He latched on to my shoulders before I could turn away. "Serena," he growled. "Stop it."

I stared back into his hazel, desperate eyes before I took in his face completely. He was so handsome. And this apocalypse—as horrible and tough as it was to make it through the past three months—only made his usual ruggedness even sexier. His hair had grown out a bit longer. Enough for him to tie it into a small ponytail. He kept his beard trimmed, but its salt-and-pepper look was even more noticeable than before in the gleams of light. Probably from the stress of it all. And he was dirty. We both were from the long day of scavenging and killing the already dead.

I took all of this in, but I immediately squashed any thoughts of anything more than a friendship with Julian. We were living in this world together, but only as survivors. Nothing more. We never were before, and we never would be in the future. I loved him, but only as my best friend.

"Julian, I don't know what you want me to say," I finally said firmly.

He took a deep breath and released it harshly, giving up on the grip that held me in place. I turned my back to him. I was just having a bad day. Weren't we allowed to have one every now and then? Especially in this broken place we now lived in? I was tough. I knew I was tough. I had come a long way in my crappy life, and there was no way it was all for nothing.

Yet, there were times when I wanted to just quit. Times when I wanted to just give up on my life. But losing Dan broke me. Watching people all around me turn into stony, unfeeling, unrelenting, flesh-eating fiends shattered me even further. It was all about surviving now. Finding resources, making it out of sticky situations alive, and protecting ourselves.

I picked up the crate again, turned around, and headed toward the door, taking one last look at the dismembered Creep I had just dispatched. Killing them actually made me feel better.

I peered out of the glass door before pushing it open. Once to my left, then my right. It was all clear. Only the three headless Creeps were outside, sprawled out on the ground. We had picked them off before entering the store, along with a few other stragglers down the road.

We got back to the truck parked down the street without any event. I clutched on to my machete with one hand, the other grasping the crate as we scurried across the street. The weight of the ax strapped to my back made me feel safer and more confident that I didn't need Julian to flank me, but he followed close, anyway. He held his rifle close to his body, his flexed arms showing muscles begging to be free from the sleeves of his T-shirt. Working out was pretty much all we did for fun these days, and it showed.

I glanced back at the small outdoor strip mall we were leaving, disappointed that this was all we managed to find. There was also a fast-food restaurant and an ice cream parlor, but we didn't even bother. There were Creeps locked up inside. And as much as the thought of a cold, creamy ice cream cone made my mouth water, it wasn't going to happen. Those luxuries didn't exist anymore.

We had ventured off farther than usual earlier in the day, heading more inland than we liked to. We were curious to see what it was like in the areas closer to the middle of Florida, more toward Orlando. It was way more congested with a mixture of Creeps and abandoned cars. Well, sometimes they were abandoned. Sometimes the Creeps were stuck inside. It was like their own personal coffin on wheels.

Runs along the coast were preferred. Hotels and resorts that aligned the beaches were sometimes gold mines. Plus, there was the reassurance that we only had three avenues of approach by the Creeps, being that the beach served as a wall. Don't get me wrong, we did have our fair share of Creep-killing, but not as much as one would think. It wasn't quite summer yet, so the hotels weren't filled with vacationers. And if there were people on vacation when the outbreak started, they had scrambled out of the hotels quickly in an attempt to get the hell out of dodge, back to where they came from.

I couldn't imagine being on vacation during something like this. It made me think about all those people that were just visiting when 9/11 happened or when a tsunami hit Thailand. Going through something like that would make me think twice about leaving the comfort of my own home again.

Honestly though, a vacation would be amazing right about now. Relaxing on an island somewhere far away, off the grid and thousands of miles away from the wretched smell of stale human flesh. It sounded like a dream. But I knew that would never happen at this point. I should even remove the word *vacation* from my vocabulary.

We hopped into the truck and made our way back to the coastline. I stared out of the window as Julian drove. It was still so surreal to watch the state of our environment around us fly past me. The once busy streets were now completely empty—of anything living, that was. There was a cluster of things strewn about on the roads. Vehicles, bikes, shopping carts, debris from buildings that were caught on fire and had exploded, street signs, light poles, which was one of the main reasons for most of the power outages around the area. People were in a hurry to leave town. Some were even turning as they drove. Accidents were occurring everywhere. Some involved taking out light poles.

The rest of the power outages happened over time. As the cities began to become overrun by the Creeps, it seemed there was no one left to man the electricity and the operating systems.

Chaos enveloped this region and swallowed it whole. It was like everything had moved in fast forward. The outbreak, the riots, the looting, the burning... We watched people turning, people killing Creeps, people killing people, people killing themselves. We even saw Creeps attacking each other. Slowly but surely, the chaos began to quiet down around us. There were less and less of the living and more and more of the dead.

But these dead weren't dead. They shuffled down the street in slow strides. Some stood around and lurked, staring off into nothing. I wanted to believe that they were actually thinking about something. Maybe about what their next move would be, where they wanted to go, what they wanted to eat. But they didn't. They just stood stiffly, jerking and twitching from time to time. The moment the smell of something living hit their noses, they were on the hunt. There were at least a few around every corner. They could be in houses, cars, stores, buses, schools...basically anywhere. Waiting. Just waiting for something with a heartbeat to cross their paths.

They could hear pretty well, but their smell perception seemed to be much more advanced. They were slow. Not as slow as a turtle, but not as fast as someone walking at a normal pace. They were strong. If they managed to grab hold of you, it was difficult to get out of their grip. I wondered where they got this strength from if they were essentially corpses, but soon I realized that it was their *need* that drove it.

They were not to be underestimated. Their pallid and decomposing skin that sometimes looked as though it were melting right off their bones and gaunt appearance had lots of people fooled. I'd seen them open doors, climb through windows, and even manage to use a weapon. It may have seemed like a toddler was trying to do all these things, but they certainly had the capacity to learn. There was proof of that displayed by Julian's daughter, Harley.

If there happened to be fresh, bright red blood around their mouths, that was when you'd better just make a run for it. It meant they had just eaten, and it was equivalent to shoveling a pound of sugar down a five-year-old's throat. Fresh food made them stronger, faster, and harder to kill.

The ride back to the house was quiet with no problems. We took the back roads from Lakeland and up south around the city of Tampa. Interstate 4 would have been the quickest route. It was the main highway from the east to west coast of Florida, but that was precisely why we avoided it. It was overcrowded with cars and Creeps.

Going through the city would have been even worse. We managed to stay in Julian's little house for about a week before the streets became too overbearing with Creeps and the non-infected trying to survive. It wasn't long before we realized there was no way we could hold it down and stay safe. I wanted to leave. Even begged Julian. But he refused. He wanted to stay in Florida and close to where it started, just in case there was a way to get help for his daughter. But he did agree to leave the city. Tampa was Ground Zero, where the initial outbreak happened and all of the riots and looting began. There was no point in staying or even scavenging around that area. We were almost positive there would be no resources left to find.

After about two and a half hours of driving, I finally felt relieved and relaxed enough to breathe steady. Stress was all I knew in this mess. From the moment we began our runs to the moment we crossed the West Bay Drive Bridge back to our house, there was a metaphorical dark cloud that hung over our heads. There were plenty of sunny days in Florida, but that gloom was always all around us.

We crossed the water to the barrier islands off the coast of the Gulf. We hooked a right and headed to our boat docked at the tip of Gulf Boulevard. Most of the population in this area consisted of the rich. There were beach cottages and large homes, mostly vacation properties. We were lucky that the outbreak didn't happen around the Fourth of July. Otherwise, they might have all been occupied.

We ran into a few people who stayed behind in the beginning, but when they began to realize that there was no help coming, they must have decided to help themselves by picking up and leaving. They all fled the island, and we had no idea what happened to them. It was the case for most of the residents in the entire vicinity, really. I'd seen the fictional stories in movies, but it was surreal to see it in real life. The apocalypse became this horrific scene of survivors desperate to stay alive. They would do anything, just like the Creeps. Even losing all their humanity and morality just to have dinner for a night. Doing things that they would have never normally done before it all happened. Violent things. Murderous things.

But, then again, wouldn't we all try to do whatever we had to do to survive? To protect ourselves and our families? This world was filled with bad people, hungry for not just food but power. It was amazing to see this unfold right before my eyes.

I glanced down at my hands and squeezed them together, pushing those thoughts out of my mind. I wasn't in the right frame of mind to think about what happened a few weeks ago. To think about *that* night.

I felt Julian's eyes shifting between me and the road as he drove, but I didn't look back at him. When we finally reached the dock and he pulled into park, I all but flew out of the cab, suddenly feeling like I needed the early evening ocean breeze in my lungs.

With an unspoken tension in the air, we unloaded the bed of the truck and filled the boat. Julian and I worked as quietly as we could when we were away from the house. Even though we couldn't help that the Creeps could smell much better than they could hear, moving around stealthily could only be beneficial to our safety.

The rich folks had quite a variety of boats to choose from docked in their boat slips. There were yachts, speed boats, and pirogues, along with some other beachy toys like surfboards and jet skis. I didn't know a lick about boats, but thankfully, Julian's dad was some kind of boat guy. Julian grew up with boats, joining his dad on fishing trips and weekends away on their own private vessel.

Our new house was on its own small island, and we needed something that could aid in carrying our supplies from the main barrier island. It also had to be something that matched our ninja-like furtiveness. So Julian chose a boat with a jet drive motor. Apparently, it was designed to be safer and more eco-friendly so that it wouldn't disturb marine life. It basically looked like a regular old fishing boat, only with the motor inboard instead of outside the water. We didn't need anything extravagant. Simply something that was quiet, efficient, and made our lives a little easier in this difficult world.

It took us no time to cruise across the water over to our tiny island. The light was dimming in the sky, but as soon as our house came into view, the constant anxiety that plagued me eased some more. It was a little disconcerting how easily one could reach us if they wanted to. This privately-owned island wasn't hidden in any way. But the Creeps couldn't swim—that we knew of—and at this point, there really weren't many non-infected people to worry about.

Julian parked the boat while I grabbed hold of the rope and wrapped it around the iron anchor that stuck out of the wooden dock. He had taught me a few nautical knots, which turned out to be easier than I'd thought.

After the vessel was secure, we began carrying the small amount of loot we were able to retrieve.

"We should probably head up the coast again tomorrow. I knew we weren't going to find much inland."

"Yeah," I replied.

We walked up the long wooden dock that led to the staircase of the large home. There were two flights before we could reach the porch that wrapped around the entire house. This was the type of house that I only dreamed of living in. It was an enormous, two-story seaside home. It was painted in a shade of blue that matched a clear morning sky, with floor-to-ceiling windows that lined the first floor. The second floor had fewer windows, but they were encased in shutters, giving it a nautical touch. At the very top was a small lookout tower enclosed in more windows, allowing a 360-degree view of the Gulf of Mexico. It was the perfect place for an easel and a blank canvas.

Whoever owned this home before was obviously loaded. It seemed to be some sort of vacation rental because we didn't find any personal items inside. There were no pictures, no food in the kitchen. Only tacky beach decorations and random artwork of the ocean and seashells on the walls. It was set up like a sort of show home, immaculately clean and untouched. The white furniture seemed new and arranged as if it were staged. It had its own private dock and its own private beach. It seemed to be ideal when Julian and I caught a glimpse of it from the main barrier island during the search for better living quarters. And we hadn't had any problems staying here. So far.

THE NIGHT

I WALKED INTO THE house first, eager to set down all the goods to take a bath. I could smell the putrid stench of the dead on me. I could smell it everywhere. All day. Even in the house. It reeked of a strong, coppery, nauseating mixture of roadkill and baby shit. The only time I got a breath of semi-fresh air was on the water or in the tub, and that was only because the vanilla-scented body wash masked it somewhat.

Julian went straight to the bedroom toward the back of the house to check on Harley. I lethargically made my way upstairs, finally feeling the weight of the day on my body. I stepped into one of the master bedrooms (yes, ONE of them). It was equipped with an en-suite bathroom, which had a step-down garden tub. The other master bedroom belonged to Julian, and he decided on that one because it was downstairs near his daughter and the front door in case of any intruders.

I instinctively slid my hand over the light switch on the wall upon entering, still not completely used to the fact that we haven't had electricity since a couple of weeks after the outbreak. Oh, what a spoiled life we lived before. I tried not to miss the convenience of it all. Instead, I told myself that this was what it was like back in the old days, when electricity wasn't even invented. People managed then, why couldn't we now? No cellphones, no computers. No microwaves to heat up processed foods. No televisions to distract us from the outside world. There was a time when I had to live that way, and it was easy for me to slip back into the pampered life of overhead lighting and warm food when I finally got on my feet. But it was definitely hard to have to go back. I didn't think I would ever have to again.

It might have been better this way. If only we could stop worrying about being eaten by the Creeps, we might have a chance of just living a quiet, simple life.

I reached inside my pocket to retrieve my lighter and lit the candle on the dresser near the door, lifting it to get a good whiff and silently thanking God we were able to loot a *Bath and Body Works* store. Believe it or not, it was untouched and hadn't been broken into. I guess no one really thought about trying to scavenge a place that mostly sold girly-scented body wash. Candles, too. Lots of floral and fruit-scented candles. I preferred the Fall smells like pumpkin spice and apple cinnamon, but anything was better than the essence of rotting flesh.

I emptied the other pocket of my jeans, which contained a multi-tool pocketknife. My back pocket was where the picture of Charlie and me lived most of the time, and I placed it on the nightstand next to the clock that didn't work. Then, I plopped down on the bed, happy to finally be able to peel the dirty, bloodstained clothes away from my body. The days of dressing all bohemian and artsy were behind me now. Cute kimonos and flowy skirts weren't very effective in these times. It was all about the durable wrangler jeans and T-shirts and tank tops. Shin guards and knee/elbow pads were also useful. Not only in preventing Creep bites, but maneuvering around places, too. There had been many instances where I had to crawl through air ducts to gain entrance into a building in order to minimize the sound of breaking glass from bashing in a window. I'd even had to jump eight feet down from a roof.

In addition to that protection, Julian came up with the brilliant idea of using leather around our arms, legs, and torso. Even our necks. He said he saw some show on *The Discovery Channel* about armor, which explained that leather would be a fine choice for its durability and ability to breathe. The material wasn't too heavy so it helped with mobility. Also, it wasn't hard to find. Leather seats from cars seemed to be the easiest way to obtain it. I guess watching hours of mindless television did account for something in this world.

After removing the last bit of my makeshift armor, which proved to be a little difficult since we had to use duct tape to secure it in place, I tore off the rest of my clothes and walked over to my own personal chemistry lab. The city's water system was cut off around the same time as the electricity, so we had to come up with something since the saltwater in the ocean just wasn't feasible. Now, this idea was both mine and Julian's—although, we might have acquired this knowledge differently. A Chemistry teacher in high school taught Julian. A homeless man with a prosthetic leg named Shaky Joe taught me. But the way we learned it didn't matter.

We each had a table set up in our bathrooms, as well as one in the kitchen. On top of it was a large, deep pot, which sat on a single burner. This pot was covered, but had a funnel connected to the cover and a long tube. The tube snaked from the large pot to a plastic tub on the floor next to it. The idea of this contraption was to turn ocean water, or saltwater, into distilled fresh water used for bathing and drinking.

Shaky Joe didn't know the name for this process, but I later learned while studying to get my GED that it was called desalination. Basically, the pot full of saltwater on the burner would boil, causing steam. This steam was then captured in the funnel, and as it cooled, would drip down into the tub as fresh water.

A process like this took some time to fill up a large plastic *Rubbermaid* tub, so I made sure to have it going all the time. Eventually, I would have to warm up the water in the cooler months, but it didn't matter much now. I'd already come to terms with the fact that a hot, steaming shower was just another luxury that I might never have again.

I watched the water roll off my skin and into the brown pool of dirty water at my feet as I poured it over me. Suddenly, *that* night from a few weeks ago flashed before my eyes. But the puddle at my feet wasn't brown. It was tinted deep red. The color of blood.

Don't think about that night, Serena.

After about thirty minutes of scrubbing the nasty away, I pulled on some sweatpants and a T-shirt and dried my hair. Brushing my hair took forever, the long knots clinging for dear life to the bristles. Dinner was my next plan before it was time to turn in and rest up for another day in hell.

I made my way downstairs and found that Julian had my same thoughts.

"How is she?" I asked, reaching around him to grab an MRE from the pantry. We lucked out in finding a few cases of these Meals Ready to Eat. They weren't exactly the tastiest, but they did the job and lasted virtually forever.

The smell of cucumber melon body wash radiated off Julian's skin and I knew that he had just bathed, too. That scent wasn't the manliest, but who cared? Another *Bath and Body Works* loot for the win.

"She's okay. If only they would stop eating all the animals, I could get her something better. I don't think that cat was enough for her today."

I carried my food and bottled water over to the couch in the living room, and Julian followed. If this world were different, you'd think Julian and I would be having a romantic dinner at home alone, judging by the candles lit all around us.

"Is she looking any worse than yesterday?"

"She's the same. Still not as bad as the others," he stated.

The last sight I had of Harley was two days ago when I poked my head into her bedroom while Julian was asleep on the couch. I caught her attention immediately after opening the door, maybe even way before then by the smell of the sweat from my pores. She was lying on the bed and she stared at me with those lifeless eyes before snapping her gritty, decaying teeth at the air. Her legs and arms flailed about, desperately yearning to tear into my flesh. But she was tethered to the bedposts by her ankles and her wrists. Julian decided to use rope because he felt the chains were just too much. It definitely wouldn't have been my personal choice, but she was *his* daughter. I didn't want to say anything.

We had no choice but to tie her up to the bed when she learned how to open the closed door to her bedroom and tried to attack her own father in the middle of the night. In a normal world, tying up a seven-year-old girl this way would have sent us straight to prison. But she was dangerous. She was no longer a tiny and cute young girl with freckles and brown pigtails. She was a monster. A monster whose skin was beginning to wear and tear from the virus. She had large bloody wounds all over her body. Her hair was thinning and falling out, chunks of it scattered all over the bedsheets. The whites of her eyes were gone.

Even still, she wasn't half as bad as most of the Creeps on the streets. We discovered that this may be because Julian had been consistently feeding her. At first, he tried regular food, but of course, she denied it. We knew exactly what she wanted, but there was no way we could feed a human to her. So the next best thing was an animal, and it seemed to keep her satisfied. Julian began keeping an eye out for them during our runs. Surprisingly, animals weren't that hard to find in a zombie apocalypse—in the beginning, anyway. Some people left their pets behind, leaving them locked up in their apartments or houses. How they could do this was beyond me, but it just made our lives a little easier. But now that the Creep population had increased and there were fewer humans, it was getting harder to find animals.

"I'm going to have to set up bigger traps and hope that I can catch something that could hold her over for a few days. The smaller animals and fish just aren't cutting it."

I finished my MRE and walked over to the wet bar to pour a glass of wine. I needed something to bring me down before bedtime.

With my glass full almost to the brim, I sat back down on the couch, stretching my legs out on the coffee table. I didn't respond to Julian's issues regarding his daughter. He didn't want to know my opinion.

"Do you want to work out with me in the morning before we go on the run?" I asked in an attempt to change the subject.

He hesitated before answering, sensing my deviation from the conversation about Harley. "Yeah, we can." The tension filled the air around us, and we both stared off into different directions. I was on the verge of calling it a night when Julian broke the silence. "Serena, can we please talk?"

I fought the urge to roll my eyes. Julian didn't deserve my attitude. It wasn't meant to be directed at him.

"Serena. Please," he pleaded.

I turned to him. "What do you want me to say?"

"I want you to tell me why you've been so distant these past few weeks."

"I'm here, Julian. I'm here," I said, shrugging my shoulders and gesturing at the room around us.

His tone got deeper. "That's not what I mean, and you know it. You haven't talked to me in weeks. Not about anything other than runs. You come home and hang around in the office most of the time. All you do is eat, sleep, and workout."

"Well, what else is there to do?"

A noticeable frustration was beginning to show on his face. "I don't know. Maybe at least try to make the best of what's happening. Hell, you could even paint if you wanted to. That used to make you so happy. I mean, I know things are bad but—"

"But what, Julian? You think I can just sit around and paint beautiful, colorful pictures?" I wanted to. I missed painting so badly. But there was too much gloom. Too much death. "Things *are* bad, haven't you noticed? The city is gone. There's no one left but us and the Creeps. Dead, raunchy, horrible things that try to eat us on a daily basis. There's no electricity, no water, and we're running out of places to find resources. We're completely alone."

"You know I don't like that word," he muttered.

"That's what you got out of what I just said?" I couldn't believe it! I understood his reasoning behind the dislike for what I called the zombies. His daughter was one of them. Honestly, I didn't mean it to be offensive. It was what a group of young teenagers called them in the beginning, and it stuck. But this wasn't about what we called those bastards!

He snapped a look back at me. His eyebrows furrowed as if he was confused. "Serena, you think I don't know that we're living in hell? We watched everything crumble around us. I was here, too. I saw them eating everyone, infecting everyone. I saw the military give up and leave us behind. I saw humans fighting humans and killing each other over the stupidest things. My daughter is a damn zombie! I have to feed her animals. Live, breathing animals."

"Then why aren't we leaving?" I asked slowly, as if speaking to a child. "We have no idea what's happening outside of Florida. We don't know if this is only happening here. But we have to find out, Julian. No one's coming for us and we can't keep trying to survive like this."

"You know I can't leave, Serena. I can't risk traveling with Harley. You're right, we don't know what's out there. And if we come across people who want to kill her, I don't know what's going to happen."

He was frightened for his daughter. I understood that. But at this point in our survival, I honestly didn't feel like there was any hope for Harley. "What if there isn't a cure? What if there is no turning back from this?"

He looked down at his hands. "I have to try. I have to stay here and hope that there's help coming and that somehow they can fix her."

I inched my way closer to him and lifted his chin up with my finger so our eyes could meet. "You don't think she's suffering? What if she wants to let go?"

I knew I was crossing a line.

Julian jerked his face away from my hand. "Jesus, Serena," he said in disgust. "Really? I can't kill my daughter."

I felt like I was hitting a brick wall. If it were up to me, I would have ended her life a long time ago. It sounded terrible, but after what I'd seen those Creeps do and after watching her day after day, constantly trying to fight her way out of those restraints in order to feed on something with a pulse, I wouldn't be able to stand it anymore. Harley wasn't my daughter, but she was Julian's daughter, and Julian was my life. Whether or not I cared about her was not even a question. In fact, I cared about her wellbeing so much that I just wanted to relieve her from the pain she so obviously dealt with every single day.

I didn't know what else to do. I didn't know how else to get to him. We couldn't stay here. What if help never came? What if there wasn't a cure? Was this how we would live our lives forever? In a city full of the undead, fighting them as they took every chance they got to try to eat our brains until one day they finally succeeded? I would rather catch on fire or die drowning than by the teeth of a Creep.

"I'm not trying to be insensitive to your daughter. I'm trying to make you realize that we need to move on. We need to at least try."

He shook his head. He wasn't budging. I slumped down on the couch, feeling defeated. But that emotion didn't last long. It quickly turned into anger. I stood up and made a beeline for the stairs but then stopped, changing my mind. It wasn't time to storm out in a huff. It was time for him to hear what had happened to me.

I turned on my heels and went back to him. "Remember when you told me to leave? When you told me to try to get out of this place?"

He didn't look up at me. "Yes, and I'm not mad at you for that. I wanted you to try to seek refuge."

"Yeah, well...I tried. I had a plan to find help for us and for Harley. But then, I came back. I came back with blood all over me and I told you it was because I had killed so many of them while I was trying to find a way out." He finally looked at me, probably wondering where I was going with my story. I shook my head. "It wasn't their blood."

"I...I don't understand."

"I killed a man. A human." My heart began to race, and my thoughts started to drift. Before I knew it, Julian was no longer in my view. I was watching what happened replay before my eyes. "I got out of the truck for a second. I had to wipe the blood and the body parts off the windshield in order to see. I had just run over a couple of Creeps who were standing in the middle of the road. Then, this man... He smelled like sweat and dirt and alcohol. He wrapped his arms around me, and my initial reaction was to scream. But it wasn't long before I realized that no one would hear me.

"He pulled some kind of bag over my head and I couldn't see. I had no idea where he was taking me. He was big. He was fat and big, and I tried to pull away. I kept punching and kicking at him, but he wouldn't let go. He threw me down onto the ground and I was finally able to rip the bag off my head. But it was too late. He had me pinned down and he weighed so much that I couldn't get him off me and I couldn't get to my knife right away and he...he started to force himself on me and touch me and..."

I wanted to finish that sentence, but it was so hard. I couldn't find the right way to explain what he did to me. I was choking on the words, trying my hardest not to cry. I told myself I wouldn't cry about it. I would never shed a tear over what that asshole did to me.

My life was never peaches-and-cream. If it weren't for the ten years I had with my brother before he died, I might have had to raise myself since the age of one. I had lived on the streets, stole, fought with old hobos who threatened to kill me over a piece of moldy garbage bread. But by the grace of God, somehow, I was never sexually assaulted or raped.

Julian stood up and began to walk toward me. "Serena, are you saying that he—"

I put my hand up, telling him to stay where he was. "I'm saying I did what I had to do. Somehow, I managed to wrestle him off me after he...and I...I killed him. I stabbed his chest over and over again until his insides were hanging out of his body. Until I could see his heart. And I got in the car and turned around and came back because I felt scared. For the first time in my life, I was legitimately scared. And I needed you, Jules. I should have never left you behind." A tear escaped my right eye, and I quickly swiped it away with the back of my hand. "I felt guilty. I felt like I was being punished for leaving you."

Julian took another step forward. He placed a hand on my neck and examined my face, as if searching for wounds or any indications that I was hurt. It happened weeks ago and the bruises that stinky douchebag left behind on my wrists and legs from throwing me around were long gone.

"Why didn't you tell me?" he asked softly, as if afraid to raise his voice. "Why didn't you tell me this happened to you?"

"Because I didn't want you to feel guilty for telling me to leave, but I knew you had only told me that because you cared and wanted me to get out."

He took yet another step forward. He looked down at me, placing his other hand on my cheek. I closed my eyes.

His skin felt warm on mine, and I tilted my head into his palm. It felt so good to be touched by someone I loved.

But then, I took a step back. "Don't."

We stood staring at each other. I knew all he wanted to do was hug me. He must have felt awful, ashamed...guilty for telling me to run away without him. But I didn't blame him. I would never blame him. He told me from the very beginning that he would protect me. He didn't break his promise. He protected me and kept me safe every chance he got when we were out there together.

"I don't ever want to talk about this again. All I want to do is get the hell out of here. I know that there are very few humans out there now, but I'm not even afraid of them anymore. I'm not afraid of the zombies, either. I'm going to continue living this screwed-up life to survive, but I have to get out of here and try for a better one. We don't know what's out there, Jules. There could be help right outside state lines and we've been sitting on our asses waiting for nothing."

"I'm so sorry this happened to you. The moment you walked out of that door—" His words were strained, his eyes suddenly bloodshot. He was clearly holding back tears. "I wanted to chase after you. You have to know that. I was so worried. I paced the house over and over again, trying to decide whether or not I should leave my daughter, chase after you, bring her with me... I didn't know what to do. But I knew you wanted to leave, and I didn't want to hold you back from a chance of possibly getting to safety or getting help. I had to let you try."

"Then let's get out of here, Julian. Together."

He ran both hands through his hair in frustration. "Serena, it isn't that simple. What if they try to take Harley away from me? What if they try to kill her? What if she gets worse? It's been months since all of this started. Someone has got to be working on a cure or something. I know you want to leave but—"

I threw my hands up. "Fine!" And that was the last thing I said to him before stomping up the stairs to the office. I slammed the door behind me and closed my eyes shut, lightly banging my head against the wood a couple of times before sliding down and falling to the floor. I rested my head in my hands, cursing myself in my mind for the way I had treated him.

The sound of something hitting the wall made me jump. Once. Twice. Three times. It was Julian's fist smashing into the wall. My fingers curled into my hair and pulled, guilt tugging at my insides for making sweet Julian this angry. He was doing the best he could. He was only trying to survive and keep his daughter safe. But I had no idea what else to do to get him to agree to leave.

I had been fighting against these monsters for months now, working out to build agility and stamina, practicing how to use my weapons the best I could to defend myself and him and Harley. There was a one hundred percent chance that I could get out of this place alone. I had confidence in myself. But I couldn't leave Julian. The truth was, if I hadn't been raped, I probably would have found my way back to him, anyway. We always found our way back to each other. Jules was the only reason I hadn't given up completely. And the reality was that he did have his daughter to worry about and he would do anything to protect her. And I would do anything to protect him.

But I knew I was changing. I knew what I needed was to get out of here. I felt like a ticking time bomb. There was an aching in the pit of my stomach. The burning madness inside of me was growing. I could feel it spreading to my limbs, my heart, and my mind.

I didn't know how to dig myself out of this hole. Out of this deep, dark existence that was now my life. Each one of us believed that we have it worse than someone else. Throughout my life, I tried not to think that way even though nothing ever went right. I never had that loving family. I never had those best friends that would do anything for me. I struggled to give myself decent things. And there was never a passing minute where I didn't miss Charlie's smile.

When that disgusting man did...things to me, my humanity completely broke apart. It was the last straw. It was the last time I would allow anyone or anything push me again—humans, Creeps, situations, evil geniuses who created experimental serums for their own, selfish purposes.

I stood up, suddenly feeling a gush of rage course through my veins. I lit the candle in the office and glanced up at the corkboard above my desk. It was a diagram. A strategically mapped layout of newspaper clippings, pictures, coordinates to locations around the world, informational articles about the outbreak and Serum Z and its timeline gathered from the Internet, and more of Dan's notes found on his laptop before the power outage.

I held the candle up, illuminating the photo in the center of the homemade blueprint. Dr. Mark Walker's sinister grin and menacing eyes stared back at me. He was the reason I lost that one chance at happiness. He was the reason I lost my knight in shining armor. The person who was supposed to be the light at the end of my dark tunnel. Dr. Walker was the reason why that sick son of a bitch violated me. He was the reason I had nightmares about taking someone's life, reliving the act of murder over and over again in my dreams.

He was the reason I ran for my life every day, avoiding being caught by a Creep and turning, or worse...becoming a meal as they tore and ripped into my body. He was the reason for this crappy world we had to live in now.

Dr. Mark Walker needed to die. And I was going to be the one to kill him.

THE
SEARCH

THERE WAS SLIGHT MOVEMENT at my feet and my eyes popped open. I immediately reached for my machete under the pillow and jumped out of bed to take the Creep-killing stance—both feet planted firmly on the ground for balance, with two hands on the handle and pulled back behind my shoulder, ready to swing.

Julian stayed seated on the edge of the bed. "Guess I should have known better."

I searched the room, alert and aware. Julian was harmless, but I was still half asleep. There was no reaching REM in the zombie apocalypse. But my adrenaline was constantly lying dormant just below the surface; therefore, it only took seconds to fully come out of my groggy state. I finally realized it was safe enough to stop threatening poor Julian with my weapon. "How long have you been in here?"

"I just sat down. I was about to wake you to tell you breakfast is ready."

I glanced at my digital wristwatch. It was eight in the morning. Seven o'clock was my usual time, when I began my daily routine of breakfast, jogging, working out, sharpening my blades, and gearing up for another day of hunting for resources.

"I overslept."

"You got to your room late last night."

"I wasn't tired," I lied. My eyelids were weighing down by the time the clock struck midnight, but I wasn't ready to give up my research for the night. I reached behind Julian to grab a T-shirt on the edge of the bed. I slept in my panties and a tank top, but my daytime clothes were always laid out and ready to be thrown on in case of an emergency. I wasn't going to let a trespassing Creep surprise me.

"Do you have any leads?" Julian asked.

"There are a few potential places. As a matter of fact, I wanted to run them by you. See if anything rings a bell."

He jabbed his thumb into his eye. "Serena, I told you I didn't know anything. I only worked with the guy for two weeks."

"We just have to be sure, Jules."

My obsession with finding this doctor was just as surprising to me as it was to Julian. A few months later and now I had more reason to hate Dr. Walker, but in the beginning, I had no idea what made me so interested. Maybe it was the desire to finish what Dan started. Maybe I felt like I owed it to him to continue his investigation on this guy. But I didn't have much to go on. Living in a world with no Internet and no news reporting was not easy. I had gotten so used to Googling everything under the sun before this all happened, that I'd completely forgotten about libraries and newspaper archives. Breaking into libraries, picking up the most recent newspapers I could find around the city, and Julian's very short employment history were all I had.

Regardless, I managed to learn a little bit about Dr. Mark Walker and his career as a physician. He had written a few books about Microbiology and doctor stuff, which I was able to find at a tiny bookstore right off the beach. I read all three, but unfortunately, it wasn't useful. It was mainly a type of textbook, teachings in Microbiology and Medicine. He'd won awards for his philanthropy and multiple charity foundations. I learned that he once had a family, but it had fallen apart after his son passed away.

Before the news stations were shut off and there was radio silence, it seemed that the world had uncovered everything: Dr. Walker and his drug Serum Z were the reason for the outbreak and this virus. The CDC figured out who Patient Zero—the man at the supermarket—was. The news outlets announced that he had chemical compounds resembling Serum Z or something similar coursing through his veins. Officials raided Dr. Walker's many clinics all over the country, including his residence, and basically detained for questioning every single person who had ever known him, but no one was able to find the shit-starter. Not him or his alleged daughter who had been known to work closely with him. Eventually, they were both labeled as terrorist fugitives.

There was some mention of Serum Z in the small amount of information that I found, but I couldn't be too sure if it was the same serum Julian remembered. The literature in medical journals mentioned that this medicine was labeled as an experimental drug and could only be used with the patient's consent.

I could feel Julian's eyes on me as I leaned over the sink and brushed my teeth in my underwear. Apocalypse or not, dental hygiene was important. My worst fear was having a toothache and no one around to fix it. And I couldn't give a crap about whether or not Jules saw my underwear.

"There's no point. I didn't work with the man long enough to know anything," Julian reiterated to me for the umpteenth time.

Listerine swooshed between my teeth before I spit it into the sink. "Well, maybe if you hear some of these places, you might remember a conversation or something."

He stood up and walked toward me. "Serena, if the government hasn't found out where he is, I really doubt we will. And anyway, what exactly do you plan to do if you found him? This guy could be dangerous."

"I don't know yet. I could give him up to the police." I was lying. I had no intentions of giving him up to anyone.

Julian stepped closer to me and reached for my hand. "You're angry. I know you are. You need something to take it out on. But it isn't your job to find this guy. We just have to survive until things get better."

I gazed back into his deep hazel eyes. A part of me wanted to give in. To see his views. To agree with him and just hang around and stay alive long enough for help to come. But the seething rage inside of me was burning. I felt anxious to do something, anything other than hang around and wait for rescue.

We stood silent for a moment before I moved away from him and walked back toward the bed. "What if we find him and he's working on a cure? What if we can get him to cure Harley?" It was a desperate final attempt to get him to agree to leave. There was a feeling of guilt that rushed through my body for exploiting his daughter, but it had to be done.

Afraid to look at him after what I'd said, I kept my eyes down and proceeded to pull my jeans on and lace up my boots.

"Well, I came in here to tell you that breakfast was ready and that...I think you're right."

I stopped breathing.

"I think we do need to move on. To find help."

He came and knelt down in front of me, forcing me to finally look at him. "I hate what happened to you when you left. I know you say it isn't my fault, but I told you that I would protect you. I shouldn't have let you go alone. I know how much you want to leave. I know you're unhappy. So I'm going to do this. With you."

"And Harley?"

"Traveling with Harley is going to be hard. But I'm not leaving her behind. I'll protect her, and you."

My lips threatened to turn up into a smile, but I wasn't ready for it. "This means a lot, Jules."

He seemed to be resisting a smile, too, but I believed it was to show me that his decision still worried him. "There has to be a compromise, though. We can't go looking for Dr. Walker right now. You have to understand that, Serena."

"It's fine. We'll figure it out later. Right now, let's just get as much as we can into the car." My plans to find the bastard weren't going to be easily dismissed, but Julian had agreed to finally leave, and I didn't want to risk him changing his mind.

"The car? You don't want to take a boat?"

"I've thought about this. If we go by land, it could be easier to find help and maybe even stock up on more supplies. Adding Harley into the equation is going to make things a little more complicated, but I really believe that we won't have any problems getting past the Cree—" I stopped myself. Bad timing to insult his daughter, just when he had finally agreed to leave with me.

"It's okay. I won't give you a hard time about it."

"Thanks."

He caressed my cheek with the back of his hand. "Serena, I just want you to be happy and safe."

His skin was rough, which was probably the result of the constant use of hand sanitizer and handwashing.

We tried to stay infection-free any way we could. Despite the callouses, it still felt nice to finally have some kind of affectionate contact with someone. It might not have seemed like a long time but in a world like this, it was easy to feel lonely.

Julian and I were the only people left around here. Technically, we weren't alone because we had each other, but there was rarely any kind of physical contact. All this time, Julian had thought he was giving me space to mourn Dan, but he didn't know about what that rapist jerk did a few weeks ago. And after that, I felt wary about being touched at all. I used to be the kind of woman who spoke with my hands, inadvertently touching whoever I was talking to during a conversation. But things were different now. And so was I.

My body wanted to be closer to him. It wanted to rest against his chest and listen to the sound of his lungs inhaling and exhaling. It wanted to hear the thump of a beating heart. The delicate sounds coming from someone who was alive. And as much as I didn't want to admit it at the moment, love and affection might have been what I needed to stop the indignation inside of me.

Julian could probably feel my body language. He inched closer to me and rested a hand on my thigh. My heart was fighting with my mind, battling with the spiritual need for intimacy of any kind and the powerful urge to stay as far away as possible to anything that could cause me pain. I knew for a fact that Jules wouldn't intentionally hurt me. I was sure of that. But I feared that if I allowed myself to get close to anyone else, then history would repeat itself, as it had always done throughout my life.

He leaned in toward me and I slammed my eyes shut. His hand cradled my cheek while the other slid up my thigh to my waist, a pleasant sensation sending chills throughout my body.

"Serena," he whispered deeply.

I opened my eyes and there he was, his lips moments away from mine. I was completely comfortable. Safe and wholly at ease. Thoughts of the new, terrifying world around us began to slowly dissolve as I gazed into his eyes. His lips parted slightly and he gently pulled me toward him. Julian and I had only kissed once a million years ago, and it was because we were both drunk and vulnerable and stupid. It was sloppy and lasted all of a few seconds. We pulled away from each other at the same time and laughed, then I turned and threw up on his couch. Not because the kiss was gross, but because the mixture of whiskey and Jello shots churned in my stomach and created an evil, disgusting alcohol baby that was fighting to escape. Honestly, the whole thing wasn't even worth mentioning again.

But maybe I needed this. Maybe I needed to do this to help me feel something...anything again. Maybe I needed Julian to remind me that—

A distressed howl followed by smashing glass forced us both to stand up and abandon the moment.

THE NURSE

Grace

MY EYELIDS FELT LIKE stones, only managing to open them halfway and long enough to see the foot of my bed. I attempted to lift my head, but it ached to even try. I was able to turn it slightly, only to catch a glimpse of a needle in my arm. My body felt like putty—like it was one with the bed.

I heard a voice. "Grace, are you awake?" It was high-pitched and girly, and I knew who it was. I moaned in response because it was all I could do. "I'll go get Dr. Kamini and let her know you're up."

A louder moan erupted out of my throat. It wasn't because I thought she didn't hear me. It wasn't because I was informing her that I understood what she said. It was because I was in so much pain that I didn't want her to go. Sonny came into view, and I whimpered once more. I didn't have enough strength to open my mouth to speak. My chest hurt too much to even breath.

"Grace," she said as she walked closer to me. I felt a hand on mine. "It's okay. I just have to get the doctor. I'll be right back."

A tear escaped my eye and run down the side of my head. I was afraid to be alone with the pain.

Her heels clanked on the floor out of the room, but it was only a second later that I heard them back inside.

"Her lips are turning blue. Let's get some food inside of her now that she's awake before hypovolemic shock sets in."

Food. Food was what I needed. The thought of blood and flesh touching my lips made my stomach flip, and suddenly, I was ravenous. I wanted to cry even more at the thought of not getting what I needed within the next five minutes.

There were hands on my body, moving and pulling me into an upright position. The pain intensified from just the touch, and I struggled to catch a decent breath.

"It's going to be okay, Grace. We've got exactly what you need, and you'll feel better before you know it," the doctor promised. It was at that exact moment that the smell reached my brain. It wasn't close, but it was coming. My mouth watered and I whined—like a child wanting something they couldn't have.

The aroma was getting closer and closer to me. My body felt awful, but the smell seemed to awaken all my senses and a rush of adrenaline surged through me.

I wanted it. I needed it.

My muscles tensed at the thought of chewing on the tender meat. I imagined the raw fat and tissues sliding off my fingertips and into my mouth, leaving behind a savory explosion of sweet and bitter on my taste buds after it glided down my throat and into my voracious stomach.

My breathing was uncontrollable now. It hurt worse than anything I'd felt before, and the rate at which my lungs moved air in and out increased. It was almost as if I was panting. The smell steadily made its way closer, but I was growing more anxious. My heart pounded in my rib cage and I could hear the thumping in my own ears. I wanted so badly to get out of bed, to reach the scent before it reached me. But I was so weak. I could barely lift my finger.

Or so I'd thought.

I closed my eyes and opened them again, glancing around and seeing several doctors holding my body down onto the bed. I was apparently fighting against them, trying my hardest to pull away from their grip. I didn't understand what was happening to me. As I searched around the room, it felt like my eyes were moving from face to face in slow motion. My vision was blurred and there only seemed to be translucent traces of people and objects. My eyes rolled with every blink.

But Sonny's frightened gaze forced me to stop and stare at her. She was standing near the door, her one arm crossed over her body. She was visibly shaking, but slightly spinning in my vision. I struggled to keep my eyesight steady. The delicious odor of blood seemed so close. Close cnough for mc to lick.

Then suddenly, a moment of clarity. My body jolted violently, and before I knew it, I could think clearly again.

I knelt over her body, hands cupped above her torso, carefully holding a pool of red liquid. I instantly pulled them apart and watched the blood splash into her empty shell. I glanced at my hands and arms. They were covered in bright red and chunks of slimy, fatty stuff. I looked down and instantly threw myself back away from the dead body that lay before me.

What did you do, Grace?

I peered up near the door and Sonny wasn't there.

"Grace? Grace, can you hear me?"

It was Dr. Kamini. I turned my attention to her. She was on the other side of the room, guarding four other doctors in a corner. I glanced back down at the dead body. She was lying on her back, arms and legs spread out. There was a large hole in her neck with veins spewing out. My eyes trailed down to her chest, which was blown wide open...and empty. Only the casing of her ribs was exposed, the bones picked dry. Copious amounts of blood pooled around her body and her white nursing uniform was now scarlet.

I had killed the nurse.

Dr. Kamini came closer, wearily. "Grace, it's okay. Let's get you back into bed."

I watched her approach me cautiously. She was clearly praying in her mind that I wouldn't attack. But I wasn't going to. I wanted to shout and cry about what I had just done. I wanted to pull my own skin apart. Cut off my own hands and arms so that I would never do it again.

But my stomach was satisfied. I got exactly what I needed, and I felt like myself again. Alive.

"This is unacceptable! Why wasn't it ready for her? This is your fault, you know that, right? We've been doing this for weeks now. You should know the drill. Her food should have been right at her bedside, ready when she woke up!"

"I'm sorry. This was a terrible mistake, and we'll be sure to have what she needs right away next time."

"Well, you better be glad it wasn't you she had attacked and eaten. We need to keep a very close eye on her. Right now, she's a danger to all of us."

I tried with all I could to stay quiet in my bed as I listened to Kate rip Dr. Kamini a new one outside my door. I hated what I'd done. It drove me insane to be considered a "danger" to anyone. And it was technically no one's fault. I understood Kate was trying to protect her staff, but Dr. Kamini had no idea what I was going to do to that poor nurse who was just trying to do her job, which was to deliver my food.

There was a knock at my door. "Grace? Are you awake?"

I couldn't believe I would actually be happy to hear Sonny's peppy voice. There was a split second when I'd thought the dead body was hers. But it wasn't. And I needed the friendly company—even if it was in the form of a narcissistic rich girl. "Yeah, come in."

She walked in hesitantly.

"Sonny, you don't have to be scared. You and I are the same. I won't eat you."

"Are we? Grace, I've never seen anything like that before."

I sunk into the hospital bed, feeling self-conscious. "What do you mean?"

She stayed close to the door. "I-I don't know. Remember when V turned? When Ian and I had to hide from him because he lost his mind and ate the other Zombrids? You were exactly like that...but worse."

I scoffed at her. "Sonny, it wasn't like that. I think it was because she had my food and—"

"She didn't have your food, Grace. It was coming, but she didn't have it."

My stomach sank. Thinking that I'd attacked her because she was physically holding my food somehow made what I'd done a little easier to swallow.

"They were trying to hold you down but as soon as she walked in, you just...you were too strong."

I stared at her, trying to read her expression. She was genuinely frightened. "When I came back from the food coma, you weren't standing at the door. Where did you go?"

"I ran out of the room."

"You didn't have the urge to eat her, too?" I don't know why I asked Sonny that. Of course, she didn't. She hadn't been drained of all her blood like I had been. Maybe I was trying to justify what I'd done. To show her that she was a half zombie, too, and she could have very well killed the same nurse.

But she shook her head and furrowed her brows at me. "No. Not like that."

I looked down at my hands. "So, what? Is everyone mad at me now?"

"We know that it wasn't you. You were starving. They're taking all of your blood for the cure. We know you wouldn't have done it otherwise."

"But?"

Sonny opened the door slightly before answering. "I'm sorry, Grace. I wanted to be here for you and help you get through this. But I can't. *We* can't. Ian doesn't want to, either."

She started to step outside of my room. "Sonny, wait! I won't hurt you!"

She didn't respond. She was gone.

Lying on my side, I gazed out of the window at the blue sky. Judging by the position of the sun, it seemed to be late afternoon. Being able to tell the time just by looking at the sky wasn't exactly something I wanted to learn, but becoming a human sundial was all I could do these days. The removal of my blood left me weak and fragile, too shaky to even hold a cup of water on my own. Once I got my human carcass fix, things were all good. But it didn't last very long. Kate said it shouldn't be too much longer before her team of scientists would finish the process of synthesizing my blood for the cure. I sure hoped it was worth it.

Before I could finish counting the birds in a flock flying over the ocean, there was a knock on my door. "Come in!"

Megan, my long-lost aunt, poked her head through the opening. "Grace?"

I sat upright in my bed and smoothed out my curls. "Yeah."

"May I come in?" she asked politely.

"Um...sure." I hadn't said a single word to Megan, or my mother, since the first time I saw them in the conference room weeks ago, and quite frankly, I still didn't want to. Even if I did, the right words would have been lost somewhere inside me. What do you say to a person, someone you trusted with every part of you, who has hurt you so badly?

Megan stepped inside my room and closed the door behind her. She was wearing jeans and a gray plaid button-down shirt, and her cowboy-style boots clattered against the marble floor of the Z lab as she went to the chair next to my bed. It was appropriate attire for farming—all she was missing was a cowboy hat. Her style was definitely different than my mother's, who usually wore slinky wrap-around dresses and closed-toe heels. Mom always looked like she was ready for the office.

When Megan sat down, I kept my eyes fixed on my hands in my lap and waited for her to say something. But we sat in weird stranger silence for what felt like forever until she finally spoke. "How are you feeling?"

"Fi—" I choked. It had been a while since I spoke. I cleared my throat. "Fine."

"They sure are taking a lot of blood from you."

I nodded.

"So, uh...I'm just going to say it. You're a freaking zombie."

I shot her a look of disbelief. What did she just say?

She smiled. "Sorry. I'm still trying to process it all. When Eve told me everything, I thought she was pitching an idea for a science fiction book or something. It was very hard to believe. But I guess it explained why she left and took you away. Or at least that's what I'm telling myself."

"What does that mean?"

"I'm still angry with her," she retorted.

"Welcome to the club."

Megan adjusted herself in the chair, bringing her legs up and crisscrossing them. She was definitely much different than my mother. I didn't think I had ever seen my mother sit so casually. "It's not really a fun club."

"No, it's not."

"I asked her about Jack, your dad."

Now she had my attention. "You did?"

"I did.

"And?" I asked, raising my brows at her.

"When she called and told me that I had to pack my bags and meet her in New Orleans because the world might end, half of me was surprised to finally hear my sister's voice after all these years. The other half couldn't wait to see her face so that I could slap it. I didn't, of course, but I did ask her a thousand questions. Questions that had been multiplying over the period between now and the last time I saw her almost thirteen years ago. I couldn't for the life of me understand what drove her away. Without a word. Taking her five-year-old daughter with her. I didn't even know if she was alive." There was an obvious heartache in the way she dragged her words. A kind of drawl that almost seemed like the actual sentences hurt her mouth. "I was damn near close to filing a missing person's report and begging the police to find my dead sister and niece, but then I received a letter in the mail, telling me that Jack had left her and she needed a fresh start. She didn't even have the decency to call me on the phone."

I couldn't imagine how devastated Megan must have felt, thinking that her sister was missing and dead. This story was only concreting the anger I had toward my mother.

"I loved you like you were my own daughter," Megan continued. "I couldn't have any kids of my own. At the time, my husband and I were trying for years. But it just didn't happen. Then you came along and you were so beautiful. You looked just like Eve and me when we were babies. You know, you vomited in my mouth once."

My eyes shifted with embarrassment from her to the floor. "Uh...sorry?" That sounded pretty gross.

Megan chuckled. "It was my own fault. Eve had just fed you, and I twirled you and held you up high above my head right after. It was your favorite thing and you cracked up laughing every time. Only this one time, you spit up right inside my mouth. But you still laughed."

I bit my lip and tried to hide my grin.

"When your mom finally told me what really happened and why she left, I still felt angry but it was more because of what you've had to deal with. I'm sorry this happened to you. I'm sorry I wasn't here to help you."

"It's not your fault. Dr. Walker and my mother did this to me."

"I know. But you can't be mad about that. Your mother loved you so much that she was willing to do anything she could to keep you safe and healthy."

"Even lie to me my whole life about everything?" I questioned her harshly. She didn't deserve my attitude because she was a victim, too, but it was hard to control it.

"Yes. She was protecting you. A mother does anything she can to protect her baby."

"Why did she lie about my dad? All this time I thought he just left us. Why couldn't she just tell me the truth about him?"

"She isn't proud about that," Megan answered. "But Dr. Walker threatened her."

"Oh, is that what she told you?" I snapped back. How convenient. The man was dead now, so it would be easy to blame everything on him.

"It is. And I believe my sister. Dr. Walker threatened to take you away with him to this island if she told anyone about Jack's death. And there would have been nothing your mother could have done. If she told authorities about you, about your condition and what you had to eat to stay normal, what do you think would have happened? Either way, you would have been a science project. Eve was only trying to let you live a normal life."

I felt like I was put in my place. What could I say to that? Megan was right—it was much better living a life full of lies than having been a ward of either Dr. Walker or a bunch of other scientists. My life would have been so different if I had to live like a lab rat.

But I shook my head in disapproval. I was still resistant. Hesitant to believe that the betrayal was all for my own benefit. "What about my boyfriend, Tristen? Was that for my own good, too?"

Megan frowned. "I heard about that. I'm sorry your boyfriend was killed."

"Did you know that Dr. Walker fed him to me?"

She nodded sadly then stood up and came to sit on the edge of my bed. I considered scooting over, afraid that it might feel awkward touching her for the first time. But when she took my hand into hers, the warmth of her baby-soft skin felt nice. Maybe it was because she resembled my mother so much.

Megan stared into my eyes, and I was scared out of my mind that she was about to give me another excuse for why Mom lied to me. I was angry that she lied about my dad, but if Megan told me right now that my mom knew that Tristen was going to die on this island, my heart would break all over again. And I wouldn't know what I would do.

"She didn't know about your boyfriend. She thought she was doing the right thing by helping to get him sent here. She thought she was giving you a gift. Eve had no idea that Dr. Walker was going to kill him."

I exhaled the breath I had been holding.

She squeezed my fingers gently. "I know you're struggling right now. I am, too. I believe Eve and understand why she did what she did, but it doesn't make it okay. So, let's see if maybe we can try to forgive her together. It doesn't have to be right away. But we have each other now and we're family. Let's me and you work on it together. What do you say?"

What *do* I say?

THE TOLL

Serena

I GAZED OUT OF the window and watched the dilapidated world pass us by. It was all so different and depressing, but I was grateful for having something to take my mind off of the almost-kiss between Julian and me. The one interrupted by Harley nearly escaping her room.

The broken buildings, abandoned cars, and overgrown wildlife made it seem like we lived in another country. In another world. When life was normal, we never really thought twice about all the little things—like who cut the grass on the median of a highway intersection? Who picked up the litter that people constantly threw out into the streets? Who controlled the stop lights? It was like secret little fairies came out at night and took care of it all while we slept.

Now, the little fairies weren't around to do those things and it didn't take long to drastically change our surroundings into a place that was almost unrecognizable. I tried desperately to understand how everything could crumble so quickly. I couldn't comprehend how one single man could virtually take down an entire city, all with one bite.

"You want some?"

Julian broke me out of my thoughts. I turned to him and reached for the bottle of water he was offering. "Thank you."

A long groan came from the backseat, and I twisted around to check on Harley. She was covered with a black blanket, only her bruised feet exposed.

"She okay?" Julian asked, keeping his eyes on the road ahead of us.

"Yeah." A huge part of me had issues with traveling with Harley, but there was nothing I could do about it, and it was the only way to get Julian to leave that damn house. And after just a few hours on the road, we managed to cross over to the east side of Florida.

"I was thinking that we should continue heading up the coast. We're going to have to stop eventually for more gas, but I think we have enough backup to get us close to Jacksonville."

Our large *Cadillac* SUV could hold a lot of fuel, but he was right. Eventually we would run out. Thankfully, there was an abundance of gas all around us, believe it or not. Siphoning it wasn't my favorite thing to do—the taste was horrendous—but the abandoned cars were a lifeline.

"You think stopping in a big city like that is a good idea?" I asked.

"I'm not happy about it, especially with Harley. But there might be resources or even refuge. If we're going to do this, we have to at least check."

I was happy that Julian finally seemed completely on board with leaving Florida. Maybe he was realizing this was our only option.

"Thank you for doing this."

He glanced over at me before resting his hand on mine. "You don't have to thank me, Serena. I knew you would end up leaving eventually, and there's no way I'm going to let you go alone this time." He squeezed my hand. I drew away after about five seconds and pretended to have an itch on my forehead. His skin was warm against mine, but I didn't want to feel it. I didn't want to feel anything.

After about another hour and a half of mostly silence and dodging Creeps on the road, we were forced to come to a halt on a narrow two-way highway. I squinted my eyes in an attempt to get a better view of what was in front of us. "Military?"

"It doesn't look like it." Two red beat-up trucks blocked the road about fifty yards ahead of us, along with two men standing beside them holding rifles. They held their weapons close to their bodies.

"Should we try to go around them?" The road was completely vacant. Grassy, flat terrain aligned the edges, and there was a line of trees a short distance away on either side of us. It would have been easy to drive around them, left or right.

Julian took a deep breath. "No. This is probably some kind of vigilante toll. We don't want to piss them off, and we aren't that far from Jacksonville. Let's just give them a canister of gas and a box of food. Hopefully that will be enough to get us through."

My heart began to race. I wasn't scared. I wasn't worried. I was ready to do this. To do what I had to do to get past these people. Julian and I looked at each other, and I gave him the go-ahead nod. He let his foot off the brake and slowly accelerated forward.

"Make sure Harley is covered up. They won't be able to see through the tinted windows."

I did as Julian said, also securing and obscuring our bag of weapons under the backseat. We didn't have a large quantity, just a few pistols, a couple of rifles, and some melee weapons courtesy of a partially looted small-town sheriff's office we found along the way.

When we finally reached the two men, Julian put the SUV in park. We both exited the vehicle at the same time and quickly shut our doors behind us in order to keep the sounds of Harley inside. I was personally glad to be away from her strained moans in my ears.

It was early morning, but the sky was still dark. The gray was a forecast of rain soon to come. I hoped we would get this over with quickly before it started pouring. There were empty bottles waiting in the trunk to be filled with rainwater.

I instinctively rested my hand on my trusty machete that was secured inside my thigh holster. I had a KA-BAR hiding inside my boot, and I knew Julian had his pistol tucked into his jeans and under his shirt behind him. We walked closer to the pair of men, one of them clad in leather from head to toe, with long, messy hair and a full scraggly beard. His sleeveless vest exposed all of his colorful ink, and I wondered if this guy was part of some biker gang.

The other man was taller and seemed cleaner and more groomed. He stood up straight with his chest jutted out in a very distinguished and confident manner.

"Well, hi there," the better-looking man called out.

I stopped but Julian took a few more steps closer to him. "Hello."

"You folks out early, huh?" he asked. There was a slight hillbilly accent hidden behind his deep, raspy voice.

"Uh, yeah. Just trying to get out of Florida."

"Why ya'll still here?" the shorter, dirtier man asked. His country accent was much heavier, and his question was followed by spit he shot out of his mouth and onto the ground. His bottom lip protruded outward, evidence that he was using a tobacco chew. Disgusting.

"You two been here this whole time?"

"Yup. We found a good place to hole up. We can tell you where it is if you're interested in staying there," Julian offered. He was trying to be friendly and generous. Maybe this would give them another reason not to mess with us.

"Why you leavin' then?"

"Cabin fever." Julian shrugged. "Just trying to see what else is out there."

The cleaner man stared at Julian a moment before answering. "Well, you ain't gonna find much. Nothing but Uglies past this point."

"Yeah, and them Jarheads ain't letting you outta Florida. You might as well turn 'round," the filthy biker added.

"Well, we have to at least try."

There was a moment of silence before the clean one glanced over at me. He inspected me thoroughly, his eyes wandering up and down the length of my body. He licked his lips when his eyes finally made it up to mine. I clenched my jaw and bit my tongue. Before the apocalypse, I hated it when men would stare me down, and now, I hated it even more. I was sure it didn't help that the makeshift armor around my torso was tightly secured. My pants were snug and my body-hugging tank top exposed my toned arms. There was a holster wrapped around my thigh and boots tied up to my calves. My hair was red and loose, long and wild. I had been working out like a mad woman and knew that my body was in the best shape it had ever been. Not that I was tooting my own horn, but I was sure a guy like this probably appreciated a woman who looked rough and tough. Hell, I could probably pass for a biker, too!

"What's your name, pretty lady?" he asked. I gritted my jaw down harder. I wasn't telling him my name.

Julian apparently wasn't okay with this, either. "Hey listen, guys. We just really want to head on out of here before the storm rolls in. Like I said, I can give you the exact directions to our house. It's off a barrier island and—"

"What's your name, girl?" the man asked again, this time with more aggression in his tone. I wasn't giving in. A roar of thunder exploded above our heads, but it didn't interrupt the hard stare we were giving each other. He was getting upset that I wouldn't speak, I could tell.

"Hey, Wade. It's about to rain cats and dogs. We should get back to the camp," the dirty man whispered loudly.

Wade didn't take his eyes off me. "We can't go now, Cooter. These folks have to pay the toll!"

Julian was one hundred percent right on this one. "Gentleman, we don't have much, but we'll give you all we've got," he lied. We had plenty in the back of the SUV.

"Well, whatcha got?" Cooter asked.

"A box of food and a canister of gas. That's all we've got."

"Let me see," Cooter demanded, taking a step toward our vehicle.

Wade stopped him with a hand to his chest. "No need for that. That should be good. But we take the girl, too."

I took a deep breath in and narrowed my eyes on Wade. I could see out of my peripheral vision that Julian was holding out his arms.

"Guys, I can't do that. She's with me. Now, you can take what we have or—"

"Or what?" Wade finally broke his stare and peered over to Julian. "We don't have to make this more

173

complicated than it is. We'll take the food, the gas...and the girl."

Julian chuckled and shook his head.

"You see that tree line right over there?" Wade asked and pointed. "I got my men back there ready to snipe you right between the eyes. So, it's up to you. You try anything stupid, you die, and we take the girl anyway. Might as well make this an easy trade."

Drops of cool rain landed on my face. I wasn't completely sure what Julian's plans were, but I had hoped he and I were on the same page. It seemed like he was on the verge of pleading some more before I stopped him.

"Jules! It's okay. I'll go with them."

"Now that's the spirit, sugar!"

I glanced at Julian, who was scanning my face, trying to search for some kind of signal or anything to inform him of my plan. But I didn't give anything away. Instead, I slowly walked closer to Wade. As soon as I reached him, he grabbed on to my neck and attempted to caress me. "Yeah, darlin'. The boys are gonna love you."

Cooter lifted his gun and pointed it at Julian with his finger on the trigger. "Don't you try nothin' stupid! Just give us the shit and get on outta here."

Julian held his hands in the air and walked back to the SUV with Cooter close behind him. I mentally willed Harley to stay silent so that Cooter wouldn't know she was in the back.

"You are one fine piece of ass," Wade crooned, running his hand down from my neck to my chest. "And a lot of woman." His hand flowed down the side of my body and to my hand that was clutched on to my melee. "You gotta let go of that, darlin'. The women at the camp aren't allowed to have weapons."

He squeezed my hand and fingers, mashing my bones together. Despite how much it hurt, I didn't want to let go. But I had to. It wasn't the right moment.

"Set it down over there," Cooter instructed Julian. Julian came over near Wade and me and set down the box and gas canister. He stepped back with his hands in the air. Then, faster than any of us could see, Julian reached behind his back, pulled his pistol out and pointed it at Cooter. Wade immediately grabbed my body and spun me around. He wrapped his arm around my neck and squeezed, then pulled out a gun and dug it into my temple.

"Put it down!" Cooter yelled.

"Let her go!" Julian hollered back.

"All right! Come on!" Wade interjected. "No one is gonna win here, fellas. You shoot Cooter, she dies!"

"Let her go," Julian repeated.

Wade whistled loudly near my ear, and I winced at the unpleasant vibration of my eardrum. Four red dots illuminated on Julian's forehead. "And you gonna die, too," he warned.

Julian held on tight to his pistol. I knew he was contemplating what to do next. Another rumble came from the sky and more raindrops fell all around us.

"Wade, we gotta get back to camp!"

"Oh, shut up, Cooter! Rain ain't gonna kill us!"

"No, but I will," I seethed, lifting my leg and reaching inside my boot in one swift motion. Before Wade could stop me, my knife was in my hand. He was still holding on to me so I couldn't turn around. Instead, I threw my hand back and felt the blade slide into his face. He let go and pushed me onto the ground. A loud yelp exploded from his throat, which caught the attention of Cooter. Cooter turned to his friend, but it was a bad choice on his part. Julian took this opportunity to shoot him in the back.

I shouted at Julian. "Get down!" He instantly flew to the ground right before the shots from the tree line were fired. Wade rolled his body against his truck, hands to his face and blood oozing out through his fingers. I hoped I got him right in the eye.

The gunfire didn't let up.

"Serena, get over here!"

The bullets whizzed by me as I made my way to Julian. He was now kneeling down and using our SUV as a shield. I glanced over at Wade. My knife was still in his face...and I wanted my knife.

Stupidly, I would admit, I crouched and dashed back over to Wade. Holding my hands and arms up around my face and head, I mentally prepared myself to feel the sudden impact of a bullet puncturing my body. But, to my surprise, I was able to reach him safely. I grabbed on to Wade's shirt to hold him straight upward and steady. He was still yelling, and for good reason—I jammed my blade into his cheek. He held his mouth open, expelling an awkward scream due to the knife that had slid through his cheek and penetrated his tongue. Red liquid rushed out of his mouth like a broken faucet.

I gripped the handle of the knife but instead of pulling out, I twisted and then pulled it away and out of his mouth, splitting his tongue and cheek wide open. He let out one more boisterous holler and tried to shove me away, but the pain was too unbearable for him. His effort no longer had any strength.

A bullet ricocheted off the truck a few inches away, and I knew it was time to get the hell out of there. But I just had to make sure Wade was dead first.

"Serena!" Julian yelled again.

I allowed Wade's limp body to fall to the ground. I pulled my arm up behind me and released it down on his face. Once, then twice, then one more time. The blood sprayed and splattered all over my arms and face as I continuously yanked the dagger out of his head, then back into it. I could hear the gunfire around me, but I didn't care. This man needed to die. He was scum, and if I didn't kill him, he would kill someone else.

Suddenly, there were arms around my body and I was being hauled off into the direction of our vehicle. Julian practically picked me up and threw me into the passenger seat. "Keep your head down!"

And right after he shouted that order, the passenger-side window shattered and blasted glass inside. I covered my head in an attempt to shield myself from the shards. The engine turned over and the tires screeched as we sped off as fast as we could.

"Shit, Serena! Are you crazy?"

I turned around to sit properly in the seat. My knife was in my hand, dripping blood and chunks of brain matter. "I needed to make sure he was dead."

"You could have been killed!"

Julian was pissed at me, but I couldn't shake the feeling of satisfaction knowing that Wade was gone. I glanced at Julian, not really sure if an apology was what I was going to give him. Wade needed to die, and Jules needed to understand that. But when I turned toward him to argue a defense for my stupid actions that could have gotten us killed, his shirt caught my attention.

"Julian?"

"What?"

"Are you bleeding?"

He glanced at the spot on his shirt near his stomach that was slowly saturating with his blood. Julian had been shot.

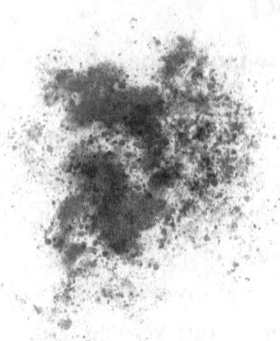

THE OBLIGATION

Grace

I HADN'T SEEN MUCH sunlight since I agreed to give all my blood away. My life consisted of feeling like death, sleeping, eating, and doing it all over again the next day. No one told me I couldn't go outside or do anything like that. It wasn't like I was on lockdown. To be honest, I just didn't want to show my face. I was ashamed of what I'd done. I had killed one of our own and that was unacceptable. And it didn't help much either when Sonny told me that basically everyone was afraid of me. Including the newcomers.

It made me feel a little better when she came back just a day after she said she wasn't coming back. Chances were that Sonny wasn't doing it out of the kindness of her heart, either. Because of her aversion to the new Zombrids on the island, she must have gotten tired of hanging out with just Ian. But she promised she wouldn't leave my side again. I wasn't sure if I was completely on board with it. Too much Sonny might actually make me *want* to eat her. Regardless, I was grateful.

I was also grateful to Ian who, for the past two months, had been coming to my room to teach me how not to kill a human. I had thought he was afraid of me because of what I'd done, but his first words to me were:

"Mate, you could have shared with me."

I had stared at him in bewilderment before saying, "What?"

"Listen, I never told Sonny I didn't want to see you— she was just being all dramatic, you know how she can be." His eyes glinted with an obvious thrill. "So? How was the nurse? Was she as good as you'd expected? Man, I wish I'd been there to partake in the feast!"

"You're sick," I said. My reflexes got the better of me and I slapped him on the back of the head for saying such a horrible thing.

"Ow! What was that for?" he said, but I shook my head, deciding to let it go. He was a serial killer, after all. And as long as he didn't act on his murderous ways, all was okay.

The whole human-resistance training consisted of a lot of meditation and focusing and "becoming one with your ability to stay grounded." In other words, just don't move. Stand still, close your eyes, breathe, and make yourself just say no.

"See, love, let me explain it to you," Ian had said, pointing to his face. "Our hungry Zombrid eyes and growls would probably scare off the prey, so we just have to wait and hope they run. If not, the overwhelming desire may or may not pass, it all depends on how hungry we are, which is why it is most effective when we haven't starved ourselves too much."

I wasn't sure if this training was going to work, but it didn't hurt to try. As delicious and satisfying as it was to eat a human, I seriously didn't want to attack anyone else.

Kate had tried to make me feel better about dining on our resident nurse by explaining why I spontaneously attacked someone. She claimed it was certainly not my fault, but the fault of Dr. Kamini and her team for being unprepared. She said it was perfectly normal for me to react the way that I did. My blood, the part of me that kept me from turning into a TZ, had been taken away. My actions were textbook (if there was a zombie textbook lying around somewhere). I was searching for what my body needed, exactly how Dr. Walker had described the process. But I still hated myself for doing it. I still hated the fact that I had lost complete control. I still hated that I felt like a monster. How could the face of the Zombrid race attack and kill innocent people? My fellow Zombrids needed to understand that it was not okay.

A knock at my door brought me back into the present. "Come in."

Kate poked her head through the crack before entering completely. "You awake?"

"Yeah," I mumbled, sinking deeper into my duvet. I really didn't want company. She pulled the chair away from the corner of the room and placed it at my bedside.

"How are you feeling?" she asked as she sat down and rested her tablet on her lap.

"I'm okay, I guess."

"Grace, I told you not to feel down on yourself. It was an accident and protocols have been set in place for the future so that it won't happen again. The rest of the Zombrids understand and know that what you did was bad. Besides, a few days have passed since then, and honestly, no one has even mentioned it."

I ignored her attempt to make me feel better. "How much more do you need?" I asked, dreading her answer.

"Not much more." She placed a hand on my arm. "We're nearing the end of trials and your blood is close to being synthesized. You'll be feeling much better before you know it."

I managed a slight smile for her.

"I came to give you some good news...and bad news. Which do you want first?"

This was not a fun game. I never knew which I wanted first. If I got the good news first, the bad news would burst my bubble. If I got the bad news first, I'd be too upset for the good news. "It doesn't matter."

"The good news is the cure. It's been weeks and our patients are showing lots of rehabilitation and stabilization. Their bodies are healing from decay, and they have nearly regained brain capacity. We're just a couple of trials away from making it official. These zombies will become Zombrids. They'll be able to live a normal life soon. Well, as normal as they can be."

"I guess your dad was wrong. He told me once you get to that dark place, you could never come back from it."

"Well, that would have been true if it wasn't for your golden blood." She winked and grinned widely. "But he could be a little bit right. We haven't had enough time to determine whether or not the mutated serum has irreversible long-term effects."

"Oh. Well, I hope he was wrong."

She inhaled deeply, as if to know and understand exactly why I said that. "Dr. Walker did whatever he had to do to get what he wanted. He wanted to have power. To be in control, all while making money. He wanted to be recognized and become a legend, like a Greek freaking god or something. He just had this belief that he could change the world. The sad part was that he really was a brilliant man. He could have done great things and might have been able to change the world if he had put his efforts into something else. He should have let Serum Z go a long time ago."

It was very hard to believe her after all that her father had done, but I understood what she was saying. As much as she would deny it, I could tell that somewhere deep down inside her, she missed her dad.

There was a moment of silence before I decided to change the subject.

"So, how is this going to work? I mean, are you just going to walk down the zombie-infested streets with my blood and hope for the best?" I knew it was going to take more than that, but I couldn't help picturing Kate running around like some kind of superhero injecting people.

She chuckled, probably finding my question comical. "I wish it were that easy. Unfortunately, I'm going to have to come out of hiding. I have prepared my presentation and I'm ready to bring it to the CDC and the government. My hopes are that everything runs smoothly. That they will agree to implement the cure and we'll start giving it to those in need. Our staff will travel the country and set up clinics in each state, with the worst ones as our top priority."

"Clinics?"

"Sadly, this cure isn't just an injection in the arm and everything is okay. We'll have to drain the patient of the mutated blood completely and replace it with the Serum Z-laced synthesized blood. It's going to take some time. Thankfully, though, the clinics will be equipped with beds and they'll have the capacity to treat hundreds of patients at a time. They'll be cured, rehabilitated, and educated on their new life as a Zombrid."

"What about food? How are they going to be fed?"

"There were a few Zombrids who volunteered to try the animal diet. It's only been a couple of months, but we've been experimenting with feeding them live animals, and so far, they are showing positive signs. And one of them is not a newly turned Zombrid."

"That's good, right?"

"It is," Kate chirped. "However, we aren't getting the same results as a Zombrid who is ingesting human remains. The differences aren't enormous, but it is enough to question whether or not this could be a problem in the future. Our worry is that if you don't get what you need, you'll eventually become a TZ. We need to make sure we're meeting the needs of the Zombrids to prevent that from happening. Now, it doesn't rule out the possibility of living on live animals *and* deceased humans. We're trying a sort of...half and half diet right now where the Zombrid is receiving something alive and dead."

I bit the inside of my cheek. "This sounds so exhausting."

"Oh, trust me. It is. But we'll figure it all out eventually, Grace. It just takes time. Honestly, I'm not that worried. Things are looking up. And if it turns out we'll need to do a half and half diet, I think people would be willing to give their bodies to science after death in order to save the Zombrids."

"I hope you're right."

Kate stood up. "Hey, you wanna go grab some Z Juice from Newport? You know you don't have to stay in here all day long."

"No, it's okay."

She pursed her lips. "Grace, you can't keep hiding from her."

"Why not?" I sassed. It bugged me that Kate knew exactly who I was hiding from. "She knew what I was, what I would eventually become. And she knew about my dad. She had so many opportunities to tell me, but she chose to lie to me my entire life!"

"How do you think I feel? My father killed people!" Kate retorted.

"Then, why did you stick around? How could you be okay with it?"

"I wasn't," she shot back. "I didn't want him to kill those people. I tried to stop him. To tell him it was wrong. But he didn't care about me. He never did. And maybe I stuck around because I thought he would one day. Your mom...she cared about you so much that she was willing to do whatever it took to protect you. She left her family, her beloved career that she worked so hard for, and everything she knew to give you a fresh start. She learned how to cook humans for you! You don't think that she knew you would find out eventually?"

"Well, yeah but—"

Kate put her hand up. "And how did you feel when you found out? How did you feel about being a Zombrid? Scared? Lonely?"

"Yes!" I shouted. I didn't mean to, but I could see the point she was making and I didn't like it.

"She tried to protect you from that as long as she could, Grace. Because she loves you. My dad couldn't give two shits whether or not I was alive. So at least you had something."

I stared into her eyes. They were welling up, and there was a glint of a tear pooling in each corner. I could feel my own eyes filling with tears as the guilt set in. Was I being too harsh on my mother? Should I join my aunt Megan in the quest of learning to forgive Dr. Eve Shelley?

Kate quickly grazed her thumb under each eye to wipe them dry. I could tell she didn't like crying over her dad. "Well, I should get back to the lab and check on those patients. I'll keep you updated on their progress and when I'm leaving to the States. You better rest up. You only have one, maybe two, more blood draws left."

I sat up in my bed as she stood and began walking toward the door. Kate turned around to face me when she reached my door. "I'm going to meet up with officials from the CDC to discuss the implementation of the cure soon. They're holed at some undisclosed location. If everything goes well, I'll be heading off with the team to Florida."

"Florida? You're going to Ground Zero?"

"It's where it started. We have to treat the patients who have had the mutated serum in their bodies longer. We don't know for certain if there's a point of no return."

Going to where it all started seemed like suicide. From the numbers on Kate's little map of the infected in that area, it seemed there was barely anyone left alive. She and her team would be risking their lives having to round up all of the infected to treat them. They weren't sure what the conditions were like there. Apocalyptic movies may have been fictional, but I imagined there was some truth to them. No people meant no electricity, no water, no food, and probably danger around every corner.

And yet, for some strange reason, I felt like it was my responsibility, too. My obligation. I was a Zombrid. I should be helping in any way I can.

"I'm going."

Kate opened her mouth to respond—probably to object—but nothing came out. Instead, she nodded her head once and stepped out of my room.

THE FAMILY

Serena

A FEW DAYS HAD passed, and I was now standing in front of a sign that read *Acadia Post Office*. After the commotion with Wade and his dipshit partner in the road, we decided to slow down our travels. My best friend was almost killed. That bullet was only an inch or two away from penetrating Julian's abdomen. Instead, it only grazed him, and I had to stitch up his wound and make sure to keep it from getting infected. Jules needed to be healthy for Creep-killing before we got to a bigger city.

Our original plan was to stop in Jacksonville to check for supplies, but we decided to keep going for Tallahassee—the capital of Florida—and stopping at as many places as we could for resources on the way there. There might be refuge in the capital, and if not, state lines weren't that far away from it.

I leaned over and peeked through the glass entrance of the post office. It seemed abandoned. No signs of humans camping out, no Creeps locked inside. I stepped back against the wall next to the door and gave Julian a thumbs up. He was parked at the corner with Harley, waiting for me to gain entry and do a quick sweep.

When I was mentally ready, I pulled on the door. It didn't hurt to check to see if it was unlocked. Sometimes, believe it or not, businesses were left unlocked. My assumption was that the employees or owner left in a hurry in the beginning of the mess. But honestly, I didn't care much to think about what might have happened. It just made my life easier when the doors weren't locked.

Unfortunately, these doors were.

I glanced over my left shoulder, then my right to check my surroundings. This was the first area in a few miles that appeared to be Creep-free. But it wasn't going to be for long, which was why I needed to get us inside. We needed to stretch out and rest up for a few hours.

There wasn't rhyme or reason to the way the Creeps traveled. Most of the time they just stumbled around with no particular destination in mind, or so it seemed. I didn't know what went on in their minds. Every now and then a horde would form and stagger about. I've tried to study this and the reasoning behind the zombies gathering together. I finally concluded that maybe this was some kind of residual human characteristic. Maybe there was still some need in a Creep's brain for social interaction. Or it could just be that they all heard or smelled something they really wanted to eat. Whatever it was, getting caught in a horde was the last thing I wanted to happen right now.

I jogged to the side of the small building and found a metal door. This door had no handle, which probably meant it was an emergency exit that could only be opened from the inside. Gripping tightly onto my machete, I continued my jog toward the back of the building. There was another door, along with a type of loading dock next to it. A mail truck was parked in front of a wide, garage-style hatch. I tugged at the door with no luck, then tried the truck entrance. Jackpot!

It was heavy but I pulled it up slowly and cautiously to keep from making any sounds that may alarm Creeps behind it. Once inside, I lowered the hatch to the ground quietly. It was pitch black, so I reached in my back pocket for my flashlight. The bright light illuminated the area around me. I started walking in slow strides with my machete held up over my head and ready to slash.

Four steps led up to the main office of the building. At a quick glance, it looked as if everything was in its place, untouched. The office door brought me to the space where the mail clerks tended to the customers, but the three cubicle-like spaces were empty. I accidentally kicked a small trash can on my way toward the counter that divided the employees from the customers, stopping immediately to listen to my surroundings for anything the noise might have alerted. Nothing.

But before I took another step, the sound of someone coughing prompted me to grip my weapon tighter. The customer area behind the counter was empty, but the wall to my left blocked my view of the rest of the facility.

There was another cough, followed by a *Shh*. Shit. There were people here. My experience with other survivors hadn't been great so far. I only assumed this time it would be the same.

"Who's there?" a male voice called out.

I didn't respond and instead began to back up toward the loading dock as quietly as I could.

"Who's out there?" the man repeated.

I managed to reach the door, but right as I placed my hand on the handle behind me, a flashlight beamed in my face and there was a mechanical sound of a gun being cocked. I immediately dropped my machete and reached for the pistol tucked into my jeans and pointed it in his direction.

"Who are you?"

"Put your weapon down," I demanded.

"Not a chance."

The light was obscuring my view of his face. I was sure mine was doing the same.

"I'm only going to ask you one more time. Who are you?"

A large part of me wanted to end his obsession with learning who I was by pulling the trigger on him and whoever else was in this place. There was no time for bullshit in this world. But the sound of another cough, a small one similar to a child, gave me second thoughts.

"Grady, what's happening?" a woman asked from around the corner of the wall.

"It's okay, Caroline! I've got it handled!"

Grady continued to point his gun in my direction. "Lady, look, we don't have much so you might as well go back to where you came from."

"Who else is here?"

"It's just me, my wife, and my kid. My kid is sick. We have nothing and nowhere to go. We're just trying to survive," he explained sincerely.

"So am I."

Grady must have been stupid because he started to lower his gun, raising his other hand in the air as if to surrender. Chances were that because I seemed to be alone, and because I was a woman, he probably thought I was just a harmless survivor, like him.

Another rule to abide by in this screwed up world: never trust anyone.

"I don't want any trouble. You looking for a place to sleep or something?" he asked.

I hesitated for a moment before answering. Julian was waiting for me in the car. It had already been a while, and

I was sure he was starting to worry. Dusk was coming fast, and we did need a place to crash. If this guy was telling the truth and it was just him and his family, bunking in the same place for the night may not be a bad idea. And besides, I could definitely take them on if I really needed to.

"Yeah. My friend is waiting outside," I finally answered.

"You guys have any water or food?"

"Some."

He lowered his flashlight and I could now see that he was nodding. "Okay. Give us some and you can stay for the night."

I swallowed a laugh. This guy thought he had the upper hand.

I ran back to the SUV. The mail truck was far enough away from the entrance of the loading dock for us to squeeze past and park inside. We grabbed some gear and resources—enough to please Grady, but not enough to make a dent in our supplies—and headed back into the post office. Julian thought about bringing Harley inside, but then decided to leave her tied up in the vehicle. We weren't sure what these people would do if they knew we were friends with a zombie.

Grady came back to the same spot we met and shined the light on Julian and me when we entered the building. We immediately handed him the supplies, enticing him to trust us even more and reducing the risk of any issues. He seemed grateful for this and guided us into a small corridor tucked in a corner. It was only as wide as a hallway of a small house and the walls were lined with mailboxes.

"It's P.O. boxes," he informed me. At the end of the small area was a woman cradling a little girl who looked to be around Harley's age. "This is Caroline, and that's Jessica."

Caroline let go of her daughter to wave. Jessica coughed and Caroline immediately wrapped her arm back around her.

"Jessica's sick. She's got a pretty bad fever. We found a pharmacy close by, and thankfully, they had some bottles of antibiotics left. We're just waiting for it to start working."

"You sure it's just a cold?" I asked with a hint of skepticism I couldn't help masking in my tone.

Grady furrowed his brows at me as if offended. "She's not bleeding or showing aggressiveness. She's not one of those...things, if that's what you're worried about."

"We're just making sure," Julian responded calmly. Grady narrowed his eyes at me before pointing at the other corner of the tiny area. I wasn't completely sure what town we were in, but it had to have been really small. This post office was nothing compared to the ones in Tampa.

"Y'all can sleep over there. These two corners give us better eyesight of the whole place, in case any of those things try coming in. We can see the street through the glass entrance from here, too. Just don't be turning any lights on when it gets dark," he advised.

Julian nodded in agreement and we headed over to our spot. We didn't bring much in with us, just our weapons, a couple of packets of trail mix, and one large bottle of water. Grady needed to believe we were just as bad off as he was. We didn't want to take the chance of him asking to tag along with us.

We both plopped down on the cool tiles of the floor.

"How's your stomach?" I asked in a low voice, peering over in Grady's direction to make sure he couldn't hear us. He didn't turn toward us and continued rummaging through the box we gifted him.

Julian looked down and pulled his shirt up, revealing his bandage. "It's sore but healing pretty quickly. Could have been worse."

I looked over at Grady again. "I'll take first watch. You can get some rest."

"Serena, I don't think we need to. There didn't seem to be a whole lot of zombies around outside, and I don't think they'll try anything," he whispered.

I watched Grady run a hand through Jessica's hair and kiss his wife. "You never know."

"Stop being stubborn and get some sleep. We don't have much longer until we get to the Capital."

Julian rested his head against the wall and closed his eyes. I tried to do the same, but my paranoia didn't allow me to fall asleep. My eyes wanted to remain wide open, as if I had no control over them. Instead, I rested a hand on the machete hoisted to my thigh and watched Grady and his family intently.

I almost *wanted* them to try something stupid.

But the post office darkened quickly, and soon the only light was the flickering of a candle in the tiny hallway where Grady and his family lay sleeping. Julian's soft snoring in the silence around me began to sound like some kind of lulling melody in my ears. There wasn't a second in the day that went by where I didn't miss Dan, but having Julian with me did weaken the agony of losing my future husband. Jules made me feel safe.

Feeling the need to see Charlie's face in that exact moment, I reached into my pocket to retrieve our picture. The edges were ripping and softening further, the usual wear and tear of a vintage photograph starting to show from constantly tucking it away somewhere. I stared at it until my eyes grew heavier, and when I felt myself fighting against my head bobbing forward, I decided to finally give into sleep.

THE STRAGGLERS

MY BODY JERKED AND my eyes popped open at the sound of someone yelling in the distance.

"Hey!" shouted the voice. I squinted to focus in the darkness. It was still night out and I felt like I'd only slept for twenty minutes.

"Shh...it's okay, baby," Caroline whispered to her daughter, rocking a moaning and weeping Jessica in her arms.

Julian stirred next to me, but I nudged him hard near his wound on his stomach to wake him up. He sucked in a pained breath of air and gave me an irritated glare. "What is it?"

"We got one of them things in here!" It was Grady, his voice carrying over to us from the direction of the loading dock. "Get over here and help me kill this thing!"

Julian and I shared a moment of holy-shit realization before we were on our feet and rushing to the back of the building. When we reached the loading dock and the SUV, Grady was standing there with his gun pointed at the window of the passenger seat. "How the hell did it get into your car?"

Harley must have somehow gotten out of the rope tied around her wrists and ankles (should have used the chains). She pressed her hands up against the window and growled and snarled at Grady. Her hot breath fogged the glass, her fingers smearing blood all over it from the wounds on her wrists. They were always torn and bleeding from her constant effort to get loose. I grabbed my machete and moved over toward Grady.

He was confused when he saw me. "What are you doing? Why are you drawing your weapon on me? There's a zombie in your car!"

Julian stepped forward with his hands in the air. "Grady, you can't shoot her. She's my daughter."

"Your daughter is a zombie? Why didn't you tell us? Why did you bring her here? My wife and kid are inside! What if she got out?"

I was eager to end his twenty-one questions and readied myself to swing my weapon. But the sound of more moaning filled the space we stood in. The loading dock door started to sway, and pings and rattles echoed off the metal from the mob of Creeps beginning to form on the other side.

"Shit! They're outside!" Grady shouted.

"You have to stop yelling," Julian warned. "Listen, let us just get out of here. We'll kill the ones that are outside before we go. Just put the gun down."

Grady took another look at Harley. "How can you let her live like that, man? How can you watch your daughter suffer like that?"

My thoughts exactly.

"You and I are two different people, Grady. You have your family, and I have mine. She isn't harming anyone. Just let us go and you won't have to worry about us...or her," Julian pleaded.

The Creeps were piling up outside, and frankly, I was getting tired of listening to this. "Julian, let's get this over with. We've got to go."

"Oh, what, y'all plan on killing me over that thing?" He moved away from the *Cadillac* and switched his attention—and his gun—to Julian.

Julian raised his arms up high in the air as if to be surrendering. "Whoa, man. You don't have to do this. We'll make sure your family is safe before we leave. And we have more food. We can give more."

In the time before the zombie apocalypse, I used to think Julian's kind and gentle nature was refreshing. The fact that he never got angry at anything could be frustrating, but mostly it was endearing. Even on my worst days, when I was pissed at the world and just wanted to be angry and gave him lousy attitude that he didn't deserve, he never returned it. He never responded with the same treatment. Julian chose to see the brighter side of things in life, always searching for the positive. But his need to spread peace had no place here. Those days were long gone. This world was harsh now, and there was no more need for compassion. Compassion could get you killed.

While Grady was preoccupied with threatening to shoot Julian, I took the opportunity to finally end the charade. Julian's back was facing me, so he didn't see when I reached over to the passenger of the SUV and opened it. Harley's attention quickly switched to my sounds and smells, but I was able to grab a hold of her ropes and allow her to exit the car. She stumbled out, ropes dangling from her wrists and dragging from her feet. I walked backward and she followed my lead.

"What are you doing?" Grady asked, holding his gun steady and taking a few steps back.

"Serena. What are you doing?" Julian repeated.

I kept inching my way in Grady's direction. Harley staggered and twitched with every step she took toward me, obviously eager to take a bite of my flesh. I glanced behind me at Grady. He was doing exactly what I wanted him to do—backing into a corner.

He switched his target. "What the hell are you doing? I'll shoot her!"

Grady wasn't going to shoot Harley. He had a daughter around the same age. He wasn't going to shoot her.

Harley nipped at the air, grinding her teeth and moving her jaw in ways I didn't think were possible unless it was broken. She wanted me so badly that I even briefly wondered what it felt like. Was her desire to eat as strong as the roaring rage boiling in the pit of my stomach? Did she want to feed on my body as much as I wanted to kill Mark Walker?

When I felt like it was the right time, I swiftly and strategically sidestepped out of Harley's murderous path. Grady had run out of anywhere to go, and before he knew it, a forceful groan escaped Harley's throat right as she leaned in and bit his arm. He instantly hollered and tried to pull away, but it wasn't long ago that Harley had a meal. Her strength was much greater. Grady was not a smart man and there was proof of this when he decided to drop his gun and attempt to rip his arm away from her teeth instead of shooting her in the face. It wouldn't have killed her, but it would have knocked her off her ass for a few minutes.

Well...shooting her was what I would have done. But I knew he wouldn't.

Harley grunted hungrily as she continued to tear at him. She jerked her head left to right, ensuring a good grip to rip away his flesh. Blood splattered and dripped everywhere in an almost comical manner. Grady tried to take a step to the side since his back was to the wall but failed and tripped over his own feet. He fell to the floor with Harley latched on. Her mouth remained on his arm, but her hands moved to his stomach. She began scratching at his shirt, causing pools of blood to appear through the fabric. This was when I knew he was done for. This virus did not stop the hair and nails from growing. Her fingernails were long, and the constant clawing and tearing at things in an attempt to break free had made them sharp and rigid.

She knew where the goods were. She knew his stomach was the way to what she needed.

I glanced at Julian. He was motionless and as white as a ghost. Up until now he had never even watched her eat the animals we caught for her meals. He said he couldn't take watching his daughter eat the flesh of something with a pulse. He would just leave her meals in front of her and step away, giving her space to do what she needed to do. But Grady definitely wasn't an animal. Harley had reached a whole new milestone in her sickness. This was her second human meal, and I had a feeling it wouldn't be her last.

A bone-chilling shrill caught me off guard, and I jumped at the sound. Grady's wife, Caroline, stood in the doorway.

"Grady!" She ran down the short flight of stairs toward her husband, but Julian finally came out of his trance in time to intercept her and hold her away. Harley had opened Grady's stomach with her bare hands and was now scooping his guts and innards out of his body and into her mouth. She savagely chewed on his insides, as if she hadn't eaten since she was born. He was no longer screaming in pain.

Caroline wailed loudly and the riotous hums of the Creeps outside grew.

"Shut her up, Julian," I demanded.

He took what I said seriously and turned Caroline around so she could bury her cries into his chest. "We need to get out of here," he whispered, as if that was going to help. The Creeps already knew we were in here.

"Backing the SUV into them will be the only way out. Jump in and start it up," I insisted. "I'll get Harley inside."

"What about her and the kid? We can't leave them here."

Technically, we could. But I knew Julian wasn't going to race out of here sans a mother and her child in the middle of a Creep horde.

The loading dock door began to cave inward as the Creeps banged on the metal. There was no telling how many were out there, but it was probably enough to knock it down. I took a deep breath in. Fighting with Jules about this was pointless, so I walked over to him, pulled Caroline's hysterically shaking body off him, and guided her toward the SUV.

"Jessica," she managed to utter out. "I need my daughter!"

"I'll get her," Julian said before running back into the post office. I opened the back door and heaved Caroline inside. She allowed herself to fall to her side and continued to cry into the seat. After shutting her door, I made my way to Harley. She was still feasting on whatever was left of Grady's torso. This was going to be tricky because I have seen Creeps switch easily from one victim to another, but I had to get her into the vehicle.

Slowly approaching her from behind, I made sure to stay quiet and not disrupt what she was doing. Once I was close, I bent down and reached for the back of her arms, pulling them behind her. At the same time, I placed my foot on her butt to push her down onto Grady's empty cavity in front of her. She couldn't stand up or move much now, and I took this opportunity to grab what was left of the ties dangling from her wrists to wrangle her. I knotted them as tight and I could, using one of the nautical knots Julian taught me, then lifted her onto her feet.

She fought relentlessly to get away. Her strength had definitely doubled since she had just eaten, but she matched the muscle that I had been working on for the past few months. If this was an adult Creep, it would have been much more difficult—if not impossible.

I opened the trunk part of the SUV and lifted her into it. To make sure she couldn't get to Caroline or her daughter in the backseat, I tied a rope around her neck and to the latch on the back of the trunk door. Julian probably wouldn't approve of this—she was basically being strangled—but I had no choice.

"Why are you putting her in here?" Caroline asked through her tears.

"Shut up," I murmured and closed the hatch softly so I wouldn't hurt Harley. As if I could, anyway.

Julian came down the stairs carrying Jessica right as I opened the back door. He placed her inside, then got into the driver's seat.

"I'm going to open the door so you can back into them," I informed him.

"Serena, you can't take them on yourself."

"You'll get most of them. I'll just get the ones that are in my way of getting in." I unhooked my machete from my thigh and pointed at the passenger seat next to Julian. "Hand me that."

He reached over and gave me my ax. "You sure about this?"

I nodded. He didn't move for a moment and simply stared into my eyes. Everything up until today had been a blur, including us. The lines between Julian and I have crossed into so many different directions, that I wasn't sure where we were headed. I loved him. He was the closest thing I ever had to family. But there were moments of affectionate need between us and moments when we didn't see eye to eye or weren't on the same page, and I didn't know if that also included our feelings for each other. When you were surviving a cruel world full of death with someone, you couldn't help but feel for them in a way you thought you never would. You were sharing something profound.

In my case, however, there were times when I felt like I was fighting this fight alone. Julian wasn't raped as a result of all of this, or had never been, and that made a world of difference. He would never understand what it felt like to be violated in that way, which caused a disconnection.

But damn it if I didn't love him...

I stared back at him. There was an unspoken exchange of emotion that transferred from his eyes to mine. I wasn't sure what it meant or if I would ever truly know. One thing was certain, though—I was completely broken, and I didn't know if I wanted to allow Julian into my war-torn heart.

I moved away from the SUV, and he frowned before starting it up. Was I scared? Not a chance. I was more afraid of what Julian was thinking than of those lifeless corpses that waited outside for us. I turned toward the door and tucked myself into the corner. With one big tug, I pulled the rusty chain and the door went up far enough to reveal the feet of the Creeps on the other side. There seemed to be more than I expected. Pulling on the chain again, the hatch slid up to about their torsos and their moans finally fully entered the area. I tugged once more with all my power to a sufficient height for the *Cadillac* to get through. This finally exposed them to the loading dock, but before any of them could step inside, Julian screeched the tires and reversed into the crowd. I was squeezed into the corner as far as I could go, and they hadn't seen me yet. But it wouldn't be long before they could smell me.

I quickly backed away from the door and watched Julian ram into about fifteen of them. Their bodies flew backwards, some rolling under the tires. This cleared most of them from the middle, but there were stragglers on either side. A few moved their attention to the car, but two of them caught a glimpse of me. The logical thing to do was to get Julian to pull back in to allow me to get safely inside the car, but I was in the mood to kill.

Before he could put the SUV back in drive, I ran to the left at the Creeps beginning to stumble toward me. With my machete in one hand and my ax in the other, I swung for the first Creep that approached me with her arms out and ready to bite. Using a cross-like motion with my weapons, I sliced at her throat, chopping her head clean off her body. Blood sprayed my face right as I remembered to close my mouth and eyes.

The next Creep threatened to get closer to me, but I kicked him away, then leaned forward before he stumbled to the ground to mimic the first move I performed on the Creep before. As he fell to the ground, two more moaned and growled close behind. I swung both melees at the same time in either direction, burying my ax into one's rotten, blistered face and my machete into the skull of the other.

This wouldn't kill them, so I pulled both arms back with all my might and thrust them forward, flinging the two Creeps off of my blades and onto the ground away from me. Julian finally accelerated forward right as I opened my arms wide and closed them into the next Creep's neck, instantly severing his head. It flew off his body and landed on the ground, then rolled away as the rest of him simply flopped down to the ground.

I opened the car door and jumped inside, slamming it closed on the hand of a Creep who tried to reach inside. Julian put it in reverse again, and we quickly backed out of the loading dock. The Creep's hand remained in the door for about another second until it broke off on its own. His body glided in midair before hitting the pavement and rolling a few times, then finally stopping on his back. I opened the door to allow the severed hand to fall off.

Taking a moment to catch my breath, I leaned back into my seat as Julian drove us to the main road. I could feel his eyes on me.

"Did you have fun?"

For the first time in what seemed like a year, I felt the sides of my mouth turn up. I glanced over at him. He, too, revealed a small grin.

"Yeah. Yeah, I did."

THE ASSIGNMENTS

Grace

IT FELT STRANGE TO be on American soil again. Not that it physically felt different or anything. It was just nice to be in a place that was familiar to me. I could never completely accept Everlasting Paradise as my home.

We left the island about four days ago, a journey I was never really too fond of the first time I did it. Three days of solid traveling by land, air, and water wasn't exactly the most fun. Although, Sonny and Ian were with me, so it made the trip tolerable. We landed in Tallahassee without any complication. It wasn't Ground Zero, but it was where Kate wanted us to be. She was still working some things out with the CDC and promised she would be here to meet us soon.

I was extremely curious to know what Florida looked like for two reasons. The first was because I had never been here before. The second was because...well...Florida was the first place to go down. It was completely red on Kate's little death map, which meant the entire state had turned. Unfortunately, we arrived at night and were immediately loaded into a helicopter and brought to the roof of some building. It was too dark to get a glimpse of the environment. There was no electricity, only glowing patches of ember here and there from where there must have been a fire blazing.

The building we entered was, apparently, one of Dr. Walker's clinics, but it really had the feel of some kind of bunker. Why would Dr. Walker have a bunker in Florida? It actually made me wonder if he was protecting himself from something.

The three of us sat at the end of a large table, awaiting our breakfast. We had been here almost a whole day, but barely saw each other because we decided to try to sleep the jet lag away after a few of Kate's employees showed us our rooms.

"This place is so sterile." Sonny visibly shivered and wrapped her arm around herself as she glanced over the room.

"They say this is one of his clinics, but I was thinking maybe it could be some kind of bunker."

"No way. A bunker would most probably be underground," Ian explained. "It kind of reminds me of a panic room, though."

Right as he said that, I completely agreed. The building was held up by what looked like thick, gray concrete walls. We hadn't seen much since we entered through the roof, only our bedrooms and this eating area, but everything was nice and neat and minimal. It was cold and lonely and very quiet.

The smell hit me long before the woman opened the door and rolled in a cart. I was able to contain myself because I'd just eaten a snack prior to leaving my room. Thankfully, I had been feeling much better since the blood draws were done, but I wasn't out of the wanting-to-eat-everything-I-saw woods yet. My eating schedule changed because of it, and I had to eat more often for the next couple of weeks. Kate and Dr. Sharma informed me that it was just a precaution because so much blood had been taken from me, and they wanted me to eat even if I didn't feel hungry. They promised that once my body regenerated every single thing it had lost, I would be as normal as I could be. Whatever *normal* even meant anymore.

I would never reject a lean piece of meat, but I wasn't going to risk attacking and killing another innocent person. So, I decided to comply with my Zombrid feeding probation.

A doctor I had never seen before entered the room and placed three trays of raw meat in front of us. The meat swam in red juice and jiggled when he set it down, evidence that it was super fresh. I wanted to wonder where it came from and why it was so fresh, but my mouth watered and suddenly it didn't matter. Sonny and Ian didn't wait one second before digging their bare hands into their plates. It didn't take me long to do the same.

I was definitely feeling much better than I did a week ago, but every time I ate, it still felt like the first time. The spongy, tough pieces of fleshy tissue hit my tongue, and I was in ecstasy. As I chewed, it was as if the meat erupted inside my mouth, releasing an astringent but saccharine taste of pure pleasure. My stomach danced in anticipation of its arrival, and when I finally swallowed, my mind drifted off into that faraway land of harmony.

But far too soon, I opened my eyes to find Sonny and Ian cleaning themselves up.

"That was amazing," Sonny purred as she fell back into her chair.

"It really was," Ian agreed.

"Okay, so what is this place? Really?" I asked, reaching across the table for a napkin to clean off residual blood and fluids.

The door swung open. "It's one of Dr. Walker's clinics," Kate said. She bumped Ian's shoulder, who was sitting at the head of the table, and pointed to the chair next to his. He glanced up at her, eyes smoky and filled with smolder. His wolfish grin practically dripped sex. She stood firm and didn't give into his wicked flirtation. Ian moved.

"He has them all over the place," Kate continued, taking a seat and throwing a folder on the table. "If you're wondering why it looks like a spaceship, it's for protection." Her eyes wandered to Ian for a split second. I knew she couldn't resist.

"From what?" Sonny asked.

"I know he didn't think a zombie apocalypse would actually happen, but maybe somewhere deep down he might have considered it. But Dr. Walker knew what he was dealing with when it came to Serum Z. He wasn't trying to protect himself. He was trying to stop anything from getting out. And anyway, Dr. Walker had a thing for efficiency. All of his clinics are like this. It's energy-efficient, durable, fire-resistant, and temperature-controlled."

Kate was poised and dressed in her usual black slacks and blazer. She must have just gotten back from meeting with the CDC.

"How did everything go?" I asked.

She took a breath in and something told me what she was about to say might not be good.

"Look, I'm going to be straight with you guys. The meetings weren't great. I got a lot of shit about Dr. Walker. Thankfully, they aren't blaming me and didn't send me to terrorist jail. Everyone is on board with the cure, but we're on a time constraint. If they don't start seeing results, they're going to take matters into their own hands."

The room grew silent. I wasn't sure about everyone else, but I was trying to figure out what they meant by taking matters into their own hands.

Finally, Kate decided to clarify. "The President and the government believe that if this cure doesn't heal at a rate that supersedes the rate of infection, then the best and only option left is to eradicate the zombies."

The silence in the room deepened. It was an ominous silence. A silence that spoke a thousand words.

"I know this is difficult to hear, guys, but we are going to make this work. We've just got to be sure to treat as many sick people as possible."

"How much time do we have?" I asked.

"I'm not completely sure yet. There'll be statistics teams hanging around here, analyzing our progress and the progress of the treatments. It took longer on the island because we were testing it out. But now that we know it works and how to do things, it should shorten the time by more than half. What might slow us down is rehabilitation and education on being a Zombrid. But I trust once we get the hang of it, things will go smoothly and quickly."

"What about flying them to the island?"

"It's a thought, but the island is so far away. And it wouldn't be able to accommodate thousands of people."

"What can we do?" Sonny queried. I was surprised to see that Sonny wanted to help.

Kate pulled out sheets of paper and passed them around to us. "Here is the schedule in which this whole process is going to work. Ian, you'll be in charge of educating and rehabilitation, along with some of our certified physicians. I'll be watching you, so no shortcuts or bullshit. They are to be taught that they cannot eat the living," she said sternly.

Ian didn't say anything, and it was probably because Kate had nailed it. In Ian's former life, pre-Everlasting Paradise, he was an undocumented serial killer. He had killed and eaten several people, including his girlfriend.

He said that his girlfriend was a mistake, but he never felt apologetic for the others. In fact, he enjoyed it. Killing seemed to be in his blood, and even though he looked like a changed man on the outside, and he had even taught me how to control my urges, we often worried the cravings were still there and that he might relapse. Maybe Kate assigned this job to him as a way to re-teach him what's right and wrong.

"Sonny, you'll be with the feeding crew."

"Oh, no! I don't want to cut up dead stuff! It's messy." She pouted.

Kate smiled. "We have our special crew of chefs for that. You will simply be supervising and making sure everyone gets the right amount of feedings. Once these TZs turn into Zombrids, they'll need to learn how to eat and control cravings. Do you think you can handle that?"

I assumed Kate asked Sonny this question because she was the newest Zombrid of us three. Newbies had a harder time dealing with their hunger pains and self-control. Surprisingly, Sonny bounced back pretty quickly after she turned, which was probably why Kate was giving her this task. There had never been any doubt of Sonny losing control around a human. I often wondered if her etiquette and well-mannered, opulent background had anything to do with her strength and willpower. Pretty little rich girls didn't get dirty.

Sonny nodded her head in agreement.

"What are we going to feed everyone, anyway?" I asked, curious about what we had just eaten, too.

"A little of both," Kate answered. "It really depends on the TZ's status. I did mention this to officials and the idea of maybe using recently deceased bodies donated to science. They actually agreed with this plan and chose to handle acquiring and delivering the bodies, which is great so we don't have to worry about it and can just focus on treating the infected."

"But, how do we know they aren't killing people for food?" I felt stupid once the words were out of my mouth. The government could be corrupt, but I didn't think they would murder people to feed other...people. Would they?

Kate chuckled. "I know Dr. Walker made us all paranoid, but I guess we just have to trust the president and his people."

"Maybe the president is a Zombrid," Ian joked.

"Maybe the Zombrids will take over the world," Sonny added.

"Let's not get ahead of ourselves. First, we have to turn all these people into Zombrids. Then we can talk about world domination," Kate mused, grinning. "What are you two doing here, anyway?" Her question was directed to both Sonny and Ian. Their presence was actually my fault. I didn't want to travel alone, so I had them accompany me. I had assumed it would be okay.

"It's my fault," I admitted. "I asked them to come along."

"Is everything under control on the island? Did you assign duties and things to the other Zombrids?"

"I did," Ian announced.

"Did you make sure to let the doctors know you were leaving?" she asked Sonny. Sonny nodded and smiled proudly. Kate turned to me. "Are the feeding schedules planned out?"

"I made sure that my mom and Megan had all that taken care of," I informed her.

She tilted her head to the side and a hint of surprise gleamed in her eyes. "You spoke to your mom?"

I looked down at my hands. "Well, I spoke to Megan," I mumbled. Kate pursed her lips. She was disappointed. In my defense, I did think long and hard about our conversation in my room a few days ago. I didn't just ignore everything she said. Between Kate and Megan, they made me realize that maybe I might have been too cruel and it was about time to consider rekindling a mother-daughter relationship. Or, at the very least, talk to my mom about everything. So I made the decision during the trip back to the States to finally break the silence once I saw her again.

"Okay, as you all know, we're in Tallahassee. You guys didn't see where you landed, but this facility is located in a sparse suburb a few miles from the city's center. The building is surrounded by fences and we have armed guards outside. We're pretty safe."

We each listened intently as Kate explained her plans. "Right now, the team is setting up the Florida Recovery Center as an extension to this building. The extra tents and beds that FEMA, the Red Cross, and the CDC contributed are being delivered and set up as we speak. They're also providing us with extra medical supplies. My original plans were to capture and treat the TZs in the Ground Zero zone in Tampa, but it seems it's too dangerous to get in there. As long as we're starting in Florida, which is where the initial outbreak began, it's better than nothing."

"What do you want me to do?" I asked. Kate peered at me and I was actually afraid of what she might assign me to.

"You'll be with me." She stood up and grabbed her items off the table.

"Wait, what are we doing?"

"We're going out to capture the TZs," she said simply, as if I was already supposed to know that.

Capture? I really didn't like that word.

THE TEENAGER

Serena

TWO HOURS. TWO HOURS of constant wailing in my ears. It took every single ounce of me not to turn around and use one of my Creep-decapitating melee moves on her.

I got it. Caroline's husband was just eaten by an adolescent, flesh-eating fiend a couple of hours ago. But these were different times now and she needed to get over it. And let's not forget about Harley, who had continuously moaned and groaned louder than she ever did before. The noise crawled up my skin like some kind of satanic ritual song. It was even harder to fight off my urges to make Julian pull over so that I could haul her out of the back to shut her up once and for all.

I glanced over at Julian. He was focused on the road, but I refused to believe the sounds coming out of this SUV weren't driving him mad.

"How far are we?" I asked. My patience was running thin.

"We're almost there. What's the plan? We just going to drive around?"

"Yeah. Assess the area. If there's refuge, you all can join them," I said hopefully. I was still trying to convince Julian that this was a good idea.

"What about you?"

"I'll be doing some research in the city." I read that Dr. Walker had a clinic or office or something here. My plan was to find as much information as I possibly could on his whereabouts. I made sure to pick up newspapers during our journey. Some of the details were the same as the ones in Tampa: articles about how Dr. Walker was a terrorist fugitive, but no one knew where he was. However, I did manage to find some different data on where he was last seen. This was all limited information, of course. The news outlets pretty much stopped reporting not long after Florida went to shit. If I could just piece it all together somehow, maybe I could have a chance. Julian was absolutely convinced I would never find him. But if I had to search the rest of my life to avenge Dan's death, and the death of my own humanity, then it would have been worth it.

The streets of Tallahassee were packed with Creeps. We tried to avoid them the best we could by taking side roads, but it all seemed just as congested. There were abandoned cars everywhere and buildings still smoking from fires here and there. Trash and random debris speckled the streets, evidence that chaos ensued at some point. Most probably during the initial outbreak.

I had never been to this city before. Dan went to college here and liked to reminisce about his fraternity days at Florida State University. And that was when it hit me. Tallahassee was home to two large colleges. It was a college town.

As the thought crossed my mind, Julian turned onto a street appropriately named College Avenue, and there they were, the buildings that made up Florida State University, along with what seemed like every single student that attended it stumbling around its campus. He jammed on the brakes and we came to a complete stop. It was early morning and light out, so we were able to see the horde of hundreds of Creeps perfectly, all wandering around aimlessly in front of us.

"Turn around! Turn around!" Caroline shrieked.

"Shh!" I yelled back. "If you don't shut up, they'll hear us."

A few of them had already spotted our SUV and began lurching their way over in our direction.

"I'm just going to back up and turn around." Julian put the car in reverse. But when he twisted in his seat and let off the gas, our vehicle didn't move. "What the hell?" He pressed on the gas again and moved the shifter into another gear, but we stayed where we were. The engine croaked, a sound exploding from under the hood as if the SUV were suddenly sick.

"Oh my God! Are we stuck?" Carline asked, voice hoarse and raspy from sobbing so much.

"We aren't stuck," I said, but inside I was really wondering if we were. The zombies might have had stronger smell than anything else, but the noise was enough to grab the attention of a few of them. About ten, maybe fifteen. "Julian, what's wrong?"

"I don't know. The damn thing won't do anything."

The zombies moved slowly, their feet dragging on the concrete in small, twitchy strides. But it wouldn't be long before they'd reach us. "I'll flank you while you look under the hood. I can get rid of most of the ones closest to us."

"Wait. Give it a minute."

The moans were coming closer, and I was now able to see the bleeding, disgusting wounds and blistering, rotting skin of the zombies inching their way toward us. Missing chunks of hair and broken, dangling limbs were just some of the characteristics these infected people now had. They were ugly monsters, and I couldn't wait to jump out of this car to slice some necks.

"I'm getting out," I declared, my fingers wrapping around the door handle and ready to swing it open.

"No! Wait a second!" Julian commanded. His voice was steady and stern. He had never yelled at me like that before.

We waited and watched the zombies close in around us. A few of them actually did reach the SUV, their hands slapping at the fiberglass hood. Julian stared at the steering wheel as if to be telepathically coaxing it to start. And when he finally turned the key, the engine roared back to life. I slammed my eyes shut and exhaled, happy to learn that we weren't stuck here, but sad that I wouldn't be able to go on a zombie-killing spree.

Loud thuds came from the back window as Julian drove backwards, followed by the entire car shifting and moving as if we had just backed onto a bumpy road.

I turned to him and smirked. "You just ran over a few."

He ignored my weird sense of humor and continued to concentrate on getting us to safety.

We circled the streets in the center of the city a few times on the lookout for any signs of human life, but it seemed there were none. Just Creeps everywhere. Julian decided to begin driving away from the downtown area, and I watched as the population of zombies and tall buildings started to become sparse. Our surroundings changed from urban to suburban within only a matter of twenty minutes.

Once we were a safe distance away, he pulled over. "We need a plan."

"What kind of plan? I mean, we don't have a specific place to go, Julian. We're winging it."

"Well, what are we supposed to do? I don't see anyone. There are no people. Human people, anyway," he mumbled. He was upset about this. I knew he was hoping for some kind of safe haven, and he was disappointed at the realization that there probably wasn't one. And there might not ever be one.

"Then we should just keep going," I said plainly.

He crinkled his forehead. "But where are we *going*? Sooner or later, we're going to run out of resources. Sooner or later, Harley is going to get hungry and I'll have to find food for her. And now we have another woman and a little girl who is sick and needs a place to rest to get better. We have to find a place to stop, restock on supplies, and just take a breather."

"Why? We can just find things like gas and food along the way."

He turned his head toward the backseat. "Have you ever killed one of them?"

Caroline sniffled. "No."

He turned back to me. "We need to teach them how to fight. We've killed so many zombies, so we know what we're doing, but you and I aren't always going to be able to protect them. They need to learn how to defend themselves."

Julian had a really great point. It was enough that we had to make sure Harley was okay. During our search for a safer place to stay after leaving his little bungalow, we continuously had to make sure Harley was either protected or hidden away in the vehicle. She had no sense of fear or reflexes. She could run off somehow or even get eaten. I had seen Creeps attack each other before, probably out of prolonged hunger. This meant that we were not only defending ourselves, but her too. We couldn't teach her how to use a weapon to defend herself. It was like we were lugging around a freaking invalid. She might as well have been deaf, blind, and mute.

"We're never going to find another place like the beach house," I scoffed sarcastically.

"I know that," he retorted. "Why are you so against finding a place to stay for a while?"

"Because, Julian, I know that it means you'll want to stay there forever. And we can't stay anywhere forever in this world, don't you get that?"

"Who says? If we find a decent place to hold down, then who says we can't make it permanent? I don't want to keep running, Serena. I could have been killed a few days ago. Harley almost got shot, and now we have two other people to protect who are clearly distraught about what just happened to someone they loved. And you..." He hesitated.

I tilted my head at him. "And me what?" I could feel my body tense and my defenses begin to loom. He held his gaze. The softness in his eyes was missing and replaced by a dour glare. He parted his lips as if to say something, then paused. I raised my eyebrows at him, mentally giving him the green light to say whatever he needed to say.

"You don't care about me."

That was not what I expected. "What?"

"Just admit it, Serena. You don't give a shit about one person in this car. All you want to do is find that doctor. You haven't cared about anything but yourself for a long time now."

"How can you say that?" I asked him. I could hear my own voice begin to rise. "I left and came back. I have been helping you take care of Harley. If it wasn't for me, Wade and Cooter would have killed you and taken all of our shit. And Grady? He would have killed you or Harley. I made sure he didn't."

Caroline and Jessica began to sob in the backseat. I wasn't sure if they knew I was the one who fed their loved one to Harley. I guess now they did. I braced myself for some kind of response coming from behind me, but there was nothing.

"You came back because you were scared. Something horrible happened to you and you didn't want to be alone."

I laughed off his accusation. "I was not scared. I could have easily just continued on my merry way after I killed that nasty bastard. I came back because I felt guilty for you. I felt pity for you. You're stuck trying to take care of Harley, and for what? She's never going to get better. You should be looking for Dr. Walker, too. He's the one who did this to your daughter." My words were mostly untrue and harsh, but his felt harsher. My chest caved at the fact that he thought I didn't care about him. I loved him! I'd always loved him.

"You don't know that she won't get better!" he yelled.

"Why don't you just kill her already, Julian!" I shouted back. "Put her out of her misery!" I said it. I finally said it and this time my words were true.

His chest moved up and down at a rapid pace. I couldn't see his mouth underneath his thick salt-and-pepper beard, but I could tell by the way the hair moved on his chin that he was biting his bottom lip. He turned his body forward, tightened his fists, and slammed them into the steering wheel. Not once, but several times in a fit of rage. Caroline yelped, and there was fear in her soft cries. I glanced behind me and saw that she was squeezing Jessica into herself as she buried her own face into the little girl's hair.

"You're scaring them," I muttered.

"Why? Why are you like this now?" he whispered. "What's happening to you is happening to all of us, too."

217

I didn't say anything and looked down at my hands. It wasn't because I didn't have anything to say. I could have told him I was like this now because I was enraged. I was furious that Dan was dead, the only person who had truly made me happy. I was furious that it took him dying for me to realize that. To realize that up until I'd met him, my life was just full of bad memories and disappointment. I hated that I loved Dan so much and that love made me depend on him to somehow erase my unfortunate past. But the crappy truth was that it would never go away. As happy as I was, it was still there. The gloom lived inside of me, and as much as I tried to escape it, it would always be there.

I could have told Julian that I missed painting, the only outlet to express how I felt. Painting beautiful and serene landscapes was my mind dreaming of what I wished my life could have been since I was a little girl hiding away from my drunk parents. I could have said that I longed for the bay, to be near it again because it was calm and tranquil, the way I had always wanted my soul to be. I was mad that this world had changed. There was nothing in it anymore to soothe my shattered past. Now, it only matched my hopeless spirit, and I found it harder and harder not to just give into what I felt seemed to be my destiny: a life that would forever be broken.

The strained moan of a Creep slipped through the crack of my passenger-side window. I peered out of it and caught a glimpse of one approaching the SUV through the side mirror. I pulled my machete out of the harness strapped to my thigh and clasped it tight. "I got it."

Thankful that this was an excuse to end the fight between Julian and me, I opened the door and stepped out. Rather than just going straight for the Creep's neck, I decided to kick his left leg. There was a cracking sound before he lost his balance and instantly fell to the ground. This Creep must not have eaten in a while. I barely kicked him, but it was hard enough to bend his leg into the complete opposite direction it should be allowed to go.

He fell onto his side. I stood over him and kicked his shoulder, hearing another break as his body flattened into the supine position. I bent down over him, grabbing his arms and placing them on either side of him. This one was very weak, but still strong enough to give me a struggle. Even so, he fought against my strength in a lazy manner. I was able to overpower him and placed a knee over each of his arms to hold them in place as I straddled his body.

He opened his mouth wide, revealing the decay and black rot of his teeth, and lifted his head in an attempt to snap at me. I put my hand on his forehead and forced his head down. His skin felt rough and scaly, and I could feel it threatening to slough off.

I took a deeper look at him, analyzing the large, open wounds on his face. A string of them ran down from his balding head to his neck and seemed to be filled with a mixture of cream-colored pus and blood. The edges of his wounds were green and gangrenous, and the smell radiating off his body had me fighting back the bile rising in my throat.

He was moving his head too much. My hand slid off his forehead, causing his loose skin to slide off with it and exposing the decomposition of the meat underneath. I flung the piece of skin off my hand and pushed his head down again. Finally, I lifted my machete into the air before swinging it down on his neck in one quick motion. It sliced right through his skin to his spine. His movements slowed down, but he was still trying his hardest to flee my restraints. With another swing, I came down again with my melee, this time severing his head from his body. He instantaneously stopped squirming.

I took a deep breath and wiped the blade of my machete on his plaid shirt before standing up. A sense of relief washed over me, and a satisfying feeling of adrenaline filled my head. I sucked in a breath of stale, putrid air and looked up to the sky. This was my escape from my broken soul now.

A strange and familiar noise from a distance quickly took my attention. I peered over at the road. The familiar sound was that of a military truck and it was heading toward us. My stomach knotted in apprehension as I stepped closer to the open road. Was it the military? Could there really be refuge?

Julian must have seen it coming, too, in his rearview mirror because he stepped out of the SUV. The truck approached and stopped right next to us. It resembled an 18-wheeler, only smaller and painted a faded green.

The passenger door opened, and a man jumped down from its tall cab. He was dressed in black fatigues and armor from head to toe. He stepped forward and approached our vehicle. I steadied myself and gripped my melee.

Never trust anyone.

"Hey!" His voice was muffled by the full-faced ski mask he wore over his head. "You broke down or something?" he asked Julian. "You need some help?"

I could tell Julian was trying to contain a smile. He was happy but didn't want to show it just yet to a stranger. My eyes drifted to the cab of the truck. There seemed to be a backseat and what looked like two women with dark hair sitting in it.

"We were just stopping to take a rest."

"You have a place to go?"

I was afraid of what Julian might say. This was no world to just accept invitations. He was so fixated on finding a "home" that I worried he would forget that.

He ran his fingers through his long hair, a sign that he was probably confused over what to say. If I wasn't here, he would have quickly told the guy he had nowhere to go and needed a place to stay. He wanted to stop running. And the only reason he was running was because of me. Because he was trying to make me happy. Because he was worried about losing me if he didn't.

I might have saved him from getting killed, but I was the reason why he almost got killed. And the honest truth was that I didn't want him to die. I knew he wanted this. I knew he needed this. I do care about him. I *do* love him.

"No!" I shouted. Julian and the masked man turned their attention to me. "No, we don't have a place to go. Please help us. We're running out of supplies. We have two sick children and a woman who just lost her husband. We have nowhere to go."

The door of the military truck opened, and the two women in the backseat hopped down and walked up.

"What's going on?" one woman asked. She was also dressed in armor and her hair was tied back into a sleek ponytail.

The woman next to her actually looked more like a teenager at a closer glance. She played with her hands in front of her, as if she was nervous or shy. Her long, curly wild hair blew around her face in the breeze.

"These folks need help," the masked man responded. The woman shifted her eyes between Julian and me, then down to the machete in my hand. She peered behind my shoulder at the Creep I had just decapitated, then back at me. She held out her hand. I was confused by this for a split second, trying to remember the last time someone offered to shake my hand.

As I took her hand in mine, she greeted me. "I'm Kate. This is my crew. We have a safe place right up the road. It's secured with a fence and armed men. We are more than happy to help you."

Julian took her hand out of mine and into his own. "Wow! That's amazing. I'm Julian and this is Serena."

Kate nodded.

"Are you guys military?" I asked skeptically.

"Not really, no. But my crew has military-trained personnel. We're working with the government."

"That sounds good," Julian said, relief in his tone. "Hey listen, we're low on gas. Do you think you can give us enough just to make sure we can make it to your place?"

"Sure. Jackson?" She motioned for Jackson and he immediately ran off to the truck. He reached up and opened the door, grabbing a red canister. He and Julian walked back toward the SUV to fill it up. I stood with Kate and the girl. We watched the guys in an awkward silence for a moment before Kate broke the ice.

"It's nice to see survivors on our first day out in town. Do you know of anyone else?"

I studied her uplifting demeanor for a moment. Her armor and skin were completely free of any dried blood or guts. Something told me she had no idea what it was like to live for almost four months in a world taken over by zombies.

"We're the only ones from here to Tampa."

Her eyes widened. "You're from Tampa?"

"Yeah."

"Wow! You were part of the first wave. I'm sorry you had to go through all of this." Her tone seemed genuinely sincere, but I still questioned it.

"Kate! We've got Seth on the radio!" the driver of the truck called out.

"Sorry," she apologized before rushing to the radio.

I looked at the girl. She couldn't have been more than eighteen years old, with a petite frame and freckles that dotted her cheeks. She seemed scared and worried and completely clueless about what was out there.

I caught her eying the dead Creep behind me.

"What's your name?" I asked.

She looked up at me with her big, brown eyes. "Grace."

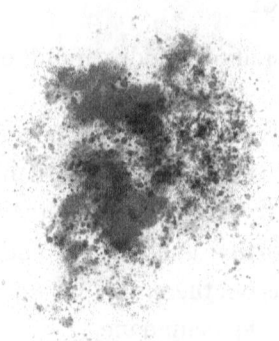

THE TZ
Grace

"DO YOU THINK IT'S safe to pick up random people off the road?" I asked Kate. I had watched enough of *The Walking Dead* to know that in a post-apocalyptic world taken over by zombies, you could never truly trust anyone.

Kate kept her eyes down on her tablet. "They're fine. But, unfortunately, they're the only survivors we will personally be helping. We need to stay focused on our mission. If we happen to see any more of the living, we'll radio in someone else to handle it."

The statement that the woman made echoed in my mind: *We are the only ones from here to Tampa.* That couldn't be true. I mean, Florida was a big state. I knew that Kate's zombie map showed it all red, but there had to be other humans. Maybe they also watched *The Walking Dead* and didn't trust anyone, either. Maybe they were just hiding and trying to stay safe.

That woman, Serena, seemed a bit scary, to be honest. She was tall and super toned, and her red hair was messy and dirty. She had an untamed glare in her eyes, as if she had lived in the woods and was just making contact with humans for the first time in a while. She was very pretty, don't get me wrong, but it was definitely hard to tell underneath the bloodstains and grime that coated her skin.

I shouldn't judge. It had been about four months since the TZs took over. Obviously, these people were doing whatever they had to do to survive. But I did see that TZ behind her. I saw his head lying next to his body, and it made me sad. That could've been Ian or Sonny...or even me. We could have been the ones that were trying to eat her. She was just defending herself.

The guards at the gate motioned for us to roll in. I turned to see the black SUV following right behind us. These people were humans and they had no idea who we were. It made me nervous for them to find out.

"Let's just make sure they're okay before we head out," Kate said before stepping out of the truck. I followed.

The SUV pulled up next to ours, and the woman and the man got out. The guy, Julian, seemed much cleaner than she did. But he was still pretty disheveled. I didn't know if it was a personal choice or not, but his thick beard looked overgrown. His hair must have been really long because he was able to tie it up into a ponytail. He, too, was tall and muscular, but he wasn't scary in the least bit. There seemed to be a kind of gentleness in his eyes.

"Julian and Serena, this is The Florida Recovery Center," Kate said, holding her hand out toward the building. "My team and everyone at this facility are working closely with the CDC, and our job is to cure the zombies."

"Wait, what?" Julian's eyes grew bigger as if he'd seen something amazing just happen right in front of him.

"You're curing them?" Serena asked.

"Yes. We have a cure. It's in the very early stages, as we have literally just arrived last night. As you can see, our team is still working on expanding the facility to accommodate the zombies we'll be helping." Kate pointed to the side of the facility, which was surrounded by workers putting up tents, pushing hospital beds around, and carrying boxes. Julian stepped closer, but Serena stood behind him, arms crossed across her chest.

"I-I have a daughter. She's sick. She was bitten and she's...one of them."

It seemed he was having a hard time revealing this. My heart sank as the worry and heartbreak in his voice pulled at its strings.

"Is she with you?"

"She's in the back. We had to tie her up. She just recently ate someone, and I don't know how long that's going to hold her over."

I peeked over to the back of the SUV and could only see another woman sitting with a young girl. That couldn't be her; otherwise, that woman's face would have been half eaten by now. His daughter must have been all the way in the back, in the trunk.

"Well, we can help her. But it's not going to cure her the way you think it is."

"What do you mean?" Serena asked assertively. "A cure is a cure. It either cures her or it doesn't."

"We really have to go, but I'll have my team explain everything to you. We have a full staff of licensed physicians who know what they're doing." Kate took Julian's hand into hers. "Your daughter is safe here and she will get the help she needs."

He looked down at Kate and squeezed her hand in return. It was as if I could visibly see the weight being lifted off his shoulders. His eyes even began to well up with tears.

She held on to his hands and smiled. "I'm sorry to ask this at such a time, but do I know you from somewhere?"

He squinted as if trying to remember, then shook his head. "I don't think so. I mean, you kind of look familiar to me, too, but I'm not sure from where."

"Huh. Well, maybe not. We have to go now. We'll be back later tonight."

We piled into the truck, and I watched Julian and Serena as we drove off the lot. He had just opened the back hatch of the SUV, and I was only able to catch a glimpse of his daughter lying down in there. She seemed to be struggling to get out of the ropes that were tied around her ankles and wrists and neck.

I turned away and instinctively brought my hand up to my neck and rubbed.

"It seems we have our first patient," Kate said. She was pleased about this, but I still felt uneasy. How was Julian going to feel when he learned that his daughter will not be completely healed? How was he going to handle knowing that he would still need to feed his daughter things with a pulse on a regular basis? How was he going to deal with the fact that she would never be normal again?

It was really how I felt about all of these zombies we were getting ready to turn into Zombrids. What if they didn't want to become Zombrids? What if they would rather die instead of eventually having to live off the meat of an actual human being? If I had the choice, I don't think I would have let Dr. Walker inject me with Serum Z. If I had a choice, I would have chosen death over a life full of constant uncertainty. Constantly worrying about whether or not I would kill again...or *when* I would kill again.

"Do you know that guy?" I asked, trying to keep my mind clear of thoughts about how this crazy life of mine all began.

"I'm not sure. I feel like I've met him before. But then again, I've met tons of people. Maybe he just looks like someone I know."

We drove down the road, which seemed to be zombie-free. But as soon as we hooked a left onto a two-way street, there they were. It was unnerving to know how close they were to the facility, and even more so when I was able to truly see them. It was exactly like a movie. Hundreds of them scattered all over the place, stumbling about with their arms hanging low at their sides. As the truck passed by, most of them lifted their heads and began staggering after us. We drove by slowly, and I wondered why.

Jackson spoke through his ski mask. "Let's try to stop in an area that isn't so congested. This way we can just get a few of them at time without having to fight them off too much."

Kate gawked out of the window with me. I didn't believe she was expecting it to look this way. The streets were not only filled with the undead, but there were debris, abandoned cars, and just plain trash all over the place. It seriously looked like a tornado had touched down, sucking up and spitting out everything in its path. I imagined what it must have been like in the beginning. People running everywhere and trying to escape being eaten alive. If they knew anything about zombies, they would have been able to call it as soon as they saw one. It would be hard to miss a zombie's characteristics, especially watching one eat another human. Everyone must have been so scared. And I hated that I was a part of it all.

"This is good right here."

The driver pulled to a stop. I glanced around outside and spotted about five of them staggering over to us. My heart began to race, and I wondered how we were going to do this. I knew how I felt when I was hungry—strong enough to push a horse over to the ground to get what I needed. How were we going to get these zombies into the back of the truck?

"Grace, you and I are going to be the ones to corral them into the back," Kate instructed.

Corral them? "How are we going to do that?"

"There's already food back there. Remember, their incredible ability to smell overpowers any of their other senses. If they smell fresh blood and meat, they're going for it."

"We're fresh," I pointed out.

"Don't worry. We have a cow that has been cut open and ready for consumption, exposing everything they want. They're going to go for that before us."

Oh, but I worried. Even though I knew what the amazing aroma of super fresh and readily available blood and guts smelled like, there was still no guarantee that they wouldn't try to chomp down on one of us on their way into the back of the truck.

"Are you ready?"

I took a deep breath in and replied warily, "Yes."

The four of us jumped out of the vehicle at the same time. I looked over each of my shoulders, scared out of my mind that a TZ would grab me. I briefly wondered what a fight between a Zombrid and a zombie would be like. I had strength, too, so who would win?

We all ran toward the back, but there wasn't a moment's time before I noticed a group of them coming our way down the street ahead of us. "They're already coming."

Jackson opened the two doors to the back of the truck, and it was as if I was suddenly slapped in the face. My stomach instantly began to growl and my mouth watered at the delicious scent that wrapped around my head.

"Grace, are you okay?" Kate whispered. She must have noticed my eyes rolling in the back of my head. I closed them and sucked in a deep and long whiff before silently calming myself and the adrenaline boiling in the pit of my stomach. I could do this. I just ate before we left. Ian taught me a lot about controlling myself. I could do this.

I opened my eyes and Kate was staring at me. "You okay?"

I nodded as I felt the pains in my stomach begin to subside. The two guards each carried a long, sword-like blade. They began to call over the TZs, who were already practically tripping over each other to get to us. I watched them. I watched as they held their arms and hands out in the air—so stereotypical. It was what we all saw in the movies. But in reality, it was much different. It was much scarier.

All five of these TZs seemed like they had not eaten in some time. They were all balding, and the skin on their heads matched the black and gray and green tint of their faces and arms. Patches of it were missing, and one of the zombies was even missing part of his jaw.

Another one, a woman who wore a sun dress that might have once been the color yellow, but now only hung off her skinny body tattered and dull, moaned her way over. Her foot looked as if it was broken, but it didn't slow her down. And as she lurched closer to us, I finally noticed her eye hanging out of its socket by a single vessel. It rested on her cheek like it belonged there.

This was what I would look like if I didn't eat?

I started to panic. I started to feel my heart racing faster and faster in my chest. This was future me! My eyeball was going to pop out of my head!

Don't have a nervous breakdown, Grace! Not now!

The guards taunted and encouraged them toward the back. Kate and I stood on either side of the truck, and as they got closer, she began to call out to them.

"Come on! Come on, guys!" She clapped her hands and motioned a path.

I wasn't sure if it was because I was scared or because I just didn't feel right calling them as if they were dogs or cattle being herded into a barn, but I stayed quiet and just readied myself for something to go wrong. As the first TZ approached Kate, I held my breath. She visibly held her breath, too.

He was going to swipe at her. He was going to grab her instead of stepping into the truck. I just knew it.

We both stood breathless and motionless as the zombie walked right past, growling and groaning the whole way. As soon as he figured out how to step into the tall truck, he immediately made his way to the cow. He fell to his knees, and with both hands, dug into its lifeless body.

Great. One down. Four to go...and about ten more that were slowly closing in on us.

The others somehow formed a single-file line of their own and made their way toward us. I held my breath again, worried that surely, this time, something would go wrong. They walked past us and began entering the vehicle, one by one. Kate watched me through them as they stumbled past her. She smiled at me. But the last one stopped. A tall, bony man covered in dried blood and other fluids stopped right in front of us.

Kate's smile quickly faded and she stood silently. She didn't move an inch, not even her eyes. The TZ lifted his face into the air and I could see his chest rise and fall rapidly. He was sniffing his surroundings. I wondered if he was confused, if he caught the smells of the cow and Kate at the same time.

The guards stood behind him and readied their weapons, but Kate bravely held her hand out as a signal for them to stay where they were. The lanky TZ's jaw began to move up and down in rapid succession, and I could hear what was left of his teeth clanking against each other. He continued to smell the air and then moved closer to Kate.

She stood still and waited, and I prayed that a breeze would suddenly shift the pleasant odor of the cow his way. But it didn't, and the TZ finally realized that Kate would be a better meal.

He hastily grabbed on to her neck and Kate's reflexes were to immediately clutch onto his arms. She began gasping for air as he squeezed her tight. She pushed away from him, swinging her head left to right to dodge the mouth that was snapping at her face. Jackson ran to them and attempted to pull the zombie away but was unsuccessful. Kate sucked in as much air as she possibly could, but she was beginning to turn red. She was clearly fighting to catch a breath. The other guard lifted his sword into the air, and suddenly, I felt the need to intervene. He couldn't kill him! I had to stop him from killing the TZ!

I rushed over to the guard and yelled, "NO!"

But before I could reach him, his sword swung across the zombie's neck. I watched as the head detached from the body and fell to the ground. I blinked at the warm, black blood that splattered my face. The zombie's hands let go of Kate's neck before his limp body fell over. Kate immediately gasped for air. I stood over his body. The TZ lay there dead, with his head several feet away from his body.

There was a pain in the pit of my stomach. It wasn't hunger. It wasn't rage. It was loss. I let myself fall to my knees next to him and rest my hand on his chest. There was no heartbeat. No movement. Suddenly, that sensation of bereavement in my stomach began to rise, and I found myself unable to fight the surge of tears eager to escape my eyes.

He was dead. Completely dead. He was me. I was him. He was a part of me. He was a part of who I was now, and he shouldn't have died. I should have saved him. I should have been able to save my own.

"Grace." I could feel Kate's hands on my back. "We have to go." I heard her words, but I couldn't possibly think of leaving him behind.

"There has to be something we can do. Can't we fix him?" I asked through my sobs.

"No, sweetie," she replied softly. "We can't help him anymore."

My chest caved in with disappointment and torment of the reality that finally hit me. He was gone for good. Kate began to lift me up and I allowed her to. The sounds of the other TZs seemed to be closer, but I couldn't take my eyes off him.

"Let's go, Grace." Kate held me steady and helped me into the truck. I pushed to my side of the seat and sunk into it, feeling the despair and sadness weighing down on me. The guard started the engine and we began to roll down the street.

"We have to get a few more. Are you okay with that?" Kate asked, concern in her tone.

But I ignored her question. "Why couldn't we fix him? How are we going to fix the ones who are missing body parts and half their faces?"

"Well, there are going to be some TZs that we just can't save, Grace. They might be too far gone."

I didn't say anything. I just stared out of the window. These people were my people. I felt it inside of me, and I needed to do what I could to save them.

THE HAIR
Serena

JULIAN WAS APPROACHED BY some doctors and they took him and Harley away. Caroline went off with some other person in a lab coat. They had to stick Jessica in a wheelchair and wheel her off. Apparently, Jessica's illness was getting worse, so the doctors were going to do whatever they had to do to fix her.

I walked into the place alone. The first thing I noticed was its thick, gray walls and lack of windows. But for the most part, the entrance reminded me of some sort of clinic. There was a waiting room and a receptionist's desk, but no receptionist. I decided to set my backpack down and sit in one of the chairs. It had been a while since I was able to just sit and relax and not have to worry about the threat of getting attacked or bitten by a Creep. But before I could take a load off, one of the three doors that aligned the back wall opened and a blonde girl walked through.

I straightened up, my sense of awareness heightening. She strolled over to me, dressed in tight, white skinny jeans and a top that exposed her belly button ring. Her long, bright yellow hair hung around her shoulders. She smiled wide and clanked her heels toward me.

Was this chick serious? We were in the middle of a zombie apocalypse, and she was dressed for a runway show? Although, I must admit, she was beautiful and practically glowing. Her skin was flawless and tan, and her facial features did resemble a supermodel.

I rested my hand on my thigh holster, mentally preparing myself for this girl to try something stupid. Then, she flipped her hair away from her shoulder in a I-think-I'm-God's-Gift-to-Earth kind of way, revealing an arm that was only three quarters there. Well, she shouldn't be hard to take down if I had to do it.

"Hiya," she greeted happily. "My name is Sonny. I hear you're with Julian and Harley and Caroline and Jessica."

I nodded and stood up.

"Great! So, you look like you need a bath." She wrinkled her nose in a disgusted but sweet manner. "And you smell like it, too."

I narrowed my eyes at her.

"We've got a hot shower ready for you. And some food. Are you hungry?"

"I could eat," I mumbled.

"Okay, just get your pack and follow me." She turned around and headed toward the door she came in through, and I followed. But after just four steps, she turned back to me. "Just...uh...try not to touch me, okay? These jeans are white and *Stella McCartney,* and we don't have a dry cleaners anywhere around."

I wanted to punch her. I wanted to knock her on her ass and rub my filthy, blood-soaked clothes all over her face.

Biting my tongue and gripping my machete tight to my side, I simply continued to follow her. We walked past the door and down a long hallway, which eventually opened into a large space that reminded me of some kind of futuristic science lab. The light was dim and there were sounds of computers and low mumblings of the people in labs coats scattered around. Glass walls were everywhere, and weird blue lights illuminated the area. The smell of bleach reminded me of a freshly mopped floor in a hospital.

We walked past all the glass and white coats until we finally reached a lounge area complete with a few couches, a television, and a pool table. As we approached, a guy stood up from one of the black leather couches.

"Ian, this is Serena. She's one of the survivors Grace and Kate found today."

The guy held out his hand. "Hello, love."

Sonny grabbed his hand and pushed it down. "Oh, you don't want to do that."

I rolled my eyes.

"It's okay. Blood and guts don't bother me," he said mischievously and winked. As far as guys with nice tans and sexy Australian accents went, he was definitely a ten. But he was clean-cut and too pretty for my taste. Besides, I could tell he was a douchebag by his popped collar and floral surf shorts. Definitely not my type.

"So, how is it out there?"

"You haven't been outside?" That was surprising, but not too much. He, too, was clean.

"Nah. We just got here."

"From where?" This made me wonder. Was Florida the only state that was hit by the outbreak?

"Everlasting—"

"Um...Ian?" Sonny interrupted abruptly. "Maybe we should get her to her room now."

The alarms were sounding loudly in my head. They exchanged glares before he realized that Sonny cut him off for a reason. But why? "Yeah, sure. I've got a meeting to go to, anyway. I'll see you around, Serena." Ian walked away with his head down in his cellphone.

"How does he have a cellphone? Nothing works here."

"Oh, it's connected to some kind of satellite or something. Come on, your room is this way."

I followed Sonny down another hallway lined with doors. She opened the second one and gestured for me to step inside. I did so and found a bed and a dresser. It was white and cold and bleak.

"This is your room. It kind of sucks, but the bed isn't so bad. I'm going to talk to the chef and get some food for you."

She was about to shut the door behind her.

"Wait!" I called out. "Where did you guys come from? Are we the only ones going through this? How is the rest of the world?"

There was a look of hesitation on her face before she responded, which was a clear indication that she wasn't going to answer any of my questions. "I'm sorry. I can't answer that. You're going to have to wait for Kate and Grace."

There was no point in asking her anything else except, "Where's Julian?"

"He's with his daughter. I'll tell him where you are. Caroline and Jessica will be staying in the tents until Jessica gets better." Then she walked out.

I took a breath in and sat down on the bed. I glanced around the room, which was pretty much empty...and lonely. It sent a shiver down my spine. There was a door that I assumed was a closet, but after flicking on the light switch, revealed a bathroom.

A light switch. Lights.

I walked to the sink and turned the handle on the faucet.

Water. Running, clear water.

I held my hand under it, feeling the temperature slowly change from cold to warm to hot. Steam began to rise and my skin began to burn, but it felt so amazing to finally feel hot water. I glanced at myself in the mirror. The steam was beginning to fog the glass, but I could still see my mirrored image.

My face was splotched with red and dirt. My hair was messy and knotted and matted. There were no changes in my physical features, but as I stared at myself in the mirror, I could see the changes inside of *me*. I knew that I was different. I knew that I was selfish and that I only truly cared about one thing: finding Dr. Walker. I knew that finding true gratification from slicing and brutally decapitating Creeps was a troubling sign. It probably meant I was on the verge of a psychotic breakdown. A therapist would have a field day with me. But I didn't care. I stared at myself in the mirror and recognized the loss and hate and anger and misery that lived inside of me, but it was mine to deal with. It was who I had become, and I was okay with it.

I stared into that mirror and there was no soul. There was nothing left of it. And I needed the world to know. I needed the Creeps to fear my soulless existence. I used to be nothing without pretend. Before this place became a chaotic mess, pretending was what kept me from drowning in a world where I just wanted nothing more but to sleep and forget where I'd come from. Forget about the overwhelming loss that constantly ate at my heart. It was all that held me together.

But I didn't want to pretend anymore.

I glanced around the bathroom, desperately and frantically in search of something. Something like scissors or a razor. I reached down into the vanity drawers, pulling them open one by one. There was nothing. There was nothing!

I slammed the drawer shut, causing the mirror to vibrate from the force. Then, I suddenly felt the weight of my machete hanging on my thigh. I reached down to unhook it from its holster, gripping the leather-bound handle in my hand and staring at the black blade covered in dried zombie blood. I raised my head up to gaze at myself again, the new me that was begging to be transformed. The more I stared, the more I needed to do this.

Grabbing a large chunk of my long, red hair, stiff and crunchy from days of not washing it, I lifted it into the air. And without another thought, raked the blade of my machete through the strands. The severed piece slipped out of my hand, and I watched it fall into the sink. I glanced back at the mirror, grabbed another chunk, and shredded. It fell into the sink. My eyes stared at my reflection again. Just a few more pieces and it would be the shortest I had ever cut my hair before. Like a pixie. Like a young boy's head. Short enough to shave off the rest whenever I could find a razor.

When I was finally satisfied with the amount of hair I'd lobbed off—and the amount of weight that was lifted off my shoulders—I began to undress. I needed to feel the hot water all over my body. After about thirty minutes of standing in the shower and watching other people's blood run off me and into the drain, I stepped out of the bathroom with a white towel wrapped around my body. Before throwing my dirty clothes into my bag and switching them for some clean(er) ones, I retrieved the picture of Charlie and me from the back pocket of my jeans. A crack appeared right between us when I unfolded it, right where the rope of the swing was. The photograph was becoming more delicate and flimsier every time I looked at it.

There was a knock on the door. When it opened, Julian poked his head through.

"Serena?"

I felt a familiar twinge in my stomach that reminded me of Dan. Sometimes, Dan would come home early from work and find me in the shower. He'd poke his head through to let me know he was home, and the sound of his voice made my stomach flutter—like a teenager hopelessly in love. I would always invite him to join me, and he would always oblige.

I felt that flutter with Julian every time he said my name. I started feeling it not too long ago. But I could never tell him.

"Yeah," I said, carefully folding the picture in half again and stuffing it inside my bag. He came in and shut the door behind him but immediately took a step back when he caught a glimpse of my new appearance. His eyes traveled from my head, down my body, to my feet, then up to my awaiting glare. Without a word, he stepped forward and touched the uneven pieces of my hair. Then, he grabbed my head and gently pulled me into his chest. I didn't want it, but I allowed it.

"Serena," he breathed. "Are you okay?"

"Yes."

"You sure?"

"Yes."

"Serena," he breathed again, this time slightly pulling me away from him. He cupped my cheek and looked down into my eyes. "Are you sure?"

I knew he was wondering if I'd finally lost it. He was probably wondering when he was going to find me hanging by a rope in the doorway.

I backed away from him and hugged myself. "I'm fine," I insisted.

He finally stopped staring and sat down on the bed, leaning forward to hold his head in his hands. It seemed he was the one who wasn't okay. My days of offering sincerity and nurturing people were long behind me, but Julian wasn't just people. I adjusted my towel to reassure its tight fit before sitting down next to him. We didn't need breasts flying around all over the place in this moment.

Before I could ask him what was wrong, he spoke. "She's going to be okay."

I didn't want to pretend to be happy anymore, but deep down, a faded pang of relief shot through me. "That's good, Jules."

He turned his head, allowing me to see his melodious, hazel eyes fill with tears. But he placed a hand over his mouth to hide his quivering lips. Julian was so beautiful in the most rugged way, but his heart was too delicate. It didn't match his appearance, and I worried so much that it would eventually ruin him.

My gaze followed his long beard up his jaw and to his sideburns, and then I watched the corners of his eyes wrinkle as he continued to cry. Part of me wanted to hold him, but that part was overcome by the indignity I felt for him. He needed to stop pretending with me, too.

"I don't know if it's okay," he admitted.

"What do you mean?"

He took a deep breath before explaining. "Kate was right. She won't be completely cured. Apparently, she's going to be half zombie."

I didn't understand. "What? How can someone be half a zombie?"

"I don't know. They have to drain the infected blood and replace it with some kind of serum-laced blood and it's going to make her half human, half zombie."

"Well, what does that mean? How does this change things?"

"The doctors said they're going to give her education and training on her new lifestyle. That she's going to have to live on eating recently deceased animals and humans, but she'll be able to control herself and live like a normal little girl."

I was furious and felt the need to stand up. "Normal? What the hell is normal about eating people, Julian?"

He lowered his head back down.

"We can't trust them!"

"Serena, I don't have a choice."

"We can't trust them. There's no way the CDC would be okay with making someone a freaking zombie hybrid that still needs to feed on humans. These people are probably some kind of scientists who just want to experiment, like that asshole Dr. Walker."

He looked up at me. "Then what am I supposed to do? Huh? You tell me."

"Stop saying that you don't have a choice! You do! We can leave. We can get out of here."

He bit his bottom lip and showed me an expression I was all too familiar with. A sign that his gentle nature ruled over everything else. He reached out and grabbed my hand, lightly tugging me toward him to sit back down.

"What am I supposed to do?" he asked in a calmer voice. "Watch her body deteriorate? Watch her hair fall out and her skin rot off? She's only seven years old. My little girl deserves a future. This isn't her fault. It's my fault. I should have been there. I should have been there to save her. And now I can. It's the least I can do."

I searched deep inside of myself to understand, to find some kind of compassion and respect for his decision. But I couldn't find it. I couldn't find the sympathy he was looking for. I didn't agree with his decision.

But I had just made my own.

"I'm leaving." The words rolled off my tongue like nothing. Julian squeezed my hand and stared intensely into my eyes. Then, unexpectedly, he leaned in and placed his lips on mine. I took a breath in and flinched. Every fiber of my body was yelling at me to push him away. Yelling at him to get off me. My mind and soul were lost in a dark, shadowy forest of despair. But there seemed to be a glimmer of something in my heart. It ignited when Julian's lips touch mine. It sparked. It hurt me to feel it because I didn't want to. But it was there. Undeniably.

As he kissed me, mouth closed and in the sweetest of ways, I fought to keep the love that wanted to surround him inside of me. The magnet that pulled me to him, the one responsible for never allowing me to leave before. His hands moved up to my face, cradling my head. His lips parted and his tongue slid across my bottom lip. He moved closer to me, and now I could feel his hard chest on mine. The natural reaction of draping my arms around him threatened to overpower my will.

Julian felt so warm. Not like that horrible man who touched me and forced himself on me. That asshole's ice-cold blood froze my skin. Jules was different. His warmth blocked the frigidness of the room. His embrace, his breath. My skin sensed his desire for me. He wanted me. He needed me. And it only showed more when the urgency of his kiss intensified. I had no choice but to finally part my lips and allow him in.

I had no choice but to finally wrap my arms around his neck.

I had no choice but to fall deep into the unmistakable love that I had for him.

I kissed him back. After all these years, I kissed him back. I pulled him to me, as far as he would go. Suddenly, it was as if he was the air I breathed. Without it, I would die.

He matched my aggression in his kiss, but I pulled at his long hair and pinched his skin between my fingers. I twisted and turned my head rapidly, ensuring that I taste every inch of his lips. Yearning for him to somehow get closer to me, I pushed him back onto the bed and climbed over him, straddling his torso and quickly leaning down to meet his lips again because they were gone too long. He ran his hands up and down my back and moaned. My mind was swimming in a pool of mixed emotions. As I closed my eyes and kissed him, flashes of my life appeared before me. My parents, Charlie, loneliness, loss, men who mistreated me, struggling to make ends meet, living on the street...

Dan appeared, dressed in his dapper suit, ready to give me a sweet goodbye kiss before work. The sense of finally feeling wanted and loved and deserved was there. It was all there. Dan had given that to me.

But so did Julian. During all this time that I'd known him, Julian had given all of this to me. Always.

I moved away from Julian's mouth and down to his neck, biting his rough skin before reaching down to the edge of his shirt and pulling it up over his head. Jules wanted me, too, but his daughter came first. She was his life, and rightfully so. Was I Julian's life, too?

I had never felt like anyone's life before. Not before Dan. Dan had made me feel wanted. But he was taken away from me. Now, all that was left was an empty shell of not only myself, but of the world around me. The darkness that lived inside of everyone, buried far down into their souls, was no longer hidden. It was the way of the world now. Their darkness was exposed. And so was mine.

I ran my fingers down his bare, toned chest, and he grabbed my wrist.

"Serena," he purred.

I ignored him and continued to kiss his body, digging my nails deep into his skin.

"Ouch! Serena!" He grabbed my other wrist and sat up, pulling me up with him. "What are you doing?"

I was drunk with a mixture of desire and anguish. But when I looked down at his chest, the blood pooling in his fresh scratches sobered me up.

"What's wrong with you?" he asked.

I hastily pulled my wrists away from him and got off the bed. I hadn't noticed that I'd hurt him, and I was embarrassed.

"Just leave, Julian."

"Not until you tell me what's happening to you. I get that you're angry, but you're aggressive. And this—" He gestured at my hair, finally acknowledging the elephant in the room. "You chopped your hair off?"

I reached down in my backpack for my clothes, and without a thought, removed my towel and dropped it on the floor at my feet.

"This is who I am now. I'm a survivor, and anything that makes life a little easier is what I'm going to do. There's no point in having long hair anymore. It just gets in the way."

Julian stared at me, mouth open and eyes wide. I could tell he was forcing his stare to remain on my face, until he finally looked away. "Can you please put some clothes on?"

The truth was that I didn't care if he saw me naked or not. I just didn't care anymore. But I started putting my clothes on, anyway. "What? Are you shy? We could have had sex, but you stopped it."

"I stopped it because you were physically hurting me, Serena. You aren't all there. Your mind was somewhere else, and I don't want to make love to you like that."

I sat next to him on the bed and pulled my boots on.

"I don't want to make love, either. There's no place for love now," I lied. There was a place for Julian's love, but I couldn't tell him that. There was no way I could. We were friends. We would always be just friends.

I stood up and secured my machete holster to my thigh before placing my hand on the door handle. "You coming?"

He didn't move. "Are you really leaving?"

"You knew it was going to happen. You're safe with these people now. I can't force you to do anything, especially when it comes to Harley. I have a mission and I'm going to follow through with it."

"You're never going to find him."

"I have to try."

He stood up and stepped toward me, forcing my back to the door. His motions were fast and full of angst, but he gently placed a hand on the door behind me, ensuring that I couldn't move.

"You love me," he stated. "You know you do."

Part of me didn't want to look up at him. But if I was going to train my mind to be stronger, I had to learn how to have willpower.

"I don't love anything anymore."

He took a deep breath and kissed me on my forehead.

"Well, I love you. I've always loved you, Serena. I need you to know that."

I quickly turned my head away from him and opened the door.

I love you.

I didn't say anything and walked out of the room.

I've always loved you, Jules.

THE CONTROL

Grace

THE SUN WAS SETTING, the sky turning shades of orange and pink and purple. I looked down at myself as my body jolted from the shocks of the military truck. I was covered in blood. It wasn't my own. It wasn't from a victim who'd succumbed to my hunger. It was the blood of the people. The people whose lives were no longer going to be what they once knew. Some of the blood was transferred from them to me while Kate and I had the unfortunate task of forcing them into the back of the truck. That blood was either theirs or the blood of something they had just eaten. But some of it came from fallen TZs, the ones we had to decapitate because they were too aggressive to handle or too close to attacking one of us.

It physically pained me every time we had to dismember one of them. My stomach churned and my chest ached to watch an innocent person—someone who never asked for this—become deader than they already were. I couldn't help but imagine my own head rolling off my body and onto the ground. I couldn't help but feel sadness for their lives ending indefinitely and never having the opportunity to become part of the new Zombrid race.

I thought long and hard all day about my responsibilities now. I vowed that I would stand behind

Kate and her plan to save the country. I promised myself that I would do whatever it took to protect my own and to teach them what it meant to be a Zombrid. The truth was that I still didn't know what it meant, but I was willing to find out. I was ready to learn and teach my fellow Zombrids.

I glanced at Kate, who was as equally covered in red.

"Today was tough, huh?" she asked. I nodded. "Well, you and I won't be on these missions every day. This task will be rotated between everyone at the facility. I just really needed you to see what it was like so you could finally understand."

I was confused. "You brought me along to teach me a lesson?"

"I know you don't like who you are. But it *is* who you are. Embracing it is the only thing left for you to do. I needed you to see that it could be worse for you. I wanted you to understand that even though Dr. Walker's plans for Serum Z were only for his benefit, there is still some good that could come out of it. You're not alone anymore. And you won't be for a long time."

She was right. I feared immortality because I didn't want to eventually end up alone. But now I had Zombrids on the island, two waiting back at The Florida Recovery Center, and about twenty future fellow Zombrids in the back of this truck. Loneliness wasn't an option anymore. Soon, there will be hundreds and thousands of people I'll be able to connect and share my life with.

"I just don't want to kill anyone anymore," I admitted.

"You can control yourself, Grace. You have that power to do it now."

I hoped that she was right.

"What about you?" I asked Kate, suddenly realizing something. "Are you a Zombrid?"

I honestly didn't know if she was or not. I would have imagined Kate telling us, but she seemed to be discreet with her personal life. I couldn't even remember ever seeing her eat.

"Am I a Zombrid?" She smiled wide and giggled. "What do you think?"

Before I could answer, the sound of a ping bounced off the side of the truck.

"What was that?"

There was another ping, then a barrage of pings quickly followed.

"We're being attacked!" Jackson yelled.

"What do we do?" Kate asked.

"Drive past!" the driver shouted.

The force of the truck accelerating pushed me back into my seat. Sparks ricocheted off the metal of the truck from the bullets, starting at the front and moving along the side and toward the back. I flinched and ducked when bullets began hitting the windows.

"It's bulletproof!" Kate informed me.

We peeked out of every window, trying to find the source of the gunfire. My eyes searched every building around us. There were businesses, a school, a post office, and shops, and zombies weaving in and out of every corner, but there were no living humans with weapons.

And as quickly as it began, it suddenly stopped.

"What the hell was that?" I asked the general audience inside the cab.

"Survivors. Enemies. Assholes. Who knows?" Jackson responded, placing a cigarette between his lips and lighting the end.

"Why would they shoot at us?" That was a stupid question. I knew why they would shoot at us. We were in a well-secured military truck. The walls were impenetrable. They probably wanted this monster truck for themselves. And any supplies they thought we might have.

Ha! I could just imagine their surprise if they happened to steal it from us and open the back hatch, only to find a bunch of TZs ready to chew their faces off.

We finally reached the gate of the facility and an involuntary sigh of relief escaped me. I was glad to be back...and ready to eat. Kate made sure to bring food during our time out, but it was only snack-sized and my stomach was now growling at me to feed it something much more hearty. No pun intended.

"I'm going to get something to eat," I announced to Kate as I stepped down from the truck.

"Okay. Jackson, get the truck to the back of the building. We need to get these patients prepped for the cure."

I walked straight into the front of the building and toward the room where Sonny, Ian, and I had our first meal, hoping there would be food ready for me in there. The two of them were in the lounge when I walked past.

"Jesus, love! Are you okay?" Ian asked, clearly concerned that the blood smeared all over me was mine.

Sonny turned to look at me. "Grace! OMG! What happened?"

My belly was now aching, and I could feel hunger spasms shooting across. Things began to spin and the ground before me was now warping.

"Grace?" I heard Ian's voice again, but I continued to focus on my walking. "She needs food. Now!"

I finally reached my destination. When I walked inside, the potent smell of fresh human flesh engulfed my personal space. Serena and Julian were sitting at the table.

I inhaled deeply and immediately wished I hadn't done that. I was trying to control my urge, but it only made it stronger.

Serena stood up almost instantly, pulling her machete off her thigh and positioning herself in a sort of fighting stance. Her wild eyes narrowed in on me, but I could feel the storm of hunger and losing control in my core and it was rising up through me. It passed up through my throat, forcing my lips to recede back as I suddenly felt the urge to threaten her with my teeth. I unconsciously released a loud hiss.

"What the hell?"

"Serena, don't do anything," Julian insisted, standing up from the table.

"What the hell is wrong with her?"

"I think she's a Zombrid."

"She *is* a Zombrid!" Sonny shouted. "Chill out! She just needs to eat!"

"Then get her some damn food before I slice her freaking head off!" Serena warned her.

I watched as she spoke, examining the skin around her mouth stretch with movement. We were feet away from each other, but the delicious scent of her blood pumping underneath that skin drove me mad. My mouth filled with saliva as I imagined tasting her. I wanted to sample her raw meat. I needed to feel the spongy tissue of her body in my mouth. I had to consume every inch of her.

I stepped forward and so did she. I hadn't realized it, but my hands were at my side, fingers curled tightly and ready to claw my fingernails into her insides.

"I swear I'm going to kill her!"

"Ian! Hurry up!" Sonny yelped out into the hall.

Julian stepped next to Serena and placed a hand on her. Good. I could take them both if I needed to, because he smelled really good, too.

"She won't do anything. She's just hungry. If she was going to, she would have attacked us already," he said softly to her. His words struck me, and suddenly Kate's words echoed in my mind...*You can control yourself, Grace.*

It was true. The old Grace would have already attacked. My expressions as far as the snarling and ferocious demeanor were uncontrollable, but somehow, I was managing to keep my actions contained. I was changing. I was able to think about what I was doing before the shadows of what I really was took over. I was reasoning with myself, listening intently to my inner thoughts—the good ones that survived and remained pure from the horrible things I had seen and done. Practicing Ian's instructions, I stood still and focused. My mouth, my stomach, every molecule in my body was compelled to ravage their bodies. But I was fighting it. I was a different person now. I still had to restrain it, but I was able to keep my hunger at bay. I didn't have to pretend to be okay with who I was anymore, and I kept myself balanced and in place, mentally repeating to myself to hold on, the food will be here soon.

And right as I began to make up a *Grace, stay where you are and don't move* chant inside my head, the sweet aroma of even fresher, raw meat finally reached my nostrils.

Sonny could smell it, too. "It's coming, Grace. Let's sit down."

Even though I knew now that I wasn't going to attack anyone, Sonny still had to shove me toward the chair. I might have been able to control my mind, but I definitely needed to work on my actions. She pushed me down and I gripped onto the edge of the table. My eyes stayed on

Serena, watching the veins in her neck pulsate with every beat of her heart.

"I'm here," Ian announced. He placed a tray of food in front of me and everything else slowly faded away.

THE SURRENDER

Serena

I RUSHED OUT OF the room and into the hall. Julian had filled me in on what a Zombrid was a couple of hours before, and I had responded with *how the hell could we live in a world with Zombie halflings*?

"Hey," Julian whispered, stepping out into the hallway.

"What?"

"You can't do that. You can't threaten them. They're helping us."

"No, they're helping you and Harley. I told you I don't trust these people. That girl was going to attack me," I whisper harshly. "And I would have killed her."

"Yes, they're helping Harley. But they're trying to help other people, too. Don't you want to be a part of that?"

I laughed sarcastically. "A part of turning people into Zombrids? Hell no!"

"Julian, Serena. Can I have a word with you?"

I turned around. Kate was standing at the end of the hall. Great. Was I in trouble because I was about to kill some half-brained teenage zombie?

Julian placed a hand on the small of my back, urging me to walk with him. We followed Kate into the lounge area where we all sat down on the couches. Kate was covered in blood and dirt and she wiped her face with a towel before speaking.

"Forgive me. Today was our first mission out in the city. I knew it would be tough, but I guess I didn't mentally prepare myself."

"It's pretty bad out there," Julian said.

"It is. But we managed to capture quite a few to begin the curing process. Did Dr. Sharma and Dr. Kamini fill you in on how it all works?"

"They did. They said Harley's blood will be replaced with new blood. Zombrid blood. But she still won't be the same."

"No, she won't. Not at first, anyway. She'll have to get used to her new appetite, heightened senses, strength, and increased intelligence. But with the education and training we will provide for her, she'll eventually learn to control herself and who she has become. Soon, she'll be the same little girl you once knew. Being a Zombrid does not change their personality—their likes and dislikes and things like that."

"What does this education and training entail? How not to kill, right?" Julian asked, leaning forward in his seat. I could tell he was nervous and worried about having to raise a Zombrid.

"The education is to teach them about what kinds of food they need to eat to keep their hunger controlled. She will be taught when to eat and how much to eat," Kate explained. "She will learn, of course, that eating living humans is not acceptable. But we have found that if the patient had a sense of morality before he or she became a human, this notion is able to be retained in their minds. They don't forget that."

"So, none of your Zombrids have killed people before?" I asked.

She paused for a moment, then replied. "Sure, they have. There may be mistakes in the beginning. A kind of falling off the wagon, if you will. But we are confident that this won't happen as often as you think, not with the food we're providing them and the training. And then, eventually, when she gets older, she'll need to consume more and often in order to stay...normal. However, we suspect that she will reach a point of total satisfaction, where her cravings will be leveled out and not continue to increase. It's something that we're exploring as the Zombrids age. This program is newly developed, but we have the best staff of teachers, as well as the Zombrids that already exist to help guide her."

"You obviously didn't teach *that* girl anything," I mumbled sarcastically, nodding toward the hallway.

She gave me a crooked glare. "Did something happen?"

"Yeah, that Grace girl almost attacked me."

Kate smiled. "I can assure you Grace wouldn't harm you. Her situation is a little different. It's because of her this cure even exists and, unfortunately, she had to endure losing large quantities of blood recently. This is probably why she showed aggression toward you. But she is recovering."

"How long is the recovery time for Harley? I mean, she has killed someone. Will she remember it? And her sores and wounds, will they be fixed?"

"Julian, your daughter is going to recover quicker than you think. She will most certainly look the same as she did before once we have given her the proper treatment. As for the memory of what she has done, the patients who have had the cure have shown limited signs of recalling their life as a TZ. If they do remember some of the unfortunate things they've done, we have therapists on call to help them."

"What about the rest of the country or other countries? Is this thing just happening here?" I needed to prepare myself for leaving the state.

"I forget that you two have been here this whole time and have not had access to the outside world. So far, the outbreak is only in the United States. Europe has not had any reports of infection. Some places in our country are worse than others. But Tampa is Ground Zero."

I had a lot more questions—like, where were they getting food for the Zombrids and how the hell did this all start and how could a bite turn you? But we were interrupted by the obnoxious Australian guy.

"Hello, mates," he greeted, jumping over the back of the couch and plopping himself right next to me. His immature behavior made my cushion bounce underneath my butt, and I gave him an irritated glower.

Kate cleared her throat and pulled her hair back behind her ear. She looked embarrassed. "Um, Ian? I'm having a meeting."

"Yeah, okay. Dr. Kamini wanted me to come get you. She said she needs some assistance with the newcomers."

She forced a smile. "Thank you. Well, it seems I must go. Please help yourselves to anything here. And please consider giving us a hand if you would like to be a part of our team. We would really appreciate it. Julian, we'll update you on your daughter's progress soon."

Julian nodded. Kate stood up and walked away, leaving us with the idiot foreign boy. Grace and the preppy blonde walked over seconds later and sat across from us.

"So, why did you do it?" Ian asked me.

I turned to him. "Do what?"

"Cut all your hair off?"

"Yeah, I was going to ask you that," Sonny chimed in. "It's all...choppy and uneven. No offense, but you look like Shaggy from *Scooby Doo* now. Do you need therapy or something? Because we've got people for that."

"Nah, love. I think it looks hot! She's a badass, I can tell."

"Well I don't care how badass you are," Sonny said, using finger quotes for the word *badass*. "But a girl is supposed to have long, luscious hair. Like mine." She flipped her locks behind her shoulder in a narcissistic manner. "I mean, even Grace has gorgeous hair, I'll admit. Unless... Wait. Are you sick? OMG! Do you have cancer? Is your hair, like, falling out?"

And these people were supposed to be smart? I turned my attention to Grace and our eyes met. She seemed shy and awkward as her hands fidgeted on her lap. Surprisingly, she opened her mouth to speak.

"Um," she said softly. "I'm sorry I was...rude to you."

"Rude? You were about to eat me," I corrected her.

"Serena," Julian hissed near my ear. I rolled my eyes.

"Well, I'm sorry I threatened to eat you. I was just really hungry, and I can promise you that I would never actually eat you."

I stood up, feeling tired of listening to these people. "Yeah, well next time you try, I won't hesitate to cut your damn head clean off your body," I warned her. I stepped around Julian's legs and walked back to my room.

I was in the middle of packing my bag when the door opened. I didn't turn around, but I knew who it was.

"What do you want, Julian?"

"Don't go," he said behind me.

I paused for a moment, taking in a deep breath of agitation. I knew this was coming.

"Please stay. I know that you want to go, but I want to help these people. I want to be a part of what they're doing. And you're tough, Serena. You know how to live in this world—we need someone like you."

I turned to face him.

"*I* need you," he confessed.

"They don't need me. There are enough guards out there to keep this place safe. And as for you, you're getting back the one thing you truly want, and that's Harley."

"But the other thing I truly want is leaving. Just stay for a few more days. Give it a chance. Please."

I grabbed my backpack and slung it over my shoulder. "Move, Julian. I have to go."

He stood up tall and backed into the door.

"You're going to block me? Seriously?"

His lips curled up into a playful grin. "You might be able to kick my ass, but I'll try to hold you back as long as I can."

I looked away from him, worried that his flirtatious teasing would make me stay or even worse, make me smile.

He gripped my hand in his. "Serena, we have been together for so long. When I saw you in that bus station for the first time, I knew I wanted to get to know you. And when I did, when I got to know the complicated, amazing person that you are, I knew I was lucky to have you in my life. Life hasn't been kind to you. I know how much you miss Charlie, how much you hate your past, how much you loved Dan. I was never able to help you before, when you lived alone on the streets. When I found out about that, I was so angry that you didn't tell me because you know I would have dropped everything to come save you. Then when you told me that man...did what he did to you... Again, I wasn't there to help you. You always confide in me, but you do it when it's too late. Let me be there for you now. Let me save you, Serena. Just give me a chance. Give *us* a chance. If you end up not really wanting to be here, I'll let you leave."

I raised an eyebrow at him. "*Let* me leave?"

"I mean, I won't give you trouble. You could just go."

A vision of myself pushing Julian out of the way, opening the door, and leaving without turning back flashed in my mind. I wanted so badly to get on that road, to kill as many Creeps as I possibly could and anyone else who got in my way. I wanted to breathe the stale, disgusting stench of the dead into my lungs, a constant reminder of who I was now and what I needed to do. Because I was always alone. My whole life, I'd always been alone.

But gazing into his eyes seemed to have an effect on my shattered soul. Somewhere lost in the mix of my crazy emotions, he was in there. Could we live happily ever after one day? Maybe. Could Julian and I actually be together? Maybe. Could I ever love myself? I don't think I ever did. There were always just pieces of myself, shards of the person I wanted to be. I tried so many times to be that person, too. But there was always something to bring me back to the damaged goods that would forever be my true identity.

Julian waited for me to say something, to finally surrender. I wanted so badly to leave...

"I'll stay for a few days."

His lips turned up into a grin. His eyes glossed over, and without a word, he wrapped his arms around my neck and pulled me into him.

I wanted so badly to run away. But I loved him. I truly loved him.

ONE WEEK LATER...

THE RAGE

Grace

I TOSSED AND TURNED in bed. I just couldn't fall asleep. A week had passed, and the events continued to replay in my mind. I didn't know why I agreed to go on two more runs to pick up TZs. Maybe it was because I felt I needed to help them. Maybe it was because I wanted to make sure they were handled with care. But we still had to kill a few of them, and I still couldn't get used to watching them take their final, absolute breath.

I needed something to drink.

I walked through the main area of the building. The scientists were still working in the lab portion of the place, despite the late hour, but the lounge area was clear. Sonny and Ian were probably sleeping, and I knew Kate was still awake and working with Dr. Kamini and Dr. Sharma on the patients in the tents.

We managed to replace the blood of almost a hundred TZs this week. That didn't sound like much, but it took a lot of work. And, unfortunately, they were the only TZs worth saving. Many others were too far gone.

Kate had asked me if I wanted to participate tonight, but I seriously just needed a break from all the blood and gore—as unbelievable as that sounded for a horror movie fanatic.

I opened a bottle of Z Juice from the fridge near the pool table and sunk my body into the leather couch.

"Mind if I join you?"

Julian's deep voice was familiar to me by now. Without turning around, I answered, "Sure."

He came and sat down on the other end of the couch. "Can't sleep?"

"Not really. You?"

He ran his hand through his long, wavy hair. "Not really."

There was silence.

"It's been raining pretty hard for the past couple of days."

I took a swig and allowed the refreshing crimson liquid to coat my throat. "I know. Sonny and Ian were freaking out because their phones haven't worked for two days."

He chuckled. "It's kind of nice to hear about people having ordinary problems for a change. You know, stuff other than trying to survive and killing zombies."

I didn't smile.

Julian noticed my recoil at his words. "I'm sorry. I didn't mean to... I'm just worried."

"Worried about what? You're safe here."

"My daughter, Harley... What's she going to be like once she fully recovers? What's she going to remember? How's she going to feel?"

"She won't remember much. I mean, she might know that she killed someone, but she won't remember everything. Our minds kind of go blank when we're eating," I explained to him.

"Have you ever killed anyone?"

His question stung me. Then suddenly, Phoebe, the doctor in the conference room, and the nurse crossed my mind. And even though I didn't kill Tristen, finding his dead body hanging in the freezer still haunted me. I'd tried everything in me to forget that Dr. Walker had secretly fed him to me...and that I had enjoyed it.

"I have," I revealed.

He turned away.

"Eating someone is bad but being a Zombrid isn't all that bad. She'll get used to it. I once knew a little girl who was a Zombrid, too, and it was like she was just a normal little girl." My heart hurt for Maddi.

"Serena and I have been wanting to ask questions, but everyone's been too busy."

Serena hadn't spoken to me all week long and it was evident that she'd gone to great lengths to avoid me. Suddenly, I felt the need to explain myself for the Serena incident, even though I was sure he already knew. "You know I didn't mean to do that to Serena. I wouldn't have hurt her."

"I know. And she knows that, too. She's just had a hard time since all of this started. She lost someone she loved, and she just can't let it go."

Love and loss seemed to be the theme of life these days.

"Do you care about her?" The sappy part of me was hoping for a love story, which was better than listening to yet another tale of loss. But he simply nodded. I had a feeling it was very complicated.

He let out a low chuckle as if to be hiding it. "She seems to think she can find the guy who started all this."

"Dr. Walker?"

His eyes widened. "Yeah."

"Well...I mean, he is the reason why all of this started. He's the reason why we're Zombrids. But he's dead now."

He scooted closer to the edge of the couch. "Wait, what? Dr. Mark Walker is dead? How do you know?"

"Because we killed him. I mean, no one knows *we* killed him. But Kate is his daughter. This is Dr. Walker's clinic."

The bewilderment in his expression made me realize he needed more info. So for the next twenty minutes, I filled him in on my personal journey and everything I knew about Dr. Walker. Normally, I wouldn't be so open to someone I barely knew, but I felt it was my duty to inform him of the origin of Zombridism, considering his daughter was transforming into one. And Julian was just so sweet. I thought maybe it could ease some of his worry.

"I knew I remembered her from somewhere," he mumbled.

"Who? Kate?"

Julian then explained his very short stint of employment with Dr. Walker and how he remembered seeing Kate once. I kept thinking about how small the world was because somehow, he found his way to us, but saying that just didn't seem appropriate anymore. The world was growing smaller by the minute.

"Are you going to tell Serena?" He had to stop her witch hunt.

"Of course. Maybe then she'll realize this is a safe place."

"SHIT!"

Julian and I both stood up, startled.

"Shit! Shit! Shit!" Kate paced the area in an apron full of blood. She was staring down at her tablet, continuously cursing at the top of her lungs.

"What's wrong?" I yelled back.

She was frantic, throwing her free hand into the air and even pulling at her hair. Julian walked over to her and put his hands on her shoulders, stopping her in her tracks.

"What is it?" he asked her in a comforting tone. But she didn't return it.

"The stupid satellite has been out for two days! The CDC and the President's people have been trying to reach us. They're pulling the plug on everything!"

A few scientists from the lab poked their heads out from their area but didn't dare come closer. Serena emerged from the hallway completely dressed, with her machete in hand. Did this woman ever just take a load off?

Sonny and Ian appeared from behind her.

"What's going on?" Ian asked.

Kate pulled herself away from Julian's grip and marched toward him. "They're ending it! They're cutting us off!"

"Well, what does that mean? We can't stay here and help them anymore?" Sonny asked.

"It means that they chose Plan B. Apparently, we weren't meeting quota," she spit out. "It means they would rather eradicate than help people!"

"What are they going to do?" I didn't want to know the answer to this. Deep down, I was hoping Kate would say that the President decided to just leave the TZs alone. Let them live happily ever after, and the rest of the humans would start a new life somewhere else. But I knew that wasn't why she was so pissed.

She snapped her head at me. "It means they're going to burn them all."

Sonny shrieked and Ian cursed. My heart fell into my stomach. Burn them all?

"They want to bomb them? Isn't the cure working, though?" Julian asked.

"Napalm, to be exact. And it is. It's working. But not quick enough, and the President feels the outbreak has reached the point of no return. We couldn't cure them as quickly as they are turning."

I didn't understand. "But we've saved so many already. They aren't even giving us a chance."

Kate shrugged her shoulders. "Yeah, well...I don't know what to tell you, Grace. We failed! And now we need to get our asses out of here!"

"When is it going to happen?" Julian asked.

"According to this," she held up her tablet, "a day ago."

"What?" Serena finally spoke up. "How is that possible? Don't they know we're here?"

"Yes, they know! Of course they know. But if you haven't noticed, there has been a severe storm going on outside and none of our satellite equipment has been working. They sent me this two days ago! It looks like maybe they were giving us a chance to respond. But since we haven't, they probably think the TZs took over our facility. They can bomb us at any minute."

The sound of metal and other things hitting the floor from the science lab rang out into the rest of the building as the scientists scrambled to pack up.

"What are we going to do?" Sonny's frightened, high-pitched voice matched the terrified look on her face.

"We're going to get the hell out of here," Serena declared.

"We better go now." Jackson came in through a pair of double doors. "The city is flooded and there's debris everywhere. We're going to need any extra time we can get to drive out of the radius of the napalm."

"What about the helicopters, mate?"

"Can't fly them in this weather. Land is the only way out, but the storm has attracted more of those things into the area. They're multiplying, and if we don't get out now, they're going to overrun us."

Kate suddenly switched into mission mode. "Okay. We need to get the ones that have had the cure out of here. Unfortunately, we can't take the patients we haven't started on. Jackson, start filling those trucks. Get the rest of the team back there to pack up as much equipment as possible. The patients come first. If it doesn't fit, leave it."

Jackson did as he was told.

"Where's my daughter?" Julian asked, almost with a growl.

Kate held her walkie up to her mouth. "Dr. Kamini, bring Harley into the lounge. Now!"

I looked at Kate. "What can we do?"

"You, Ian, and Sonny, gather your things for now. I just need you three on that truck when we're ready to leave."

We all went our separate ways. I ran down the hall and into my room, cramming every item I owned into my suitcase. I kept looking down at the clock on my phone, watching the minutes count down and I didn't know why. We didn't know when it would happen. This place could go up in flames at any moment. I really had no idea what napalm was other than what I'd seen on *The History Channel*, but I knew that it basically torched everything in its path for miles.

I fought the tears that wanted to surge out of me as I gathered my belongings. We could have changed the world. We could have saved so many. But they barely gave us a chance. And now all of those innocent zombies—the ones that could have been a part of our new race—were going to burn as if they meant nothing at all. They were complete strangers, but I could feel the heavy loss bearing down on me.

My mother popped into my head, and I suddenly wished that I could hug her. My heart hurt for the way I had been treating her, and I realized right then that I wanted her back in my life.

As I searched through my phone contacts for *Mom*, I remembered that I changed her name months ago. The anger over her lies had been so strong that calling her Mom just pissed me off. So, I had decided she wasn't worthy of it and changed it to the name that *I* had known my whole life.

Grace Shelley: *I'm sorry for everything, Mom. I want us to be okay. I love who I am, and I love you.*

The weather had been bad for days, and I was almost certain our phones were still out of service. Sending that message, though I wasn't sure she'd receive it, made me feel closer to her. But barely a minute later, my phone dinged.

Veronica Shelley: *I love you too, Gracie. We are going to be okay. I can't wait to see you.*

I smiled and held my phone to my chest. I knew we had a lot to work out, but we had to start somewhere. I quickly tapped the edit symbol and changed her first name to Eve. Then, I backspaced her whole name and changed it to Mom. Right after that, I edited my own name, changing my last name to Romero. When I got back, I planned to urge my mom to change our last names back to Romero, in honor of my father, Jack Romero. I was immortal, and I wanted my father's name to live on.

Ian and Sonny walked out of their rooms at the same time I stepped out of mine, and we headed back to the lounge with our bags in tow. Sonny grabbed my hand and squeezed.

"I'm scared, Grace," she whispered close to my ear.

"It's going to be okay," I whispered back and squeezed her hand tightly in return. I spotted Serena and Julian standing on either side of the room. They hadn't really spoken to each other all week, either. He loved her, and she loved him. You could tell. But they were having some kind of disagreement in their relationship, and I didn't know why. Something told me it was her fault. She was so closed off. So distant from everything. A twinge of pity for him flowed through me. It must have been so hard to feel connected to someone so broken.

Everyone worked as fast as they could to get the trucks loaded and equipment packed. But the minutes were flying by, and we could all feel the end dangerously closing in on us.

Kate came in. "Okay guys, I just feel like I need to say something before we go."

"Kate, this isn't the time for a toast," Ian chortled, but I knew he was serious.

She ignored him. "I just want to say that we tried to fix this. We tried to cure those in need. We weren't able to help nearly as many as we'd hoped, but...we tried." This was a woman who never showed an ounce of emotion— even as she watched her own father die in front of her. But Kate was choking up as she spoke. She truly believed in this cause, in the creation of a Zombrid race, and she worked her ass off to get here.

"We're going to take these patients to the island with us, to the Safe Zone, to teach them what it means to be a

Zombrid, and we won't give up trying to cure anyone we can. We are good people, and I will never let my father's name cast a shadow over what we are."

My jaw dropped. What *we* are? Her eyes found mine and the corner of her mouth turned up.

"I'm sorry, who is your dad?" Serena interrupted.

"Serena." Julian tried to take her attention away from Kate's answer, but it was too late. I realized right then that he hadn't had the time to tell her.

"My dad is Dr. Walker."

Instantaneously, Serena pulled a gun out from behind her with one hand. She pointed it straight at Kate and raised her machete up high in the other hand. "Your dad is Mark Walker?"

"Serena!" Julian shouted.

"What are you doing?" Kate asked as she took a step back in surprise. She clearly had no idea why Serena was pointing a gun and a knife at her.

"Where is he?"

"Serena, please!"

"Shut up, Julian! Where is he?" she repeated.

"I-I...he's dead!"

"You're lying!"

"He is, Serena. He died," Julian confirmed. "Now put your weapons down."

Ian stepped up near her. "You do realize there are four Zombrids surrounding you, right? We can take you down, love."

Serena kept her gun pointed at Kate, but her machete moved to Ian. "You step any closer to me, and I will chop your damn head off," she hissed through clenched teeth.

I would never hurt her because I knew how much she meant to Julian, but I took a step forward with Sonny to show that I stood behind my fellow Zombrids.

Kate held her hands out in surrender. "My dad was a terrible man. He harvested humans. He killed people. He was planning to try to make millions off of Serum Z. He didn't care about anything but himself, but I'm not like him. I simply want to help people. Please."

"You think that we can live together in a world with zombies?"

"Not zombies. *Zombrids*. And yes, I do believe Zombrids could co-exist with humans. We can make it work. I can show you."

"I don't want to see anything! It's because of your dad that everything is going to shit. You have no idea what we have had to do to survive. You have no idea what it's like to watch someone you love turn into a monster."

"Serena, we're all going through this...together. You aren't alone."

"Bullshit! Every last one of you is a sympathizer." She pointed her gun at Julian. "Including you!"

Dr. Kamini walked into the lounge, holding Harley's hand. Serena quickly pointed her gun at the doctor.

"Dr. Kamini, stay where you are," Kate demanded.

"Daddy?" Harley called out. She was not completely well, but she was on her way there. Julian stood on the other side of the room, several feet away from her.

"Baby! Stay there!"

Serena's attention was focused on Harley. I suspected that she was surprised to see Harley's appearance now after what she'd been used to. Harley still had a long road of recovery ahead of her, but she was completely different compared to the hungry, growling, decomposing little girl from just a few days ago.

Ian took this opportunity to intervene. He swiftly reached over and pulled Serena's arm, twisting it behind her back. She cried out in pain as he forced her to release the gun. It fell to the ground and Ian kicked it over to Julian. But her other arm was free, and in one rapid motion, she swung her blade across Ian's face and lifted her foot, smashing it into his stomach. He stumbled backwards, blood pouring out of his cheek from the enormous gash that now took up most of his head. Sonny immediately ran to his aid, but Serena stabled her stance and reared up to charge back at Ian. I ran toward her, fearful that she would kill both Ian and Sonny.

In my mind, somehow, I pictured exactly what was about to happen. And I couldn't understand why she was about to do it. Why was she about to kill two people who were only trying to help her? Sonny and Ian had done nothing! They were innocent. None of this was their fault, and I wasn't about to let her end their lives.

I knew that technically none of this was my doing. I didn't kill Dr. Walker's son. I didn't come up with the idea for Serum Z. I didn't inject people around the world. But the truth was, I was the beginning of it all. I was Patient Zero and the reason why we were all here. It had to start somewhere, and it started with me. It was my responsibility now to make sure people didn't try to harm us. I had to protect my kind.

I reached Sonny and Ian before Serena could.

"Serena, please! Don't do this!" I begged. I was buying myself time. I knew I could take her down. I was stronger than her, but I was planning my attack in my head.

"Get out of my way! They need to die! You all need to die!"

Sonny was huddled over Ian. The sound of Harley's sobs echoed in the room. I held out my arms in front of her, praying that she wouldn't take another step closer.

"This is no one's fault but Dr. Walker, and he's dead. We're all just normal people. We are all in this together."

Serena snorted. "We are not the same. You're all a bunch of monsters! Now, get the hell out of my way!"

She lifted her machete high up into the air. I dug my heels into the floor and just as I decided to lunge myself at her, a gunshot rang through my ears.

THE
BOMB

Serena

THE BURNING STARTED AT my shoulder, but quickly radiated down to my hand and up to my neck. It knocked the wind out of my lungs, but it didn't stop me. It didn't stop the strength and the force of my momentum from swinging my machete at her.

I was so angry. The adrenaline coursed through my veins like a freight train without brakes. Grace's body, ironically, gracefully tumbled onto the floor. My attention went straight to my arm. The bullet didn't exit. I could feel it lodged inside of me, and it hurt like hell. But I didn't care. I had to finish her off. I had to severe her head from her body.

I stood over Grace's body and raised my injured arm up above me. But before my blade could collide with her neck again, my body was catapulted into the air. Again, the air was forced out of my lungs as my body slammed against the ground. Julian lay on top of me, his hand pinning my weapon down.

"We have to go now!" I could hear Jackson's voice from a distance.

I looked up at Julian and watched the storm passing through his eyes. "What are you doing, Serena?"

"We have to kill them! You should have killed Harley a long time ago," I managed to say under the weight of his body.

"Everyone, let's get out of here. We don't know how much more time we have!" Kate called out. "Sonny, grab Ian. Jackson, let's get Grace!"

Julian continued to stare at me.

"Get off me," I seethed. I thrust my hips up in an attempt to bounce him off. But he didn't budge. "Get off me, Julian!"

He didn't say anything. I could hear their voices gathering together as they were getting ready to exit the building.

"Julian! What are you doing?"

Finally, he turned me onto my stomach, grabbed both my wrists, and pressed them together against my back. "Jackson! Bring over a zip tie!"

"Are you kidding me?" I mumbled into the floor. I tried to wiggle my way out from under him, but his weight wouldn't allow it.

"I can't let you hurt anyone else!" he yelled. He was pissed.

I could feel the blood rushing out of my shoulder and hoped that it would drain me. I hoped that I would bleed out right where I was, and that I'd fall into a deep, dark sleep. No more pain, no more loss, no more surviving in a universe that clearly didn't want me in it. And hadn't for a long time. I kept fighting for so many years. I'd fought my way through every obstacle God had thrown at me. But maybe I wasn't supposed to fight anymore. Maybe this was my final battle.

The ground shook. My face and body were still planted firmly on the floor. I squinted and wondered if my mind was playing tricks on me. But the ground beneath me shook again, followed by a low, continuous tremble.

"What is that?" Kate asked.

The pressure from Julian's weight lifted, and I was hoisted up on my feet. The ground started to shake violently, and everyone stumbled.

"It's the bomb!"

Julian pushed me up against the wall, then ran toward his daughter. Cracks ran up the concrete walls and pieces of the ceiling started to rain down all around us. The lights flickered and the fixtures detached, dropping and shattering glass on the floor. I watched Julian grab his daughter and throw her over his shoulder. Jackson had Grace's head and Kate had her feet. They were shuffling her body toward the door. Ian had an arm dangling over each of Sonny and Dr. Kamini's shoulders.

I glanced up. Larger chunks of building material were coming down now. Julian ran back toward me, and I prayed that he wouldn't get hit. Our eyes met when he reached me. The storm in his eyes was gone. The softness was back. The sweet, kind heart that beat in his chest reflected through his glare straight at me. His benevolent soul spoke to my inner core, and in that moment, I knew for certain that I loved him more than I ever believed I did. And I needed him to know. I needed him to know before we died.

"I love you!" I called out to him.

Everything shook but somehow, someway, he held out a steady hand and cradled my cheek. There was no place for us to go. This bomb was going to kill us, and I just wanted to be in Julian's arms.

With my hands still tied behind my back and Harley still slung over his shoulder, he leaned down and kissed me. I closed my eyes and kissed him back as the world crumbled all around us.

THE SURVIVORS

Grace

I COULDN'T BREATHE. THERE was a weight on my chest, on my ribs, that was constricting the oxygen to flow freely in and out of my body. My eyes fluttered open, but I immediately shut them when I felt what seemed like sand scratching my corneas. There was a burning smell in the air, and I could hear crackling and flames around me. My arms didn't seem to be held down by anything, so I rubbed my eyes and opened them. The sky was above me. A gloomy and cloudy, smoke-filled sky.

I ran a hand down my torso, only to feel a hard metal object on top of me. Glancing down at my body, I realized it was the casing of a fluorescent light fixture. On top of that was a large scrap of what used to be the ceiling. The light fixture must have stopped it from crushing my body.

Suddenly, claustrophobia set in and I needed to get up. I needed air.

I thrust my hips in an attempt to move the debris off me, but it didn't help. I tried again and again, maneuvering my body in different ways. After trying for what felt like forever, I was somehow able to gain leverage by lifting the edges of the light fixture upward. This was enough to slightly slide the piece of concrete off the metal, which allowed me to wiggle my way out from under it.

When I was finally free, every part of my body began to throb. I rolled onto my side in agony, feeling every inch of skin, every bone ache. My arms and hands were bloody, and I could feel the pieces of glass moving around underneath my skin from the lights that fell on top of me. But it was nothing compared to the immense pain coming from my neck. I hadn't felt it until I started moving, and it made me wish I were dead.

I peered down at myself. The entire left side of my body was covered in a mixture of blood, white dust, and black ash. I brought my hand up to my neck. It didn't feel like it was gushing anymore, but there was certainly an enormous gash. Flashes of Serena's machete popped into my mind. She could have decapitated me. She could have killed me for good, but my head was still attached to my body. I didn't die. I won't die. I was a Zombrid, and I'd get better.

I tore a portion of my shirt off and wrapped it around my neck wound. Then I climbed out of the pile of rubble that had buried me and took it all in. The building was completely gone. There were no walls, no ceiling, no roof. Dark smoke flowed all around me, causing a haziness in the air. It was hard, but I was still able to see through it. The inside was now the outside. The trees that once surrounded the building were gone. The trucks and cars that were parked outside were on fire. The tents that housed the future Zombrids were demolished. I couldn't even tell if it was day or night.

Then, there was a sound. A moan. It was close by.

"Hello?" I called out and coughed. My throat was so dry and filled with junk.

Again, another moan. It was coming from my right. I shuffled through the mounds of debris.

"Who is it? Say something! Let me know where you are!"

More moaning. It was coming from my left this time.

I hurried over to the first moan. There was a slight movement under a pile of concrete in front of a large metal door frame that was somehow still standing. I'd hoped that I would have the strength to lift the blocks off whoever it was. I hadn't eaten and lost a ton of blood. But when I started to pick up the pieces, it seemed I had just enough strength. And it helped that the person underneath was helping me, too.

I removed a piece and uncovered a sliver of golden hair. It was Sonny. I picked up the pace and frantically shoveled out the heavy blocks as fast as I could. When her face hit the warm air, she gasped.

"Grace!" She coughed.

"It's okay. You're okay, Sonny. Just breathe." She seemed to be fine once I was able to help her out. All limbs, minus one arm, were intact. She was bleeding from some cuts, but nothing major. It was time to move on to the next moan, which had multiplied by two.

"I'm going to help whoever is over here. You go help whoever is in that corner," I instructed Sonny, pointing in the direction of the moan that was the farthest away from me. She nodded and stumbled through mountains of wreckage. I followed the noise and worked fast to uncover another person.

Kate sucked in a breath. "Gra...ce," she choked.

"I've got Harley over here!" Sonny called out. "She's okay. She's bleeding but she seems okay."

If my memory served me right, that meant we were still missing five people. My chest caved at the idea of anyone of us dying. So far, we had three Zombrids alive and well. Ian had to be somewhere.

I helped Kate out of her hole and made sure she was all there before running to Sonny and Harley. "Did you hear anyone else?"

"No, I don't hear anything," she said. Harley looked dazed and confused, but she clung onto Sonny's waist.

The sounds of crackling embers filled the space around us. I glanced around and focused on the noise. The place was a disaster. Everything was gone. Buildings down the block were obliterated. There was literally nothing left. The President called in the napalm, and it destroyed everything in its path. If it wasn't for Dr. Walker's concrete facility, we would have all been cremated.

Panic, or maybe hunger, threatened to force tears out of my eyes, but I choked them back. It wasn't the time to freak out about what we were going to do now that there was nothing. My biggest priority was to find more survivors.

"Ian! Can you hear me?" I called out. I knew that we were still missing the humans. I knew that they probably needed more help than a Zombrid. But Ian was one of our own. We cared about him. We needed him.

I remembered Serena and him in a standoff before the building blew up. I remembered Serena swinging her machete at him. I remembered there was blood, but I didn't think she killed him. She couldn't have killed him. He had to be okay.

"Julian is here!" Kate yelled. "Looks like just a broken arm."

"Where...where's my daughter?" he asked immediately.

One human saved. Two more to go and one Zombrid. Well, I wasn't sure if I wanted to find one of the humans. I mean, Serena did try to kill me. She *could* have killed me. And maybe I didn't mind dying a few months ago, but I didn't want to die now. I wanted to fight. Fight for who I was. Fight for my fellow Zombrids. She tried to take my long life away from me, but I wanted my immortality.

"Shit!"

"What?" I asked, rushing over to Kate. Julian was now with Harley, checking her body and nurturing her shock.

"It's Dr. Kamini," she said grimly as she knelt down in front of a pile. I glanced down. Dr. Kamini was completely covered in building material. Her hair was matted to her face with blood and ash. Her eyes had rolled to the back of her head and her mouth hung open; a trail of red liquid had leaked from the corner. She was dead.

My stomach flipped, then a terrible spasm shot across it. It was awful, but Dr. Kamini's fresh blood demanded my attention. Kate looked up at me, brows furrowed, and bit her bottom lip. There was no doubt she was thinking the same thing. It was the first time I'd ever seen the need in her eyes.

"Maybe we should find everyone else first," I suggested. She nodded and we began searching together.

Once Julian made sure his daughter was okay, he asked Sonny to keep an eye on her and began his search for Serena. That woman tried to murder me, but I felt his urgency to find someone he loved underneath all of this horror. Kate and I climbed and shuffled around the piles. It was truly unbelievable—like a war zone. I wondered what the rest of the city looked like. I wondered if all the TZs were gone—my heart ached at the thought. They were probably gone, and they'd never get another chance at life again.

I squinted my eyes. Movement. It looked like one of the cinder blocks was moving. "Did you see that?"

"Yeah. I think someone's over there," Kate said, rushing over.

We reached the spot. I couldn't begin to understand where we were exactly. I didn't even know if this was still the same room we had been in before the blast. It all looked the same—smoky and gray and blown to pieces.

"There's someone over here!" Julian called out a few feet away. "He's...he's not..."

My heart pounded. It was a *he*. It could have been Jackson or Ian. But Kate and I combined our strength and removed the blocks from where we were. There were feet, legs, a torso... I knew who it was. It wasn't a man's body. It was a woman. Her body armor. Her red hair. It was Serena.

We moved a piece of rubble that had Serena's arm pinned down. "Are you okay?"

She coughed and winced and groaned. She was clearly alive, and I didn't know how to feel about it.

"Julian, Serena is here!" Kate shouted. He jumped up from the body he'd been uncovering and hurried over to her side. If the person he was helping had been alive, he would not have left him half buried. Julian had a bigger heart than that.

Kate switched with Julian and practically crawled toward the body. I didn't move. I was too afraid. It could be either Jackson or Ian, and as bad as it sounded, I hoped that it was Jackson. He wasn't a main character in our story. Ian was. Ian had to be okay.

"No!" Kate cried out.

I slammed my eyes shut and prayed.

"Damn it!"

It was him.

"Is it Ian?" Sonny asked, fear in her tone.

"Yes! It's him. It's Ian."

I stumbled over to Kate. She was crying and struggling to lift the concrete blocks off him. My heart broke at the sight of her body shaking with every sob—a mixture of grief and intense hunger. And as we exposed his crushed and crumbled body, we learned what had ended his Zombrid life. His neck was severed. A sharp, metal beam had sliced right through him. His head was detached from his body, and there was no saving him. Ian was gone forever.

I felt Sonny's hand on my back as she knelt down with us, and we all huddled together and cried over our friend. It wasn't fair.

It took us a little time, but we were finally able to find Jackson. He had been hit by falling debris and didn't make it through the blast, either. Kate, Sonny, and I knew that there was no way we could move on without something to curb the cravings. So, we feasted on Dr. Kamini. Harley seemed to be going through some kind of mental shock, but Julian was able to coax her into getting food in her belly. It would only be best for her. We had no idea how long it would be before we could find food again. Thankfully, Jackson's body was available to dismember and stow away for future feedings.

We pulled Ian's body out of the wreckage. There was no way we were going to leave him in the middle of a destroyed city. And so we stood around him, silently prayed, and burned his body. Once he was turned to ash, it was time to figure out what to do.

"I think we should just try to get out of Florida," Kate said as she rummaged through the remains of the building. We were trying to find anything of use for our journey.

"Where can we go?" Sonny asked. Harley's arm was wrapped around her waist and her face was buried in Sonny's hip. It seemed like she might have grown attached to the blonde bombshell that I once called my nemesis.

Sonny didn't look like she cared that a little girl clung to her as if she were her mommy, either. In fact, her only arm draped over Harley's back, comforting her. Watching Sonny and Harley made me happy. Maybe Sonny could actually start to care about something other than herself.

"We could just try to get out of Florida," Julian proposed.

"What about the cure?" I asked.

Kate glanced over to me. "We lost most of the synthetic blood. We have some on the island, but we'll need more if we want to help the TZs." She raised her eyebrows, waiting for some kind of approval from me. She meant that she would need more of my blood, and I was perfectly willing and ready to give it to her.

"Of course. I'll do whatever I have to," I told her.

"We don't even know if there are any more TZs out there," Sonny pointed out.

"I know," Kate said. "We need to get back to the Safe Zone, reconvene, and discuss our next plan."

"If we can find a phone or something, I can get Daddy to come get us. He was in Europe last time we spoke, but he'll send someone right away."

Kate held up her satellite phone. "I had it tucked inside my pants. I don't know if it works, but it didn't get crushed."

Sonny, Kate, and Harley fidgeted with the phone. I peeked over at Julian and Serena. We made a makeshift sling for Julian's arm. Serena wasn't in terrible shape, but she was shot in the shoulder before the building collapsed, by Jackson we later learned, and there was an enormous knot the size of a golf ball on her forehead. Her ankle might have been broken, too.

I watched Julian hug Serena with his good arm. He held her close to his body and leaned down toward her ear. He was whispering something to her as she gripped onto his shirt and chest—almost as if she *needed* to. She didn't have that hard, menacing look she had before. Her expression was softer. Her eyebrows furrowed and she seemed to be sad. Maybe even contrite.

A tiny part of me wished that it was Serena instead of Ian. She tried to kill him. She tried to kill me. But I couldn't be that way. Hate had no place in our world—especially not right now. We needed to band together. The humans and the Zombrids had to come together to make it all right.

I walked over to her. She dropped her hand and turned toward me. She opened her mouth to say something, but I stopped her.

"I forgive you."

Serena searched my eyes for something—I didn't know for what. Maybe she thought I wasn't serious.

"I forgive you for trying to kill me. I get it. You were scared of us. But you don't have to be anymore. We have to help people now. Are you willing to help us?"

Serena looked down at her hands. I wondered if she would have the audacity to say no after everything we'd just been through. But when she glanced back up at me, a tear had escaped her eye.

"I'm sorry," she said. "I'm so sorry I did that."

"Will you help us?"

The tears fell from her cheeks and she took me into her arms.

"Yes," she whispered into my ear.

"Okay, gang," Kate said behind us. "We've got to find higher ground to get a signal on this thing. Let's get out of here."

I pulled away from Serena and smiled. "I'm a Zombrid and you're a human. Let's go save our people."

ACKNOWLEDGEMENTS

To my husband, my biggest fan. Thank you for encouraging me all those times I wanted to give up.

To my editor, Precy Larkins, I didn't realize how much I needed you. Thank you for your expert help and guidance. And for being a friend.

Murphy Rae, my cover designer with Indie Solutions and Elaine York with Allusion Graphics—You lovely ladies are truly magical, and you made the pages of this series resemble an actual book on a bookshelf. Truly a dream come true. Thank you for patiently working with me.

To my readers, thanks for following Grace's journey. I hope you all enjoyed this story as much as I have enjoyed telling it.

Don't ever forget who you are. Be kind to yourself. And learn to love your flaws. We all have them. We're only human, after all;)

ABOUT THE AUTHOR

J.Q. Davis is from New Orleans, Louisiana. She has a bachelor's degree in healthcare but chooses to pursue her dreams of being a writer. Her husband is a retired Marine (23 years!) who works with surgical robots. They don't have kids but spoil their pups as if they were real little girls.

Her other interests include exercising, listening to indie music, watching anything even remotely related to horror, and reading young adult novels. She is also a video gamer and secretly dreams about being a professional ice skater, volcanologist, and a stop-motion animator.

She is excited to continue this journey through writing and hopes that her readers enjoy her books.

Follow J.Q. Davis on:
Twitter: @JoJoQD
Instagram: @authorj.q.davis
Website: www.jqdavis.com